Advance praise for *Murder in Sugar Land*

"Absolutely superb! David Crump describes the reality of a trial better than anyone. After 30 years as a trial lawyer and 14 years as a trial judge, I have had the same experiences. And Crump nails it. This is a book you simply cannot put down."

— Judge R. Terence Ney
Past President, State Bar of Virginia

I0526321

"David Crump knows his material and characters well! He has written yet another excellent legal thriller."

— David Beck
Past President, State Bar of Texas

"Crump steers his readers through our judicial system as only a practitioner and professor of law is able to do! This is a fascinating story crafted with characters who are so vivid and real that you are faced with the terrible conflict of not wanting to put it down, while realizing it will end too soon if you don't."

— Bill Balleza
News Anchor, NBC-TV Channel 2

"Each of David Crump's novels leaves me looking forward to the next. His characters are each so unusual, they are almost Faulkner-esque. I highly recommend this one!"

— T. Gerald Treece
Legal Commentator, CBS-TV Channel 11

"I was immediately drawn in by the characters' dialogue! I love a novel that begins, in essence, like a play."

— Sharon H. Gehbauer
English Literature Teacher, High School, St. Agnes Academy

"The story takes you behind the scenes and behind the bench. It's a fun courtroom drama in classic Crump style!"

— D. Hull Youngblood
Past Chair, Board of Directors, State Bar of Texas

"This is the most realistic courtroom novel you'll find today, so grab your seat at the defense table and watch the legal chess match unfold!"

— Gary Taylor
Pulitzer Prize Nominee Journalist
Author of true-crime bestseller *Luggage by Kroger*

"An intriguing story about our criminal justice system, by someone who has been there and done that!"

— Richard Alderman
"The People's Lawyer," ABC-TV Channel 13

"As a successful lawyer who has fought complex legal battles, David Crump succeeds as an author of bestselling books because he knows what he's writing about."

— Lynne Liberato
Past President, State Bar of Texas

MURDER

IN

SUGAR LAND

MURDER
IN
SUGAR LAND

David Crump

QP BOOKS
New Orleans, Louisiana

Published in 2013 by QP Books.

ISBN 978-1-61027-182-0 (pbk.)
ISBN 978-1-61027-183-7 (ePub)

QP BOOKS
Quid Pro, LLC
5860 Citrus Blvd., suite D-101
New Orleans, Louisiana 70123
www.qpbooks.com

Cataloging-in-Publication Data

Crump, David.

    Murder in Sugar Land / David Crump.

        p. cm.

    ISBN 978-1-61027-182-0 (pbk.)

1. Trials—United States—Fiction. 2. Law Firms—United States—Fiction. I. Title.

PS3549.R383C2 2013

833' .24—dc21
2013441322
CIP

Author's Preface

Most novels about lawyers are not about lawyers. They distort the picture. This story is different, because the main character is the American system of justice, the way it really is. The plot in a novel should grow out of the characters and their conflicts, and this one grows out of the character of American justice, which pulsates and shakes with internal conflicts.

But every story requires concessions to the demands of fiction. Real-life courtroom dramas are built on tedious work, and so a good courtroom novel requires what writers call "dramatic compression." This story is no exception.

Still, this is a story that shows reality. The critics have picked up on this, in describing my other novels. The word is, those stories show courtrooms the way they really are. And so does this novel, the one that you're reading. I've added a Postscript at the end, to describe the compromises that the conventions of fiction have required. But for now, imagine that you're a new associate in the law firm of Robert Herrick and Associates, assigned to a case that will become a big adventure. And all you have to do, to get started, is to . . . turn the page.

MURDER

IN

SUGAR LAND

1

PROBABLE CAUSE

Okay, Brianna. Lift up your hands, and let's get these bracelets off."
At that, Brianna Edwards, Jail Inmate No. 2476, raised her arms, rigidly locked together. "Ooof. These things, these handcuffs . . . they're always too tight. Can't you people come up with something softer?"

"It's part of the deal, for folks in jail. Everybody gets treated the same way. Bad, that is. But that's good, because everybody gets treated the same way."

The jailer pointed down at the floor. "Now, watch this step here, Brianna, where the linoleum is broken. We don't want you to fracture your hind end before you get your pretty self outta the holdover cell."

"Wow, this light is bright, here in the courtroom." The door pulled back to close, and Brianna shielded her eyes. "Or rather, I guess it's just dark back there in the holdover. . . ."

She stopped. "Hey, look! There's Delia!"

"Well, Brianna, why don't you just sashay over there and sit yourself right down, next to old Delia? Right there . . . yes, in that jury box. This morning, there ain't no jury, and that's where we gonna put all of you fine folk who gotta see the judge."

And so, Brianna hustled over there. "Dee-li-a!"

"Bree-anna! I haven't seen you in what seems like fifty years." Delia Marchand, Inmate No. 2477, spread her arms wide.

"It's more like twenty-four hours, but I have to agree with you." Brianna pursed her lips. "Time grinds slowly, since we got arrested."

"It's not as much fun as it's cracked up to be, in this jail."

"It's not fun, you mean . . . here in 'stir.' Isn't that what they say, 'In Stir'?"

1

"Or, maybe, 'in the Calaboose.' That's what they say."

"In the Can. How 'bout that, 'in the Can'?"

"In 'Time Out.'"

"In the 'Palace of Perjury.'"

"In the 'Hall of Broken Dreams.'"

"Well, anyway, the answer is: Noooo, it's not fun, here in jail." Brianna put on a philosophical look, as if she were disclosing a deep truth. "In fact, it's what I'd call just . . . generally crummy. This jail isn't even vaguely okay."

"And it's not for a good reason, even." Delia shook her head. "It's all because of a guy. A male of the species. Whenever two girls are having trouble, it's usually a man who's caused it. "

Brianna grinned mischievously. "But you know, Delia, it mighta been worth it . . . if . . . *if this particular guy'd had a bigger dick!*" And both women threw their heads back and laughed at that: at how strange life could be, and at the paradox of this moment.

But instantly, they flinched when they heard the judge's voice. He sounded bored, but at the same time, the words cut like a knife. "You two 'ladies'"—and the voice made it clear that 'ladies' was not what the judge meant at all—"You two 'ladies' are in *my* courtroom. One more outburst like that, and you gonna be watching this courtroom amusement through a gag and a face mask. Do I make myself clear?"

Barely above a whisper, Delia answered: "Yes . . . sir." And from Brianna: "Yes . . . yes, . . . your honor."

And then . . . there was silence. The silence lasted for what seemed like forever, but it probably was less than five seconds. Then:

"Brianna Edwards." The clerk's voice carried the same bored-but-official tone. Brianna pulled herself to a standing position and trudged from the jury box to face the judge, in the same place that she had seen occupied earlier by other jail inmates. Without intending to, she adopted a helpless posture.

The judge sounded bored, again. "Brianna Edwards, you're charged with *solicitation of capital murder.*" He looked up at Brianna, with a curious look, quizzical but without sympathy. "As of now, bail at two hundred." He spat out the next words. "That doesn't mean two hundred dollars, young lady. It means two hundred thousand. So, Brianna Edwards, have you got a lawyer?"

"Not yet. But I . . . I've spoken to someone. I'll . . . I'll have . . . a lawyer."

"No lawyer." The judge made a movement with his pen. And then, he clicked his laptop. Brianna wondered why he needed both, but immediately, she jerked herself back to the present, because the judge was still speaking. "Sit down, Brianna Edwards."

The judge called everyone by their first and last names. This way, Brianna realized, he avoided using just first names, which would have sounded too friendly, and he also avoided calling inmates by 'Mr.' or 'Ms.,' which would have lent these prisoners too much of an appearance of dignity.

"When we go through the probable cause stuff, Brianna Edwards," the judge continued, "you'll be represented by the public defender."

The judge already had made it plain, by body language, voice tone, and explicit words, that he considered the "probable cause stuff" to be a colossal waste of time. There would be later hearings to determine, for each inmate, whether probable cause justified prosecuting that inmate in a trial, including the grand jury's decision on an indictment.

"But first, the Supreme Court says we've got to wade through this early probable cause hearing, within a day or so from when you got arrested." This hearing, the judge had explained, was only a "rough approximation." A minimum amount of evidence would do. A police report would be enough, if it wasn't too silly. "It's just to find out whether the State has enough evidence to hold you in custody, or whether we've got to release you."

Brianna already knew the answer to that. She wasn't going to be released. Not a chance.

And anyway, the "probable cause stuff" consisted of a few whispered words for each inmate. The prosecutor would summarize the police reports with a voice you could barely hear. The public defender would say almost nothing. He spoke seriously on behalf of barely one inmate out of every ten, because there wasn't much to say at most probable cause hearings. The judge had made sure that all of the prisoners understood. It was a charade, ordered by our remote, out-of-touch Supreme Court.

Brianna sat down, dejectedly.

Suddenly she turned. "Delia!" Her words were whispered but urgent. "Delia, what were we thinking, you and I? I mean, about what we did. Why'd we do something that stupid?"

"I've been wondering the same thing." Delia wiped her hands on her jail-issued courtroom dress, which sported a vague bluish green color punctuated with garish yellow stars and bright crescent moons. "We didn't kill anybody, we didn't even hurt anyone, and yet here we are, treated like mass murderers."

"But . . . I mean, .Delia . . . how did we get here, in this awful place? How did we get . . . into . . . *this* mess? How?". . .

"I. . . I wish I knew."

And they both thought back to that earlier time. Before the crime. Before all their conspiring, and before jail.

Six months earlier, when it had all started. . . .

2

SIX MONTHS EARLIER

I t had started one summer evening, when they were standing, innocently enough, in the apartment they shared. Brianna was frustrated. "Delia, have you seen my red blouse? The sexy one?"

"I can't tell you whether I've seen it, because it's somewhere under all the other stuff on the floor." Delia's answer was cheerful, but it hinted at a slight feeling of disgust.

The floor was a chaotic mix of underwear, denim, poly-cotton, natural fibers, and hosiery. Exuberantly, it presented every color in the rainbow. The two chests-of-drawers were empty, except for a few straggling pieces of lingerie dangling out of randomly skewed drawers. Brianna picked through the layers of cloth and lace.

"Someday, Brianna, you've got to clear this stuff off the floor and do a wash. Two thirds of this stuff is yours, you know."

"Delia, why don't you go gargle with razor blades and get off my back?" Brianna laughed. "Besides, you've got the two-thirds part wrong. Two thirds of this junk is *yours*, you ass-aching floozy."

"Listen to you, Brianna. You speak like a true expert on being a floozy. I guess the floor is a good organizational system for clothes."

"Well." Brianna looked around. "I need to find it. I need that red thing."

"Why? What's so important, that you need it for?"

"Alan. You remember. I've got to go meet my guy Alan. And it's important that my appearance is, well, 'fetching,' if I can use a word we don't use much anymore."

"This Alan, he's that important?"

"Yes, indeed."

"Why's that? What has Alan got that every ordinary guy hasn't got?" Delia's skepticism oozed out of her words. The unspoken message was, "Brianna, you always pick guys that turn out to be bums, and here we go again."

"Six foot two, eyes of blue." Brianna was happily immune to Delia's implied insult. "Just like in the song. 'Cept even better. Alan's got what you might call your basic sex appeal."

"Awww, come on." Delia was laughing, now. "You know what they say. Beauty is only skin deep. Especially on a guy. It doesn't mean there's anything worthwhile underneath."

She looked at Brianna and saw her struggling to answer, because, yes, that was a good point. Brianna was naïve, sometimes, and she came across that way, because even though she was in her mid-30's, she stood just five feet two inches, and she looked impossibly young. Her big blue eyes contributed to that impression. So did her blonde hair, especially in the short and sassy cut she favored. In fact, Brianna usually tried to make up for her naïve appearance by careful grooming and by wearing conservative clothes.

Now, she blinked, as she wondered what she thought about what Delia had said. She was still looking for the red blouse as she tried to answer.

"Well, yes, but Alan . . . well . . . So far he's been a fine guy, too. Not just good-looking. He's been good to me. It sounds corny, but it's nice. I mean, he opens the door every time. Which is old fashioned, but I'm surprised about how happy it makes me feel, after so much of the opposite from other guys. He's respectful, and he doesn't use four-letter words in every other sentence. Like you do, Delia."

"Oh! Wow! And what does Saint Alan do for a living? Or does he survive on alms like the other members of the Cherubim?"

"He's in the oil business. The only down side is that he's from out of town. But he comes here all the time to meet with the other branch of his big company."

"And what do you and Alan talk about all the time? Your basic oil patch stuff, I guess. Blowout preventers? Drilling mud? Geophysical maps? I hear they use a lot of salty brine in fracking those wells."

"Not as much salty brine as you put out, Delia."

Delia had to laugh, at that. Her hair, hanging down her back, was as dark as Brianna's was light, and it always shook when she laughed. She seemed to tower over Brianna, even though she was just five feet six; it was the height difference that created that impression. Now, she looked even bigger to Brianna, as she waved her arms to show mock concern.

"So, what kind of chatter does Alan come on to you with? That is, if it's not drilling mud? I wanna know!" She waved her arms to show mock concern.

"Oh, we talk about all kinds of things. I can't even remember. We just seem to be on the same wavelength."

"The same moonbeam, in your case."

"Maybe. I've never met a guy I thought was so close to what I want. We've talked a lot about how it was like, back in college, dealing with fraternity guys. And with final exams. Just silly stuff. But Alan and I, we really get along."

"That's always nice. And rare." Delia sighed. Her voice showed a hint of envy.

"All right! Look! Here's my red blouse. And it's even clean." She studied it. "We've got a good organizational system here on the floor."

"Good. You can put off the big job."

"What big job?"

"Picking the clothes up." Delia looked serious, as if she were analyzing an important assignment for her roommate, but then . . . she laughed.

*   *   *

Fifteen minutes later, Brianna was dressed and ready. "But whoops, I almost forgot. I've got to call Robert Herrick."

"Who's that?" Delia wanted to know.

"Robert Herrick. My boss at the law firm. The head lawyer. The law firm is called, 'Robert Herrick and Associates,' and it's his law firm."

"It sounds like a one-man operation. How can this guy Robert Herrick afford a big-time legal assistant like Brianna Edwards, I have to ask?"

"No, actually, it's a huge law firm. It's named after him because he started it. His firm has lots of lawyers, all representing injured people, all trying to recover something for the little guy who's been crashed into, or malpracticed on, or defrauded; but I'm not sure exactly how many lawyers we've got by now, because we've grown so fast. Robert Herrick has been the President of the Bar Association and president of just about everything else, because he's a pretty successful guy."

"How come he puts up with you, then?"

"He's also a nice guy. He doesn't treat underlings like hired hands. He's that rare combination: a boss who's really made it big but who never talks down to me. I really feel like I'm part of something important there." She was dialing the number. "Hi, Robert? You said I needed to phone you to touch base. About when to start in the morning. When do I need to be there, I wonder?"

A pause. Then: "Oooof. Robert, you're really going to be there that early? . . . Okay. I'll put together the briefing book. . . . It's not every day that we have the opportunity to host a meeting with that supreme sleazebag, Jimmy Coleman, the bad guy from the big law firm. . . . Yes, I'll be there. . . . Yes . . . awake!!!"

Another pause. "Yes, I know this case. This is an unbelievable case. It's horrible, and the defendants are guilty as sin. And I know: Jimmy Coleman will be there, using every underhanded Rambo lawyer guerilla theatre tactic to derail us from making our case. I'll be ready."

* * *

A minute later, she hung up. And she laughed. "Good thing you've given me special permission to ignore the floor for now, Delia. I've got to get to the law firm early tomorrow. Big day. Big confrontation, in a big case."

Delia smiled. "But right now, you've got a big night, from what you've been saying. A big night with Alan."

"That's right. So, I've got to be versatile. I've got to act like a big-time legal assistant by day, working at my law firm. And I've got to be a big-time sex symbol at night, tonight."

Delia laughed. "Dream on. But yes, you can put off that big job, of picking up the clothes."

"Right." Brianna adjusted the scoop neckline on her red blouse. "I'm putting off everything, Delia, 'cause I'm out of here. Alan, baby, here I come. You lucky guy!" And she looked into the mirror approvingly.

"He's probably no good, in the end." Delia laughed. "You know how it goes, Brianna, in your love life. Never any good choices."

"Careful." Unexpectedly, Brianna's eyes were heavy and wet. "I'm still sensitive."

"Oh. Sorry."

"That last guy I fell for, I don't even want to say his name. He ran around on me unmercifully."

"I know. I'm sorry. Maybe Alan is different."

"Maybe so." Brianna made the effort to brighten her eyes. "I hope so. I need it."

"But you know, Delia," she said, on the way out. "As perfect as he is, there's something about Alan that bugs me. Something that just doesn't seem right. Like, maybe he's not really the type of guy he acts like, or maybe . . . he's not who he claims."

She shook her head. "Oh, well. Every guy has secrets. Every guy disappoints you, sometimes. But . . . I'm not the type to mess up something this perfect, or at least, something that *seems* this perfect."

3

THE LAW FIRM

The next morning, Brianna was there, at the law firm, before six thirty.

"Good morning, Brianna," said Robert Herrick.

"Good morning," she replied to the boss, while shaking off her drowsiness.

Robert Herrick's law firm occupied the top two floors of the Chase Bank Tower. Houston's tallest building. His office, where he and Brianna stood now, was spacious, and the dark parquet floor was covered by the most beautiful oriental carpet Brianna had ever seen. The furnishings were elegant: plants and flowers under the greenhouse-style windows, a mahogany desk with matching desk chairs, and paintings by Picasso, Mondrian, and Wyeth. Outside, the downtown buildings sprawled toward the south, in shades of gray, brown, and white. Off to the west, the greenery along Memorial Drive stretched past River Oaks and Tanglewood, and there, it faded away into the distance.

Tom Kennedy came in to sit by the desk. He was Robert's favorite partner, the one he worked with most.

Tom shook his head. "Mr. Escondido's case is really tragic."

Brianna handed both lawyers the preparation file. At the top, there was a newspaper headline that screamed out, "Botched Operation: Surgeon Removes Wrong Lung from Dying Patient!"

The subtitle went on to say, "Doctor Left Larry Escondido's Diseased Lung in Place, But Cut Out Healthy Organ." Robert winced.

"Poor Mr. Escondido," he said, referring to the patient condemned to die—who was also his client.

"The question is: how is this doctor going to cover up his mistake?" Kennedy assumed that the doctor would weasel out of responsibility. He would lay it off on someone else.

The telephone rang. The voice on the other end was wispy. "Yes, Mr. Escondido," said Robert.

He paused. "You're asking, what's happening today? Well ... it's called a *'deposition.'* I'm going ask Doctor Kapritska questions. The doctor who removed your lung. No, we won't be in a courtroom.... The deposition will be right here, in our law office, in a conference room. There will be a court reporter, and a videographer, and Doctor Kapritska will have to answer my questions under oath. This is how we find out the story the other side is going to tell. And yes, I want you to be here, if you possibly can."

The conversation ended quickly. Then, "Let's get down to business." Robert studied the deposition outline. "What's the best way to talk to this doctor? Do we refer to this disaster as a 'pulmonectomy' and use technical language, or do we just say, 'Doctor, you cut off the wrong lung, didn't you?'"

His voice was anguished. "I'm sorry." He looked down. "This case gets to me. Sometimes, I'm not analytical, and I identify too emotionally with the plaintiff."

He looked thoughtful. "It'll be hard on Mr. Escondido today. But when I asked him, he said he wanted to be present. This Doctor Kapritska will have to look at the man he's condemned to death—and maybe he'll tell the truth."

*   *   *

An hour and a half later, they sat in the conference room. It was quiet, but there was a sense of impending struggle. A battle was about to start, a bloodless but vigorous conflict, around this conference table.

Robert, Tom, and Brianna sat together with Larry Escondido, who slumped in a massive wheelchair. And next to Mr. Escondido, there was a pile of tanks, monitors, filters, pumps, and other technology, all connected by a maze of wires, and all managed by an attendant in white clothes. The lifelines of a dying man, who was here as a lawsuit plaintiff.

Jimmy Coleman, from the law firm of Booker Bayne, sat on the opposite side. Booker Bayne was one of the biggest firms in the world, with more than a thousand attorneys—in Houston, Washington, Los Angeles, San Francisco, New York, London, Frankfurt, Hong Kong, Singapore, and other financial centers. Four of those lawyers from Booker Bayne sat next to Jimmy, unnecessarily billing over two thousand dollars an hour.

"Doctor Kapritska," Robert asked the witness—the physician who had removed the wrong lung—"do you know what a 'deposition' is?"

"Objection. Form," interrupted Jimmy Coleman. "It's an improper question."

"You can answer the question," Robert said to the doctor, firmly. He explained to the witness, "Objections don't usually stop the questions, in a deposition; the court reporter just takes them down, so the judge can decide about them, some day—if the case is ever tried."

"Yes," said the doctor tonelessly. "I know what a deposition is."

"Then you know that I will ask you questions, and Doctor, you will be testifying under penalty of perjury, with the court reporter taking it down. And your deposition can be used at the trial. It can be seen on video by the jury. You know all of that?

"Objection. Form!" Jimmy Coleman's voice sounded like sandpaper.

"Yes. I know that," said the witness indifferently.

Brianna remembered what Robert had told her, when she'd started work years ago. "One purpose of a deposition is to contradict the witness if he changes his story during the trial. But sometimes the witness explains away the contradiction by saying, 'I didn't understand what was going on.' And it's helpful for the jury to hear the witness say that he did, actually, know how the deposition would be used."

But now it was difficult to ask questions, with Jimmy Coleman barking objections.

Slowly, while ignoring the interruptions, Robert got the witness to talk about his training and experience, about preparations for Mr. Escondido's operation, and about the roles of every nurse and doctor involved. The questions and answers bristled with anatomical jargon: the "costal surface," the "oblique fissure," the "subclavian vein." And repeatedly, Jimmy Coleman rasped, "Objection! Form!"

Finally: "Let's take a break. Mr. Escondido has to have a procedure."

"What's Jimmy Coleman up to?" Brianna asked. "What are all these objections about?"

Tom Kennedy knew. "Confusion. It interrupts the thought process. The witness can give an evasive answer that says nothing, and it's harder to follow."

Robert usually tried to stay on good terms with his opponents, but Jimmy Coleman made it difficult. "It's like, whenever we represent somebody who's hurt bad, the defendants know they can make it harder by hiring Jimmy."

*   *   *

"Okay," said Robert, as they waited for the deposition to start again. "We have a new settlement offer from Jimmy. They'll pay two million dollars to Mr. Escondido."

"It's not enough, of course," said Tom Kennedy. "But it's progress."

Robert sighed. "I'd trade it all away, if Mr. Escondido had his good lung back."

"Stay focused, Robert!" Kennedy smiled. "And don't get emotional."

"I'm not going to get emotional," said Robert Herrick, but he sounded doubtful.

"Aw, come on. You don't fool me. You always want to fight for the injured plaintiff against those rich, powerful corporations." Kennedy smiled again. "I'll never forget our case with Mrs. Polk. It showed me how much you identify with the little guy."

"What about Mrs. Polk?"

"We tell this story here in the office." Kennedy's grin was as wide as a courtroom. "Back when we represented Mrs. Polk, Robert, you interrupted a deposition you were taking in another case, a completely unrelated case, so you could socialize with your other client, Mrs. Polk. Who was a cleaning lady. And the witness in the deposition was the CEO of a Fortune 500 company that you were suing, but heck, that didn't stop you. 'Hello, Mrs. Polk, how are you? Are you back to a hundred percent?' And you kept that pinstriped big shot waiting, while you chatted with this cleaning lady about her grandkids, her church, and her favorite barbecue joint!"

"Yes. I remember." Robert laughed. "But see, I'm fond of Mrs. Polk. She's a friend. Besides, the deposition turned out all right, because when I met with Mrs. Polk, it distracted the pinstriped guy."

"Oh, yeah?" Kennedy's eyebrow arched.

"Yeah. When I went back into the deposition, the atmosphere changed. That CEO spilled his guts. It happens. The big shot has to wait because of one of the little people, and it disorients him. After Mrs. Polk, that CEO gave me all the answers I needed to bury his sleazy company."

"Gee. Maybe you ought to hire Mrs. Polk to interrupt all your depositions."

"I just wish I could have given Mrs. Polk back a husband with a healthy body." Robert sounded subdued. "I'd rather have that than all our financial success."

And of course, the financial success had been amazing. Today, the firm called "Robert Herrick & Associates" had more than a hundred employees, including twenty-six lawyers, thirty paralegals, and an audiovisual studio that made videos for use in court. And Robert had built all of it—after coming out of law school with nothing but debts. He had refused the huge salary that every firm in town had offered.

And now, the big-firm lawyers treated him with respect when they agreed to settlements in the millions. His clients loved him. He didn't just analyze an injury in terms of dollars; he felt it, the same way they did, and they knew he would fight for them.

But Tom Kennedy wasn't finished. He wanted to represent more banks and insurance companies: the clients who could pay up front. "So, Robert, how come you're already emotionally involved in Mr. Escondido's case?"

Robert smiled. "You got me, Tom! I'm a bleeding heart." He shook his head. "But you're right. I've got to stay focused on the case for Mr. Escondido. And not on my emotions about it."

4
THE SETTLEMENT

When the deposition started again, Robert asked about his client's remaining life. "Doctor, how long do you estimate that Mr. Escondido will live?"

"Objection. Form." Jimmy Coleman was still here.

"I don't have any idea." Jimmy had coached this doctor well. He wasn't going to admit anything.

"Mr. Escondido is condemned to death, isn't he?"

The witness looked away, with no expression. "Mr. Escondido will die eventually, just like everyone else, but we don't know when that will be."

"Have you given any thought to Mr. Escondido's quality of life?"

"Objection. Form."

"Of course. But as a surgeon, I don't think about what happens when things go wrong."

Sometimes, an innocuous-sounding answer is helpful. The defendant didn't think about the life of someone he'd injured? Or rather, someone he'd killed? The jury would have to hear that answer.

Suddenly, Larry Escondido struggled to speak. He could barely whisper. "I . . . am . . . so . . . tired. . . ."

Even Jimmy Coleman got the message. "We'd better take a break again."

*   *   *

The break ended. Time to re-start the deposition. Robert stood outside the conference room, talking to Brianna Edwards. It didn't have anything to do with the deposition, but this was Robert Herrick.

"So, Brianna, what is it that makes you think that this boyfriend of yours . . . Alan, is that his name? . . . What makes you think Alan isn't who he claims to be?"

"It's just a feeling." Brianna was embarrassed.

"Herrick, what the hell are you doing?" Jimmy Coleman waved his arms. "Doctor Kapritska is ready to go."

"I'll be a moment. Just wait." Robert's voice was firm. "So, Brianna, what gives you this feeling?" He was projecting empathy toward Brianna, but he was also trying to get analytical answers.

"Alan is just so . . . *secretive*. He doesn't tell me anything about him."

"And this is a boyfriend you feel committed to? Like, he might be . . . 'the one'?"

"Well . . . yes."

They talked for ten more minutes, with Robert learning very little. Brianna was aching with uncertainty, but she didn't know much herself.

"Herrick! Let's finish this deposition!" Jimmy's voice sounded like hailstones on concrete.

And finally, Robert sat at the big, inlaid-wood conference table, once again.

He looked at his notes, just for effect. "Doctor Kapritska, you used the phrase, 'when things go wrong.' Things sure did *go wrong* for Mr. Escondido, didn't they?"

"Objection! Form." Jimmy sounded like a bullfrog, but with a little higher pitch. When a lawyer hears his opponent use his own witness's words, he knows there's trouble.

A pause. Then, hesitantly, "Yes."

Robert sensed the opening. "Doctor, you were negligent, weren't you?"

"Objection! Form!" Jimmy yelled.

"I don't know," said the doctor miserably.

Sometimes, the best strategy is to act like a bull in a china shop: forceful, insistent, hammering away. "Doctor, let me ask you again, because yes, certainly, you know, and you know for sure! *You . . . were . . . negligent!* Weren't you!" It wasn't really a question.

The witness looked down at the table. And then, painfully: "Yes."

"And that's what caused all of this, wasn't it?" Robert's words sounded like a pile driver.

"Objection! Form!"

"Y . . . yes."

*   *   *

The deposition was over. And so were the settlement negotiations that came out of them.

"Ten million dollars. That's a victory." Tom Kennedy looked relieved at the offer from Booker Bayne. "It's a large amount, a very large amount, after the legislature passed those tort reform laws. But Mr. Escondido will have huge medical expenses, and he may live several years."

"It's not as much as Mr. Escondido deserves. But under the law, it's at the upper end of what we could ever expect. And when you get paid an amount that's at the upper limit of what you can expect, then it's malpractice not to settle."

"You did the impossible, Robert." Brianna was amazed. "And Jimmy didn't offer it out of the goodness of his heart."

"No. Jimmy Coleman doesn't have any . . . *'goodness'* . . . in that ramshackle heart of his," Tom Kennedy snorted. "He'd probably still have denied that this doctor was liable."

Robert nodded. "Yes, absolutely. He would have denied all responsibility. In fact, he had a defense of what we call 'proximate cause' up his sleeve, the whole time."

"So, he would have claimed that . . . Doctor Kapritska's negligence didn't really 'cause' this tragedy?" Kennedy was trying to figure it out.

"That was Jimmy's theory?" Brianna was even more amazed than Kennedy.

"Right. Jimmy planned to lay it off on another doctor, the intake physician, who had the job of marking the patient beforehand." Robert shook his head. "Surgeons have a way to prevent this kind of mistake. Simple, but it usually works. The physician most familiar with the patient uses a felt pen to write directly on the body. He writes something like, *'This side,'* and he draws an arrow, right on the body. But Jimmy told me, off the record, that he was going to claim that the marking was too vague, too misleading, and that's what really caused the mistake."

"And let me guess," Brianna said. "That particular doctor, the one who did the marking, he probably doesn't have any insurance. That's why Jimmy wanted to lay it off on him."

"Right."

Kennedy smiled. "But Jimmy's defense fell apart . . . when Doctor Kapritska told the truth. When he admitted that he'd caused it. I guess the doctor forgot his memorized lines. Robert, you helped him forget."

*　　*　　*

Later, when he and Kennedy were alone, Robert said, "You know, Tom, on a different subject . . . I'm worried about Brianna."

"What? . . . Why's that?"

Robert told his partner about Alan, or as much as he knew.

Kennedy looked surprised. "Yes. . . . Yes, that's strange."

Suddenly, it dawned on him—what Robert had done. "Robert, you talked with Brianna out in the hall . . . and made Doctor Kapritska wait . . . just like you talked to Mrs. Polk about her favorite barbecue joint . . . and then, just like making that pinstriped CEO wait for Mrs. Polk, and he finally told the truth, you made this doctor wait for your legal assistant, and then Doctor Kapritska told the truth too. Did you . . . Did you . . . ."

He looked at Robert. "Did you pull off that same trick, again?"

"I'm not telling." Robert laughed. "I'll take the Fifth Amendment. But I'll tell you what. I wish we didn't have the ten million, and Mr. Escondido had a healthy lung, instead."

He paused. "And also, I wish I could stop worrying about this boyfriend of Brianna's. And worrying . . . about what this guy Alan might do."

5
THE TELEVISION VERSION

I t was ten o'clock in the evening. At the Herrick household, edges of the calm darkness outside were filtering through the heavy shutters across the windows in the living room. The television started showing the local news.

Robert sat beside his wife, Maria, as trumpet sounds from the television announced the beginning of "Action News." The screen showed a picture of the city skyline, and then images of the anchors, plus the sportscaster and the weather announcer, scrolling smoothly across the screen. They all flashed million-dollar smiles, and all of their names were displayed underneath.

"Good evening, friends!" the anchor said heartily. "I'm John Moreno, and this . . . is . . . Action News!"

First, there was a story about a shooting in a bar near Highway 59. It was followed by coverage of a fire that had destroyed a home. And then, to Robert's surprise, there was a story that was familiar.

The screen behind John Moreno filled with a stock image: a doctor, or probably a model, wearing a green surgeon's mask and holding a scalpel. The doctor-model held the scalpel high, unnaturally high, and it had a menacing appearance.

"We don't usually carry medical malpractice news," the anchor intoned, "but this is a story we've told you about, before. And believe me, friends, it's a tragic story."

The scene behind him changed, and an image of a courthouse appeared.

"Regular viewers of Action News can all remember that we told you about a man named Larry Escondido. And about his operation. And also, about the lawsuit that grew out of his operation. Mr. Escondido went into St. Barnaby Hospital for what seemed like a routine operation."

"Robert, this is about your case!" said Maria excitedly.

"Except that it wasn't a 'routine' operation," Robert answered.

"Mr. Escondido needed diseased lung tissue removed," the anchor went on. "But what happened was a terrible mistake. Dr. Lawrence Kapritska removed the lung tissue. The trouble is, he removed it on the wrong side."

"It was the entire lung!" Robert shook his head.

Maria put her hand on his arm, gently, as if to say, "It's al-l-l-l right, Robert."

The background changed again, and it showed file footage of Mr. Escondido in his wheelchair. "We've told you this much of the story, before. Mr. Escondido survives today, barely, with one lung—his diseased lung—and meanwhile, he's lost the use of his one good lung, because of the operation."

The anchor raised his voice. "But Action News has learned, it may not be Doctor Kapritska's fault! Sources close to the investigation, and court papers, tell the real story. The body markings that guided Doctor Kapritska were put there by another physician, whose identity the papers do not disclose."

The doctor's image with the menacing scalpel reappeared, as John Moreno went on. "And those markings told the operating physicians to operate on the lung they actually operated on. The instructions were wrong, and they told Doctor Kapritska to do exactly what he did, in cutting the wrong lung!"

"Good grief," said Robert. "I guess it's not hard to guess who those 'sources close to the investigation' might have been."

"But now there's a new twist!" John Moreno announced excitedly. "Action News has learned that Doctor Kapritska has settled the case with lawyers for Mr. Escondido."

"That's correct," Robert said. "It's nice to hear a correct statement."

Maria smiled. "Shhhh. Let's see whether 'Action . . . News' messes it up. But Robert, don't worry about what they get wrong! It won't affect anything."

The anchor was wound up, now. "According to Jimmy Coleman, the lawyer for Doctor Kapritska, the settlement is what he calls a 'protective settlement.' A settlement of the kind that lawyers sometimes make, even when it's not legally necessary."

And there, on the screen, was Jimmy Coleman, speaking. "A jury trial is expensive, even when the likelihood of the jury going against you is small. Doctor Kapritska is a fine doctor. We settled it because he can't sit there in a long trial, for months on end, and ignore all his patients. He'd have to fire everyone in his office, and he'd have to cancel his operating schedule. It's a protective settlement, this settlement we made."

The anchor reappeared. "The amount of the settlement, we're told, is confidential. It hasn't been disclosed."

Robert shook his head. Jimmy had made it appear as though he had settled the case for a tiny amount, just to avoid the time that a trial would take. And also, he had gotten it across that Doctor Kapritska, his client, was a fine doctor, who wasn't responsible for this tragedy.

The news switched to another story, about a school bond issue. This was probably the story of most interest to the most people, but here it was, after Jimmy Coleman's self-interested puffery.

Robert's wife, Maria, had to laugh once again. "That malpractice story is about as accurate a story as their priorities are accurate—priorities like burying an important story about school bonds and children's educations and taxes, all behind a fire, a shooting, and what amounts to a commercial for Jimmy Coleman's client. But don't let it get to you, Robert. You did a fantastic job for Mr. Escondido."

"Well, if Bill Balleza or Dave Ward were doing this story, they wouldn't have let Jimmy Coleman foul it up."

Maria smiled again. "You're my strong man, and you don't like injustice, even if it's only injustice in news stories that aren't completely accurate. Which you don't expect them to be, in the first place." And finally, with that, she made him laugh. But not for long, because he was still seeing Larry Escondido's image in his mind.

"Oh, well," he sighed. "We've settled that case. There's nothing more I can do for poor Mr. Escondido. And I've got to move on, because I have plenty of cases coming up, where my other clients need help."

But his voice showed that he was still thinking about the man with one diseased lung.

6

DELIA AND ANDERSON

Back at the apartment, there was the usual chaos. Tonight, it was Delia's turn to dress up, and to look all over the floor for clothes.

"So, Delia, who's this guy you've been seeing? This guy Anderson?"

"He's really interesting. He's from out of town too, just like your guy Alan. Brianna, this time I need that red thing. That blouse. I need to borrow it from you."

Delia laughed. "That is, assuming it's actually yours. I can't remember. Maybe it's mine."

"It's mine, dummy. But all right, if you can find it on the floor. It's there somewhere, in our official storage system."

"It's not on the floor. It's hanging up. I took it to the cleaners, because I foresaw this moment coming."

"Now, aren't you providential!"

"Yes. Absolutely. That's me. Always planning for the future. So, here it is, the red blouse. It'll be sexier on me than on you."

"In your dreams, Delia."

"No. In your nightmares, Brianna. You're not all you think you're cracked up to be." And both women laughed.

"Well, okay, Delia. Shimmy for us a little bit in that shiny, sexy red blouse. . . . . Hmmm. No, not as good as I'd look. Kind of pathetic, in fact." Brianna shook her head, in mock concern. "In fact, I may need to get that thing back from you. I wouldn't want my blouse to learn any ugly habits."

"Brianna, baby, I make this thing look hotter red than you do, by about a hundred degrees."

"Okay. I'll leave you with your illusions. So, where are you and Anderson going?"

"To a concert at Verizon Theatre. Group called 'Moe and the Lawn.' I hear the lead singer is named Moe, and he's the band leader. The rest of the guys in the band, naturally, would be . . . 'the Lawn,' I guess."

"Moe and the Lawn? That's corny. But it's got that home-made sound. They must have stayed up all night to think that one up."

"More likely, knowing how these things work, it was ten minutes and a pitcher of beer. Anyway, Anderson's going to take me to dinner first. At Gino's. You know, that place near downtown. Near the Verizon."

"And afterward?"

"Well, maybe it's time to let Anderson take me home and see if he's any good."

"Mercy me! And where's that? Home, I mean?"

"He usually ends up staying at the InterContinental on the West Loop. You know, he's from out of town. That's what I told you. And that's pretty close to Orinoco Oil's headquarters, and it's a real luxury hotel."

"Where's this magical guy, this Anderson, come from?"

"Some place I've never heard of, way up north. And he's also in the oil business, just like your guy Alan."

"I guess we just have got the same kind of taste in guys, even if I am the better looking one of us." Brianna laughed. Delia, for her part, looked puzzled and tossed her long black hair around, just so she could communicate to Brianna that she had it wrong, about who was better looking.

7

MARIA

The day after Delia's big night with Anderson, Robert Herrick was in his office, at the massive mahogany desk, with Tom Kennedy facing him. They were doing what they called "intake": deciding whether to accept one or two of the dozens of new cases that other lawyers referred to them every week.

They had celebrated their success in the Escondido case all too briefly. Now, it was on to another task: the task of deciding which new cases to take. The task of building for the future.

"Wait a second, Tom." Robert Herrick looked puzzled. "This next case, you said, is what we call a 'Title Seven' case? About sex discrimination, right?"

"No. Age discrimination." Robert Herrick's partner smiled, because this opportunity was unusual.

"But our plaintiff in this . . . ahhh . . . Age Discrimination case . . . . Ahhh, Tom, what was it that you said she, our potential client, does for a living?"

"Well . . . , she is what some people would call an . . . 'exotic dancer.'"

"An exotic dancer?"

"Yep."

"And she's been discriminated against because of her age? Allegedly, at least?"

"That's right. The referring lawyer is Albert Hodge. You know, he's connected with a lot of these . . . dancers . . . the ladies who labor in this . . . industry. This particular lady, she's named Aviva. She's forty-two. And she's still . . . dancing. Or at least, she wants to. We have an expert witness who says she still can."

"An 'expert witness'? An expert in . . . exotic dancers??"

"Yes, and a pretty good one, too. This guy was manager of The Stork Club for more than ten years. He's our expert witness. And in his professional opinion, this lady is still good at it. His report says, and I quote: 'This here Aviva, she can stand up to the kids.'"

"Wooo." Robert Herrick threw his head back. His expression said that he was struggling to reconcile his distaste for the classy sleaze of the topless bars that sprouted here on so many local street corners, with his distaste for mistreatment of working people. An "exotic dancer" was a working stiff, wasn't she? And she could be ... discriminated against, couldn't she? Just like anyone else? Herrick looked at Tom Kennedy. "What's our evidence of age discrimination? What did we get from Albert Hodge?"

"Well, they've demoted this Aviva to being just a waitress. And Aviva says ... she says the guy in charge told her, 'Aviva, it's because you're over the hill. Aviva, you are too old.'"

"Uh-oh. That's against the law."

"Well, yes, but ... It's only against the law if, in fact, he did say it. *If* he said it. I mean ... if he said it, number one; and if a jury thinks he meant it, number two; and if she isn't actually 'over the hill,' number three; and if the jury believes he didn't really think so, but just demoted her because she was forty-two, number four. But ... if he actually demoted her honestly, for a reason that had to do with her, ahhh ... job performance ... then, there's no case, and it doesn't matter whether he was right in thinking that, or whether he was wrong. That's a lot of hoops to jump through."

Kennedy paused. "And naturally, the guy denies he said anything about her age, or anything remotely like that."

"Naturally. Lots of hoops to jump though, and at the very beginning, there's a he-said-she-said. Which we'd have to get over. Why can't anything in a lawsuit ever turn out to be clear-cut? I mean, if you watch *Damages* or *Perry Mason*, it's always a sure thing."

"I'm sensing that you want to move on." Tom Kennedy smiled, again. "Yes, it's about people's rights, and justice; but at the same time, you can't right every wrong. You've got to have at least a minor amount of evidence."

"Right. Call up Albert Hodge and express our regrets." It was always hard to refuse to get involved in righting an injustice—or even what could be, might be, called an injustice—including the demotion of a topless dancer; and Herrick's voice showed this ambivalence. But choices were what it was about. "If we charge off at every case, like Don Quixote and Sancho Panza charged at windmills, we won't be able to charge at the ones that really count. Even after all these years, it's hard to tell, sometimes."

They both looked out the floor-to-ceiling, greenhouse-style windows toward the west, where Buffalo Bayou threaded through a broad greensward toward the Galleria. Kennedy sat at one of the three desk chairs and looked over the stacks of expanding files that covered the surface in front of him. The beautiful oriental carpet that surrounded them was full of crescents, diamonds, circles, and bands, all in a riot of colors, and the geraniums flowered in shades of red and pink.

Robert Herrick had been phenomenally successful. But to the legal community, he still was known as the "Famous Lawyer for the Little Guy." And he still thought that way.

It was Herrick that broke the silence. "Tom, you remember the problem with Brianna Edwards?"

"Of course. The problem of the possibly fraudulent boyfriend, Alan." Kennedy shook his head. "Brianna's unusual, I guess—kind of a clueless Valley Girl, you know, and really messy with her surroundings—but she's smart, and she works hard, and I wouldn't necessarily say she was exactly . . . strange. But this problem is strange."

"You know, Tom, I'd like to do something to help Brianna."

"Robert, you always want to help, even when it's not sensible." Kennedy looked amused. "You're the lawyer for the hopeless case. You like everybody, and you want to get involved, even when it's sure to backfire. Like now."

"I guess so." Robert Herrick looked uncertain.

"It's your tragic flaw, like the main guy in a Greek drama."

"Maybe we can put one of the investigators on it. And at least find out who this Alan is. Just to give Brianna some peace of mind. She's going crazy over this, you know."

"That's you, Robert Herrick." Kennedy's grin was as wide as a federal courtroom. "That's you. I suppose you learned your manners at Harvard." He pronounced it "HAAAH-vud," the way they do in Massachusetts.

Robert Herrick had gone to Harvard on a baseball scholarship. After that, and after a time in the Army—as a cook, of all things—he'd gone back to school, at the University of Houston Law Center, where he'd finished at the top of his class. His twenty-six lawyers handled commercial cases, now, as well as personal injury claims, almost always on the side of the injured party: the injured plaintiff, or the wronged small business. The defense lawyers who paid his clients huge sums all liked him, and they referred to him as "The Baby-Faced Assassin," because of his youthful looks. And his ability to beat them at trial.

"Keep out of it, Robert," Kennedy laughed. "Don't make it worse. You'll only screw it up."

As if to punctuate Kennedy's advice, the telephone buzzed. The intercom.

Donna de Carlo's voice came over the line. "Robert, it's Maria. The lady known as the red-headed Cuban. Your . . . beautiful . . . *wife!*"

"My wife always calls at the key moment," Robert smiled. "Right when we're having an uninterrupted good time. It's like she can sense when there's a party, and she wants to be there too."

Maria Melendes had floated to Florida from Cuba when she was a child. Her father was a prominent dissident—a wealthy doctor—who had escaped from Castro's prisons. Her journey to the present had featured many twists and turns.

Robert pushed the button on the telephone. "Hi, sweetheart. Always nice to hear from you."

His smile widened. "But Maria, I hope that this time it's not one of your pranks. Like the time that you called up and pretended to be a Supreme Court Justice. Or the time that you told us about that serial killer, . . . only it took a while before we figured out that it was a joke, and the guy wasn't really on the loose. Or the time that. . . ."

"Lucky you!" Maria Melendes said, in her bounciest tone. "I don't plan any of these things. Not this time. Next time, watch out."

Maria Melendes was the first woman Robert had been able to care about since his first wife's death. Even now, as he thought about it, he reached toward the heavy gold frame that held his favorite picture of Patricia. She'd had ovarian cancer and died after more than seventeen years of marriage. Whenever there was a moment of uncertainty, Robert would extend his fingers, involuntarily, toward her portrait.

"Maria, we're grateful for your newfound maturity." He laughed. And so did Maria. And Tom.

Maria Melendes wasn't a timid sort. Quite the opposite. She was an assistant district attorney, and she had an unusual job in which she was referred to as "The D.A.'s Official Killer." When a capital murderer got the death sentence and the appellate courts affirmed it, that was only the beginning of the journey, because a seemingly endless loop of habeas corpus petitions and stays of executions would start. Proceedings in state courts and federal courts, and in trial courts and appellate courts, with the Board of Pardons and Paroles getting into the act—and the Governor, too, needing to be informed about every case and occasionally granting stays.

Maria, then, would inherit the gut-wrenching responsibility for representing the State. And getting the execution carried out—or trying to. Or, in some cases that called for painful judgments, "confessing error," which meant agreeing with the lawyers for the condemned prisoner and joining in the request to the judges to throw out the death sentence. Good judgment about when to give up, and agree with the defense, was an important part of the job.

Sometimes the convict would make eleventh-hour claims of innocence, based on doubtful evidence that his lawyers would claim they had just discovered. And it was essential to be able to recognize the unusual cases in which these claims had some remote possibility of being legitimate. But if the story was fraudulent, Maria's job was to say so, all the way up to the Supreme Court.

And the job included fielding flack from Hollywood types like Kenny Rogers or Danny Glover, whose ignorance was deep enough so that they thought they knew when some "other dude" had really committed the crime. To that part of the world, Maria Melendes was a force of darkness.

Now, she quietly said to her husband, "Robert, I just heard that the Fine Arts Museum is going to have an exhibit featuring Jules Olitski. And I don't know why I didn't find this out earlier, but it'll be there for a while. Robert, I really want you to take me there. Pleeease."

"Jules Olitski!" Robert wrinkled his nose. "He follows the 'blob' theory of art. The way he paints . . . well, there's this squared oval of yellow, right above a rounded square of turquoise and another blob of orange. That's the guy you're talking about?"

"Careful. I think he's great. And I'm not so sure about you." She laughed. Maria Melendes laughed a lot.

"Well, Jules Olitski isn't as bad as Jackson Pollock." Robert rubbed his chin, thoughtfully. "You know, that abstract-expression guru, Jackson Pollock, who puts his canvas on the floor and drips messy smears of paint across it. Olitski? He's not as bad. He's also not as bad as Rothko, either: the guy who does just black canvases, black blobs, without any color. At least Olitski has blobs that come in different colors."

"So, I guess that means you'll take me, then?"

"Not right this minute. We're in the middle of something."

"No, silly." She laughed, for the umpteenth time. "The exhibit isn't here yet. You'd better not be working every night for the rest of the year."

"All right." He sighed, a painful, henpecked kind of sigh, but he laughed at the same time.

Maria's unusual history included growing up in suburban Miami and learning English there. Before she was twenty, she left home for Las Vegas—and made her living as a showgirl. Her experiences there motivated her in an uncommon way to seek justice against people who preyed on other people. After working her way through law school, she naturally gravitated toward the District Attorney's office. Her happy-go-lucky, prankster personality was the product of all these experiences.

Tom Kennedy spoke up, now. "Maria, it seems that there's peace in the family, since Robert's promised to take you to the art museum. And so, maybe you can solve another problem for us. You remember Brianna Edwards? She's got boyfriend problems. A vague sort of boyfriend problems. We don't know just what sort, because she doesn't know, but she's asked for help from your husband, which would mean Robert, here. Because, well, I guess . . . Robert is everybody's Father Confessor."

Kennedy chuckled. "It seems Brianna's got some circumstantial evidence that her boyfriend is not who he seems. Heck, the evidence is kind of thin, but he may even be two-timing her. And Robert says he wants to help."

"Robert, I know you." Maria's analysis of the situation was immediate. "I like Brianna Edwards, but I know you. This isn't likely to be something you can solve." And she said the same thing that Tom Kennedy had said earlier. "Robert, if you do anything, you'll just screw things up. Don't make it worse."

"Well . . . all right." Robert Herrick looked doubtful. "But Brianna's the best legal assistant I've ever had. And . . . well, I'm worried about her."

8
BRIANNA AND ALAN

T hank you, Alan." Brianna was breathless as she got out of the car with her boyfriend. "This was really fun, even if I'm a little heady from the wine. In fact, that's how I know it was fun."

"You're welcome, Brianna." Alan was, in fact, six foot two, with eyes of blue. Brianna looked at him while they waited for the elevator. He looks great, she thought. Dark blue suit. Blond hair. Well cut mustache and small beard. Light blue eyes, almost gray. "I liked it too. I really enjoy your company, Brianna. You're kind of a smartass."

"Thank you . . . I think. I'm a . . . smartass?"

"Well, I guess I should have said you're 'quick and clever.' But that just means the same thing. It's a compliment. Smartass is virtually a require-ment for me, because I'm one too, you know."

"Okay. Thanks." She laughed. And then, she turned wistful. "But . . . Alan. You know I could fall for you. And I know so little about you. You wouldn't string me along, would you? You're not married? You told me. But I want to be sure about that."

"No and no. Do you want to see the divorce papers?" He unlocked his room, at the InterContinental Hotel.

"No. I'm sorry. I . . . I want to see something else. And do what we both want to do."

He looked at her, startled by her intensity.

"Alan, you know I love you. I want to be with you. I want to give my-self to you."

Now he was fumbling, badly. And breathing a lot. Unbuttoning the buttons on her blouse took him forever. Then: "Alan, baby, this bra opens in the front. It's easier than you're making it."

"Oh. Okay." Quietly.

And at that, with her breasts swaying, she knelt. She fumbled, too, but less, fumbling because of the wine.

His body stiffened, and he made a noise. He could handle it only for a moment, until he lifted her to her feet, then lifted her off the floor, and now, she cried out, partly in pain and partly in anticipation, as he began to move with her. She climbed, climbed, climbed . . . until it all seemed ready to burst, and she was screaming, and his body shuddered.

Afterward, he lay behind her, with her facing away from him, and with his arm around her. They both were quiet, so quiet that they heard slight, muffled noises from the street, of traffic passing. It was odd to hear those sounds, but not unpleasant.

Brianna stirred slightly. She started to say something, but then thought better of it. Then:

"Alan, honey?"

"Yes, baby?" Softly.

"I told you about Delia. My roommate. She's dating a guy named Anderson. The next time you come to town, could we get together with them, Delia and Anderson?"

"You mean an old-fashioned double date?"

"Yes."

"I don't know, Brianna. For now, I'd just like to keep you to myself. I'd rather not."

Again, she was quiet. For a moment. For what seemed a long time. Just thinking. Her mind raced. She closed her eyes. Then:

"Alan, remember what I said. I could really fall for you. Heck, I *am* falling for you. I love you. I don't do this with just anybody. I may already have fallen for you! In spite of myself, in spite of being careful about *not* falling for you." She hesitated. "You're sure there's not somebody else? And you're not married?"

*   *   *

Five minutes after Brianna was gone, Alan was on the phone. "Carlos? You're going to bring me the usual 'gift box'? I know, I know. It's a pain driving this stuff back to Ohio, making that long trip instead of flying, but it's not going to be forever. And the money's worth it."

He paused to hear the answer. "Good."

Another pause. Then:

"You know, Carlos, it's not just for cover. Oh, I mean, yes, these two women, they're good cover. But they're also a lot of fun." He laughed.

"Sometimes, I almost feel bad about taking advantage of these two," he went on. "This Brianna, she's all lovey-dovey and all over me, and she keeps telling me how delicate she is. She's had a slew of boyfriends who've trashed her. She even confided to me that she was molested for years by a Catholic priest when she was little, and it still affects her. She wants me to tell her about me, and how much I love her. Good luck, with that."

He snorted. "Anyway, back to business. Bring the gift box, Carlos, and I'll meet you in the garage. It's parking space B-56 this time."

9
BETRAYAL

L ater, back at the apartment, Delia had a shocked look on her face. But it was a resolved look. A look of painful acceptance.

"Well no, Brianna, I guess nobody can be absolutely sure about this. Or about anything. In college, I studied the so-called 'skeptical philosophers,' and there were some of those skeptical guys who were pretty smart, and they said that you can't ever know anything for sure. Not even whether you are 'you.'

"But it's pretty clear, in the real world," she went on, helplessly. "Your Alan and my Anderson are frauds. I . . . I don't see a way around it. I've got to believe it."

"The son of a bitch." Brianna looked down at the floor.

"Look here. I Googled the guy. Under one name, and then the other. And nothing came up. And then, I Googled both names. And his last name. 'Anderson Alan Blackburn.' And I also put in 'Ohio,' where our so-called Alan and so-called Anderson both live, by amazing coincidence. And, Bingo. There is an Alan Anderson Blackburn who is a vice president for Orinoco Oil, in Findlay, Ohio. And that's one of the biggest oil companies in the country, and they've got their main headquarters here in this city, and obviously, he comes here all the time on business."

"Still . . . ." Brianna was holding onto hope, just like a penniless would-be zillionaire who buys a lottery ticket after the jackpot shoots above two hundred million.

"Well, it took a lot more searching. But here's what I found. This Alan Anderson Blackburn works for Orinoco Oil, and he has a Ph.D. in mechanical engineering from CalTech."

"You don't have to remind me. That's the same degree my Alan has."

"And my Anderson."

"And 'our' Alan Anderson. They're . . . the same guy."

"I just can't believe it."

"Neither can I. But we've got to believe it, because it's true."

"I just can't believe it."

"Well, I fished around that web site, and it's pretty well hidden, but there's a picture of this Alan Anderson Blackburn. And guess what? It's my so-called 'Anderson.' And . . . ."

Brianna stared at the picture with one eye closed, squinting, trying not to look. "And, yes, it's my so-called Alan."

"We've been had. We've both been doing all kinds of, well, intimate . . . stuff . . . with the same guy, when we wouldn't have done any of it if we had known that . . . we were both having sex with the same fraudulent guy, for goodness sake!"

"He told me there was no one else. I begged him to tell me."

"He told me the same thing. And wait. It gets worse."

"How could it get worse? Do I even want you to tell me?"

"No, you don't. But here it is. The guy's married. Got a little sweetie named Gwen stashed away in Findlay, Ohio. Actually, 'Gwendolyn.' That's her real name: Gwendolyn. It says so, right here on the website."

Silence. Then:

"I want him dead." Brianna practically shouted the words.

"I do too."

"I'm serious."

"So am I."

Brianna shook her head. "I'd like to shoot him. I'd like to strangle him. I'd like to drown him. I'd like to do a lot more to him, all slowly."

"But the trouble is, we don't know how to do any of those things." Delia shook her head. "You and I, we couldn't do those kinds of things."

There was a long silence. Then, from Brianna:

"I went to school with a guy who dropped out. Elmo Naughton. He's been in all kinds of trouble. But Elmo's one of these bad boys with a heart of gold, if you know what I mean. And he owes me. I bailed him out once and helped him go straight. For about two weeks."

"His name is Elmo?" Delia laughed. "Elmo? Brianna, did you hang out with Bert and Ernie too?"

"Yes, it's a dumb name." Brianna laughed too, in spite of her pain. "But yes, it's Elmo. And if he heard anybody making fun of it, he got violent. But I bet that wacky Elmo can get the job done. He'll help us teach Alan Anderson Blackburn a real good lesson."

They looked at each other. Finally, Delia said, "Should we really do this? Not really, but we can pretend."

"I want to do it right now, while I'm still mad enough to do it. But you're right. Let's just scare the hell out of him."

*   *   *

Across town, Robert Herrick was with his family. He wasn't aware, yet, of what Alan Anderson Blackburn had done to Brianna and Delia.

That evening, in fact, he made chicken Cordon Bleu with artichokes and glazed carrots. "I'm always amazed that you know how to do this kind of thing," Maria said when she was alone with him in the kitchen.

Robert just laughed. "I didn't learn it at the body shop." He had told her about growing up in New England—in Providence. He had worked at an automobile body shop to make ends meet while he lived alone with his mother.

"And I'm sure you didn't learn how to cook at Harvard."

"I learned it in Da Nang, of course." He laughed again. "In Vietnam. Most of the time I was a platoon leader, and I did search-and-destroy missions. But there was a time when I was in Da Nang, stationed as a . . . cook. They drafted me from law school to make me into . . . a cook."

"But it's not very macho, now, what with you baking a raspberry soufflé!"

"These aren't things I would have made in the army. There wasn't much Cordon Bleu, and not many soufflés."

"Well, macho or not, I appreciate your attitude. I even stopped going out with Cuban guys, right after I met you, Robert. You know, because I told you how it was. They're too macho, Cuban guys. Some of them have attitudes toward women that are . . . well, different from what would be ideal, let's just say. I decided I would go for the soufflé type."

"That's certainly what I am. That's my identity. The soufflé type." And they both laughed, and they went in to join the others.

Robert's mother, Rosalie, was there. And his daughter Pepper. The family knew that you'd better not call Pepper by her real name, Cynthia, because it was long past being out of fashion with her. Jonathan, her new husband, was there with little Robert III, the baby. And finally, there was Robert Herrick Junior, whom everybody called Robby, so they could distinguish him from his father, the original Robert Herrick.

After dinner, everyone adjourned to the living room. The kids had their eyes glued to the television, because football was on. Jonathan and Robby understood football because they had played it, but Pepper just kept saying "unnecessary roughness!" after every play. Then, she realized that Maria was almost like a visiting professor of football. Maria could make it interesting.

"See, Pepper, that's what's called a suicide pass." Maria pointed. "The quarterback drifts to the right with a play-action fake handoff like that. And then, he turns and throws it across the field, deep to the left, to the receiver who's on a fly pattern toward the flag."

"A suicide pass? Why's it called that?" Pepper wanted to know.

"Well, Jonathan and Robby know what I'm talking about, but I guess it's not obvious. First thing, it's suicidal because it's a slow-developing play. The pass rush from the defensive end and the cornerback is likely to sack the quarterback, and usually, all you have is a running back or at most a fullback to block out there on the right side. Second, the quarterback has to turn around and throw across his body. Not an easy thing. Third, he's got to throw it over all of the defenders, and it's suicidal because if he doesn't get sacked, he's likely to get intercepted."

"Why's anybody want to do it, then, if it's that suicidal?" Pepper wanted to know.

"Surprise. It has the advantage of surprise. Strategies in war, in chess, or in football, all involve surprise. If it's done right, even if it involves a lot of confusion and weakness and risks, the suicide pass can fool the other team, because the defensive guys follow the quarterback while he goes to the right. And a suicide pass can go for a big gain, just like what we just saw."

Now it was Robert who was impressed. "I'm amazed that you know this kind of stuff."

"I guess it's because of the same randomness of fortune, in my life, that taught you how to make a soufflé, in your life." She laughed. "But Robert, as I always tell you, you look really corny in that apron that says, 'Kiss the Cook.'"

"Well, as I've always told you, one of my clients gave this to me after one of my favorite cases. And as I've also told you, I've never gotten around to getting a more 'with it' apron."

"I guess you're not very *with it,* even for a parent," Pepper said, and everyone laughed. "Good thing you've got Maria. She's more with it, I'd say."

Since everyone was laughing, Pepper added, as she sometimes did, "And Grandma is more with it, for a grandma!" But no one particularly laughed at this—they never did, no matter how many times she tried it—and Pepper looked disappointed.

"And that brings up something else," Grandma Rosalie said. "I've asked you this before, but I've always wondered how you turned out to be so 'with it,' Maria, after you came to the United States from a different language, and different culture, and different set of values. How?"

Maria's eyes watered just a little at that. And Robert said, "Her father believed in the total immersion theory of education. He didn't suffer fools gladly, and he didn't put up with what he called 'spoiled kids.'"

He looked at Pepper. "Hear that, kid? I'm not going to put up with any 'spoiled kids' either."

The remark struck Pepper's barely post-adolescent sense of humor as rip-roaringly funny. She started laughing and almost couldn't stop. "Daddy, that's just . . . ridiculous."

"I suppose your parents wanted you to become an American, Maria," Rosalie said. "And to adopt a new way of thinking . . . this country's way of thinking."

"Not at all," Maria said quickly. "They went through a lot. I think it was hardest on my mother. She had been a proud society lady, and here she was, beginning with nothing, in a country where her speech was confused and halting. She worked in laundries and hotel housekeeping. She did everything possible to hold onto her Cuban heritage. And to make me remember it. She gave money to anyone who worked to make Cuba free, and she shopped in the Cuban markets, and she bet on the jai alai games.

"Whenever it came up, whenever there was something about America that wasn't good, that wasn't perfect, they had a standard line, my father and mother. They said . . . 'It wasn't that way in Cuba.' It was as if they were saying to me, 'This is where you come from, and you owe respect.'"

Improbably, Maria had moved to Nevada years ago, after growing up in Hialeah, just north of Miami. She had made her living in Las Vegas . . . as a showgirl. Her background was so unusual for an assistant district attorney that newspapers and magazines had done feature stories about her. Some of them were embarrassing, such as the one that showed her in costume, smiling sweetly from behind a mountain of red hair, feathers, faux pearls, and blue-mauve-and-rose eye shadow so thick that it showed hills and valleys, wearing pink satin and sequins and plenty of bare skin. The caption had said, "Maria Melendes: The Showgirl Who Turned Assistant District Attorney!" She found herself constantly explaining it to co-workers who loved to tease her: "Look, it was a family show! We weren't exotic dancers. We were *showgirls*. We were like that big dance troupe in New York, on Broadway. You know! We were like the *Rockettes!*"

Robert stared at her.

She is so different from me, he said to himself for the hundredth time. Maybe I can say these are healthy differences, but she is so opinionated, and so different. Instead of being a Democrat like me, she's a conservative Republican. She's incredibly neat, and except for having a housekeeper, I'm not. She's enamoured of those silly little romance novels, and they turn me right off. She loves stuffed animals, and I think they clutter the place. I'd like to sleep on Saturday afternoon, and she'd rather play tennis, or ride a horse, and have me come with her.

And for the thousandth time, he looked at her again. The dusky cork-screw curls of sunset-red Cuban hair, falling in little ringlets that hung down below her shoulders. The perfect white, almost translucent, Hispanic skin that shimmered in the late light. The big almond eyes, so bright and glittering. The cheekbones that managed to be both high and soft, in a shadow slightly more rose-colored than the rest of her. The full, round lips. . . .

Then, suddenly, he was aware that she was looking back at him, and she smiled. She was beautiful. The room felt warmer, and his stomach felt that familiar puddle in it: the sensation that he had every time he looked at her.

"Tell us again about how you met each other!" demanded Rosalie.

"No," said Robert. "Not again."

"Of course," said Maria, ignoring him. "As you know, it was at a bar. I'm kind of ashamed of that. But it was one of those Bar Association get-togethers, which just happened to be at a bar. And I had this green dress on, which he's told me he liked because it set off my hair. I don't have it anymore because I wore it out, that green dress, wearing it for him. Anyway, he walked up to me, and he said, "Hi! Who are you?' That was his masterly pick-up line."

"The direct approach," said Pepper approvingly. She'd heard it all before. And she said the same thing she always said when she heard the story: "Daddy, I didn't know you had it in you."

And they all laughed. Robert laughed with the puddle still in his stomach.

10
NOTHING THE LAW CAN DO

The next afternoon, Robert's cell phone rang. "Hello." Here in the stadium, he didn't have time to see who was calling.

"Robert? . . . Robert Herrick?"

"This is Robert Herrick."

"Robert, this is Brianna Edwards. You got my email, right? And you told me to call."

"Oh. Okay, Brianna. Let me get out of this area a little bit and get someplace where I can hear you."

"Where are you? What's all that noise?"

"It's the season opener. University of Houston Cougars against the University of Texas Longhorns. Baseball. I'm at the baseball stadium. And it's full. There are people, like, hanging from the sky. All yelling."

It was well known that Robert Herrick had gone to the University of Houston for law school, and that he was one of the school's biggest financial contributors. Less well known was that he had pitched in college baseball. His team, at Harvard, had gone to the College World Series. When the Cougar baseball team had heard that, they had made spitting noises of a kind that, in baseball players, is a sign of respect. "He pitched in the College World Series!? Wow."

"And so I try not to miss the season opener for the Cougars," Robert told Brianna, with a smile. "It's my school."

"Well, I hope they win. Big Time. And Robert, I hope you can help me, too, and help me Big Time."

"Brianna, I'd do whatever I could for you."

"What can I do about this guy, Alan Anderson Blackburn? What he did to me and Delia has got to be illegal."

"Well . . . ."

"Isn't there something I can sue him for? Like, he impersonated someone else! I looked it up, and that's a crime."

"No, Brianna, the crime is 'Impersonating a Public Servant.' If somebody pretends to be a police officer and pulls someone over to the side of the road, it's a crime."

"But isn't there a civil lawsuit for this?"

"In the first place, he didn't 'impersonate' anyone. And anyway, no."

"Well, you're the best lawyer I know. I guess you must be right."

Even after practicing law all these years, Robert Herrick still made an impression on women jurors. They seemed to respond to his youthful good looks, with the shock of dark brown hair that fell over this forehead. And men were impressed that he could articulate his final argument at the end of a long case, without notes, and keep everyone's attention. He was rich beyond most people's imagination, but he worked, still, because he liked making things turn out right. And he was frustrated, now, that he couldn't make things right for Brianna Edwards, who had done a good job while working in his office.

Brianna wasn't ready to give up. "There's this civil claim for 'intentional infliction of emotional distress,' you know."

Robert Herrick cringed. "Yes, there is. And after I got your email, that was what I thought about. But it's the hardest kind of claim to prove in court. Immediately after I thought about it, I knew it wouldn't work. Still, Brianna, I got one of the associates to look into it. She went through the cases, and she found absolutely nothing like this. And you can see why."

He searched for the right words to tell Brianna how impossible it was, but to show he understood how she felt. "They call them 'jilted girlfriend' cases. Pardon me for saying that, because I know you got mistreated, and it really hurt you, but my point is, any judge would say, 'this is just another "jilted girlfriend" case.' And the judge would say, 'If everybody sued whenever a boyfriend didn't tell the truth, the courthouse would be overrun.' I realize that that's not exactly your situation, and this is a case of a guy who mistreated two women who knew each other, but it's the same principle."

"But . . . it's not fair."

"I know. I'm sorry. The law doesn't always make things turn out so they're fair. There are more trashy things that people do, where the law can't help, than there are trashy things where it can help. The law just doesn't right every wrong."

"But . . . it makes you want to take the law into your own hands. I understand why vigilantes do what they do, after going through this."

As the conversation wound down, and they said goodbye, Robert thought to himself: "I didn't like the way that 'vigilante' comment sounded."

*   *   *

"What did Mr. Herrick say?"

"Nothing, really." Brianna's eyes suddenly were heavy and wet, again. "It's time for me to go to my volunteer station at the hospital. You know, at the ICU. The Cardiac Intensive Care Unit. It'll take my mind off things, when I'm dealing with these families of heart transplant patients."

"But wait!" Delia was really concerned, now. "You didn't answer me. What did he say, your lawyer?"

"Exactly what we thought he would say. There's no way to sue Alan Anderson Blackburn. But . . . listen, Delia. . . . I've got to go."

"Okay. No way to sue him. So, I guess . . . we go to Plan B."

"Maybe. I don't know. I don't care about Plan B, right now. . . . Delia, please: ask me later. Because . . . I am so . . . unhappy. Alan's all over my heart. I still love him. And I hate him. In the back of my mind, I think I was hoping that Robert would have some legal way of getting it all straightened out, so that . . . Alan would be faithful. Crazy, I know; but that's what I was thinking."

With an effort, she cleared her eyes. "But I've got to get over it. And Delia, look: I've got to go."

"I understand. It's nice, what you're doing, Brianna, volunteering at that hospital. Giving something back. The stories you've told me about the Cardiac ICU are just amazing. I still can't believe what you said about what happens when someone dies—that you're the first one to really talk to the widow, when a guy dies there. You're the first one to talk to the woman who's . . . lost her husband?"

"That's right. It's hard. Best way to talk to her, I've found out, is not to even try to talk to her, or get her to talk, because after all, her husband has just now died, poor woman—whoever she is. No matter how tough she seems, I just hold her hand."

"Wow."

"Then, I talk to the other people in the family. The kids, usually. They aren't as hopeless as their mother, because even if Daddy is gone, they still have their companions, in their own lives—unlike their mother. They're full of grief, but they can talk, and usually, they want to. And their mother—she usually wants to *hear* them talk, even if she's not talking, even if she's not listening—instead of talking herself. She doesn't want to talk."

Delia was thoughtful, hearing that. "I never would have figured that out. Never."

"I usually ask the son or daughter, who aren't really kids of course, because by now they're grownups, to tell me what their Daddy liked to do, what he talked to them about, what they learned from him—and what he was like. But not in the past tense. I say, 'What is he like, your Daddy?'"

"Go ahead and go." Delia smiled. "I won't ask you what anyone was like—anyone in your past. It's the past . . . just the past, and it's gone. And you're a beautiful lady, Brianna. You're wonderful. Just remember that."

"Well, but a lot of times you keep telling me, Delia, how messy the floor is. I make the floor messy."

And both women laughed at that. Brianna walked to the door, and Delia said, after her, "You're wonderful. Just remember that."

11
PLAN B

At the office, next day, Robert smiled at her, but it was a forced smile. "I'm sorry, Brianna."

"I know. You've been great, Robert. You're one of the few people I've been able to tell about it. About Alan, I mean. And it's so strange, telling you about it, because you're my boss."

"Well, but that's not what matters in this situation!" He laughed, and after hesitating, she did too.

A little more seriously, he said: "There are a lot of things that the psychologists can tell you to do about this kind of thing. You should go and see one."

"No. Thank you . . . but No."

"Well, that's the reaction a lot of people have. And if that's your reaction, Brianna, I've found that it's not useful to try to talk you into it."

"I don't want to keep dwelling on the story of my being fooled by this worthless guy, even if it involves just having to tell it to a psychologist. I just want to get my head straight, myself. And I can do it."

He looked at her skeptically. "Brianna, I've had cases where psychologists have been important witnesses and consultants, and they can tell you how to deal with betrayal. You want to lash out, is the problem, and you can't lash out, and that makes you feel helpless. There's some standard advice that might do you some good. I'm not a psychologist, and the standard advice sounds corny, but it fulfills people's desires to take action and stop feeling like victims.

"Here's what works, Brianna, or so I'm told: doing something disrespectful to an image of the person who's wronged you, something to lift yourself mentally. Something as simple as taking a picture of the guy and pasting it to the bottom of your shoe. With every step, you're in control—

symbolically, at least, and symbols are what counts, here. I know, I know; it sounds crazy. But—the professionals—well, they tell me it helps a little, at least for some people. It's a matter of taking back your freedom of action, or your control over your thoughts, I guess."

"I'd like to do more than that." Brianna's eyes clouded. "I'd like to do . . . well, a lot more than that, to this man."

Robert stared at her for a moment. "Listen, Brianna. I don't want you going off the deep end. I don't want you doing something that's going to hurt you."

She made herself smile. "I won't go off the deep end. Don't worry. Robert, you're great. Thanks. I can't tell you how much I appreciate it."

*　*　*

The day lengthened, and Brianna had trouble getting through it while holding her tears back. The shadows lengthened, and the traffic was clumping, and then finally, she drove home. She had to think hard about her driving, to be able to control herself. It was like watching a movie of herself driving home to the apartment—she was that disconnected from herself.

*　*　*

"Baby, I understand," said Delia. "I'm hurt too. I wasn't into him as much you were, Brianna, but remember—I gave myself to him, too."

"It just doesn't seem to get any better. They say time heals all wounds, but I guess this one is going to take a lot of time."

"You need to do something to take back control of your thoughts. Even something that's just symbolic."

She was startled. "That's exactly what Robert said. He said, 'do something.'"

"So, we go to Plan B."

"Plan B. We want him dead. So we . . . do it. Or pretend to."

"Right. We take it all the way through. Almost."

"Delia, you and I don't know how to do this. We don't even know how to hire someone to do all of this, what we want to do. But—you remember my friend Elmo Naughton, that I mentioned?"

"Right. The guy with the wacked Muppet name."

"He's constantly in trouble, but he loves me, and I've helped him, and he's messed up his life, like I said, but he knows how to help us do this."

"This is going to be a big acting job. It's going to be hard, but if we do it right, we can get right up to the edge of it, just as a prank, but not quite, and we can scare the wits out of this worthless Alan-Anderson-Blackburn buzzard."

*   *   *

They both were quiet. And they sat and stared at nothing. And at the telephone. And at nothing. And finally, Brianna spoke.

"You and I have a reputation as pranksters. This is one of our bigger pranks." She picked up the telephone.

"Well, it will teach him a lesson. The world can't work this way. He lied and lied. And he knew he was sleeping with both of us, playing us against one another."

"Of course he knew." Brianna shook her head.

"He gave us two different names, for goodness sake! And he success-fully avoided seeing us at the same time, like on a double date. He knew, and that probably gave him a bigger charge."

Brianna's eyes clouded, and her mouth compressed. "He shouldn't get away with it. It's beyond making me mad. It makes me crazy. It makes me hurt, and I'm seeing all kinds of starry, fuzzy, reddish haze wherever I look, because I'm so hurt and so mad, and it's the kind of thing that . . . we gotta *do* something about."

She scrolled the telephone and pushed the button. There was a pause while it rang.

"Ahhhh . . . . Hello? Hello?"

"Hello? Is this Elmo Naughton?" Brianna's voice was too loud. Too angry.

The voice on the other end of the call seemed to come from a long dis-tance away, very slowly. "Who . . . is . . . this?"

"Elmo, it's Brianna Edwards." She looked at the phone, disgusted. "Elmo, are you messed up again?"

Elmo, in fact, had been stringing out lines of cocaine with a plastic pen with writing on the side, which advertised: "The Pink Pussycat Lair. Best Gentlemen's Club Ever." He put the pen down and took his eyes off the white powder, and he concentrated, so as not to seem "messed up."

Brianna asked again, "Elmo, are you messed up?"

"Oh, no, no, noooo. I'm never doing that again." He sniffed and held his head. "I learned my lesson about that a long time ago."

"Good." But Brianna was skeptical, and she let it show in her voice.

"Brianna, I owe you. You know I'd do anything to make a good impression on you."

"Okay. I'm going to let you do just that. We need to break somebody's knees. Actually, worse. And you know the kind of people who can do it."

There was a gurgling sound at the other end of the line. And a long silence. Then: "You want me to help you hire a hit man? Brianna, this doesn't sound like you."

"I know. How much does it cost?"

Elmo Naughton held his head again. And sniffed again. "It varies, and it can go as little as a few thousand, or up to hundreds of thousands. It's like anything else. You get what you pay for."

"We're only in the market for a few thousand, I'm afraid. It's just me and Delia." She heard Delia's words again, in her mind: "We're going to need to perform a good acting job."

"Let me see what I can do and I'll get back to you." He hesitated. "You've got to be really sure, about something like this. You want to kill this guy?"

Once again, Brianna thought, "It's got to be a good acting job, even if we're not really going to kill him."

He asked her again. "Brianna, you really want to kill this guy?"

A pause. Then: "Yeah. . . ." Her voice trailed off.

Brianna stabbed at the "End Call" button. She looked at Delia and frowned. "I didn't like the sound of Elmo Naughton's voice," she said, again too loudly.

12
HABEAS CORPUS

Five hundred miles away, Maria Melendes was carrying out her duties as "The D.A.'s Official Killer." She sat inside the fortress-like building in downtown New Orleans, where the Federal Court of Appeals has its headquarters.

There are no jury boxes here. That's because there are no jurors. There are speaker's stands for the lawyers, and there are long benches, impressive and heavy, for the judges to sit behind. The judges' work is simple, in a way: they study trial records, to decide whether trial judges have followed the law. It's antiseptic, and sometimes boring.

But this is where justice ends, in most cases. This is usually the court of last resort.

Maria's duty today was unpleasant. For an appeal, most of the lawyer's time is spent on research. Writing a brief is hard. The oral argument is flashier, but contrary to impressions made in Hollywood, the written brief is 90 percent of the job.

And Maria was here for a high-pressure case. It sounded innocuous: *Eddie Ray Bonner v. The State of Texas*. But the crime was gruesome. The jury had returned a death-penalty verdict, and if anyone was a fit subject for that, it was Eddie Ray Bonner.

*   *   *

Suddenly, a law clerk opened the back door with a series of *bang!* Sounds—three loud, ceremonial blasts, made by striking a steel knocker. He followed with an old-fashioned cry: *"Order in the court! Everyone rise, please!"* The three judges seemed to carry with them all the prestige and power of the oversized flag that hung behind them, as they marched majestically to the bench.

"Be seated, please," said the chief judge pleasantly. And then, in a monotone, he called the first case, which had a funny-sounding name: *"The Seagoing Vessel Known as 'The Tillie B.'"*

The judges listened, then, to a pair of lawyers who argued fine points of trial procedure about a collision between two freighters near the Mississippi coast, one of which was, of course, the "Seagoing Vessel Known as The Tillie B." If these lawyers thought the name of their case was funny, they didn't show it. They fought passionately about the law of the sea.

Next, there was a product liability case about a water heater that had caught fire. Maria was troubled to learn that it was easy to start this kind of conflagration. All you needed to do was to store petrochemicals near your gas-burning appliance.

Finally, the chief judge announced Maria's case: *"Eddie Ray Bonner v. Texas."* Her opponent would go first. The chief judge looked toward the counsel table and called the defense attorney's name: "Mr. Stanley."

The lawyer for the condemned man stood. "Lawrence Stanley, your honors, for Eddie Ray Bonner!" His voice was crisp and firm.

Maria listened as the defense lawyer gave a sanitized version of the crime. "The State's evidence allegedly showed that Eddie Ray Bonner killed a woman named Sally Ryan, and also Thomas Ryan, her six-month-old son."

Apparently, Maria thought, that's the way the defendant would like to describe it.

"But that's *not the issue!*" the defense lawyer went on. "Someone charged with a capital crime has a right to a trial with a proper jury. And in this case, the jury was selected illegally. The trial judge struck a potential juror off the panel in violation of the Supreme Court's decision in *Witherspoon v. Illinois.*

"And as your honors know, removing a single qualified juror from the jury panel is a *Witherspoon* violation. This court has to reverse, if even one potential juror was disqualified. Just one, who shouldn't have been removed."

The defense lawyer held up pages from the transcript. "There was one potential juror—a Mrs. Pamela Effinger, 68 years old—who reacted emotionally when the trial judge mentioned the death penalty."

He continued, "Ms. Effinger shed some tears, in fact. But the trial record shows that the trial judge continued to question her, rapid-fire, and this wasn't the right way to handle a frail woman who was under so much pressure. Ms. Effinger obviously felt harassed, and the trial judge lost patience, and he disqualified her—wrongly, we say."

Lawrence Stanley lifted a finger, to signal that his next point would be devastating. "I calculate that Ms. Effinger was considered for less than five minutes. Less than *five minutes!* With a man's life at stake."

"Well, that's not exactly like the *Witherspoon* case," said the chief judge. "How is it, that you say this is a *Witherspoon* violation?"

After Lawrence Stanley attempted to respond, the judges unleashed a concentrated series of questions. The lawyer answered each one by saying that the treatment of Ms. Effinger was "analogous" to the disqualification of potential jurors in the *Witherspoon* case.

The judge on the right side was puzzled, still. "But those kinds of jurors, who were wrongly disqualified in the *Witherspoon* case—they were jurors who promised that they would follow the law, even if they disagreed with the death penalty. Isn't that different from a juror who only cries, and can't say anything?" He touched the briefs in front of him. "Wasn't this lady simply unfit to be a juror?"

Exactly, Maria thought. But Lawrence Stanley was doing a good job for his client. The analogy, he kept explaining, was that Mrs. Effinger's tears and crying were brought on by the pressure she felt. "But the record doesn't show that she couldn't follow the law."

*   *   *

Finally, the defense lawyer's time ended. Maria stood up and walked quickly to the speaker's stand.

She opened the single manila folder on which she had written her notes. There were no papers in it. There were only handwritten notes on each leaf of the inside of the folder.

She stood still at the podium for exactly five seconds. Her manila-folder technique allowed her to do it smoothly. No fumbling to detract from her arguments. Nothing to suggest uncertainty.

"Counsel for Eddie Ray Bonner has acted as though this were the first time any judge has looked at this case." Maria's voice carried an accusing edge. "That's wrong, of course. Eddie Ray Bonner's death sentence has been reviewed by twenty-three judges before this habeas corpus case. Not to mention, twelve jurors.

"In the second place," she went on, "Congress and the Supreme Court have been clear in saying that we don't have an endless loop in which we forever retry, reconsider, and rehash every trial in an unlimited series of habeas corpus petitions. They've said this until they're blue in the face, but it won't mean anything until it's enforced by this court."

She lifted a paper that she had laid to the side, just to emphasize that she was quoting, now. "There is an Act of Congress about this. The Act says that at this point, from the remote position of this appeal, you cannot reconsider a claim already decided by a state court, and here are the exact words, *unless* the prisoner's claim was an . . . '*unreasonable* determination, in light of the evidence.'"

Maria looked up. "You didn't hear that from Mr. Stanley. The law says that you can only reverse if the state courts' decisions were *unreasonable*. There has to be an end, somewhere."

The chief judge agreed. "That's right, of course." But still, he seemed worried. "Maybe the trial judge should have tried harder to keep this potential juror. He dismissed the juror for 'unfitness.' That's a pretty general ground."

"Of course it is, your honor," Maria said immediately. "But it has to be. The law has to recognize a general category of jurors who are 'unfit' to serve, because some jurors react in bizarre ways. And this juror was extreme.

"When Mrs. Effinger heard that this was a capital case, well, she immediately started crying. She didn't answer a single question. The trial judge asked whether she wanted a break. More tears. The trial judge asked whether she wanted water. More tears. The judge took a break. Mrs. Effinger was still crying, a half hour later."

The judge on the right spoke, now. "This trial would have required a pretty strong stomach. It's gruesome. Does that have anything to do with the . . . '*reasonableness*' of excusing Mrs. Effinger?"

"That's right, your honor. The gruesomeness of the crime matters. Usually, we don't deal with the facts of the crime, in habeas cases. Just with procedure. But this time, the facts are important."

Her face contorted. "The evidence showed that Eddie Ray Bonner raped this poor woman, Sally Ryan, chosen at random. In her own home. Then, he strangled her.

"And the evidence showed the panic, the terror, and the torture that must have overwhelmed Sally Ryan's mind. While her baby was right there. While she was dying, Sally Ryan must have known what was going to happen to her baby. And the crying lady, Mrs. Effinger, would have had to feel that emotion, too.

"Then, after some violent acts and sexual acts on Sally Ryan's dead body"—Maria's face compressed again—"Eddie Ray Bonner dismembered her, and he burned the body parts. And then, he buried the body parts in the pasture. And he threw her baby, her helpless baby, into that shallow grave, before he closed it."

The courtroom was silent. It was an unreal silence. Maria continued: "This particular lady, this Mrs. Effinger, would have been unfit to hear any case. But especially this case. It just was not ... *unreasonable* ... for the trial judge to decide that she was 'unfit' to be a juror in this horrifying case."

She fielded questions from all three judges for what seemed forever, but really, for what was probably ten more minutes. Finally, a red light flashed on the podium. Meaning, "Stop."

She sat down, exhausted. Now, the court would recess. The judges would go home without thinking much more about Eddie Ray Bonner. Or Sally Ryan, or her baby.

But some day—on some date between tomorrow and an unknowable number of years from now—the judges would write an order deciding the case.

Maria shook hands with Lawrence Stanley. He had been handed a difficult task, doing his job as a public duty, with little or no pay. This kind of legal work was hard on both sides.

13

THE CALL TO THE HOMICIDE DIVISION

've looked all over our apartment for a pen or a pencil," Brianna announced. "A pen or pencil, so I can write down this phone number I just got."

Delia hesitated. "A pen or pencil? I don't know, Brianna. Look in those funny-looking drawers in the end tables, maybe."

"The ones by the couch?" Brianna carried her cell phone with her while she searched for the elusive writing instrument she needed. "Nothing in this drawer, on this side."

"Which side are you on?" Delia was in the bedroom, and Brianna couldn't hear her clearly. "Well, it doesn't matter which side you're on. Whichever side it is, try the other side."

"Okay. Trying the other side."

"Good idea. You're a smart lady."

"A little less sarcasm, please, Miss Know-It-All."

Brianna bent to reach the drawer in the matching end table. It stuck. She yanked it. Suddenly, the drawer flew out, and the contents scattered.

There were several pens. And a pencil. But there was something else that grabbed all of Brianna's attention. Her eyes bulged.

There was an envelope wedged in the corner of the drawer. The handwriting was familiar. Instantly, she saw that it was Alan's handwriting. Or Anderson's, if you looked at it from Delia's point of view. Or Alan Anderson's, if you looked at it from the perspective of the information they had found on the internet.

"It's an envelope from my Alan, my beloved Alan, addressed to Delia," she whispered to herself. Her eyes suddenly were wet.

There was a crumpled letter that stuck out of the envelope. Without thinking, she unfolded it and smoothed it.

By now, there were tears running down Brianna's face. She saw Delia's name. Again without thinking, she read on. Her heart was in her throat. She thought, "Alan, I loved you. What are you doing now?"

She read the words. Loving affectionate words, but not addressed to her. "My beautiful Delia." The same thing he said to me! "My beautiful Brianna," he called me! Her thoughts pounded; they hammered in her head. Then, she read, "You're my one and only." The same corny expression he used with me. But this isn't written to me.

And then, "I want to make love to you again, my Delia. Right now." Brianna's tears were interfering with her ability to see the handwriting. She brushed her hand over her eyes.

Alan's letter went on, in familiar words. "Is it all right if next time we see each other, we rush on over to where we can be alone, and we make love first thing?"

"Just what he . . . said to me," Brianna whispered to herself. "And the next time I saw him . . . we did."

She dropped Delia's letter on the floor. And she stood still. A hot wave flashed over her. She felt a despair so deep that she could barely look at Alan's letter any longer. From the bottom of a well, from a dark hole of loss, she looked up at the ceiling. And then she braced herself.

She whispered, "Alan, you can't be allowed to get away with what you've done to me."

*   *   *

The Houston Police Department's Homicide Division is at 51 Riesner Street, on the edge of downtown, in a disheveled, outdated building. When the call came in, Detective Derrigan Slaughter was discussing football with his partner, Donnie Cashdollar. Slaughter was a huge, courtly African-American officer, always perfectly dressed, this time in a black pinstripe double-breasted suit with a solid silver tie.

Detective Cashdollar, on the other hand, was exuberantly—if less elegantly—decked out in a green jacket, ill-fitting blue pants, a maroon-and-gold striped shirt, and a red tie with little irregularly spaced yellow stars. It was a kind of trademark, the resplendent Slaughter with the sloppy Cashdollar, and by now, everybody at the Cop Shop expected this duo to exhibit their well-known contrast.

"They done ripped they britches, our football team, letting that defensive end go." Derrigan Slaughter glowered at the stupidity of the Houston Texans. "Ain't gonna be no pass rush at all, this season."

"You wait and see. This new guy is going to take over, and he's gonna do as much as the old guy did. That new guy, Whitney Mercilus, you know."

"Yes, he be 'Mercy-less,' this Mr. Mercilus. And he be a really big Neee-grow." Derrigan Slaughter said it just for fun, because he liked wordplay, and in spite of being black himself, he liked bugging his partner a little with edgy language. He also liked proving that he was beyond worrying about race, which Cashdollar wasn't, quite. "But this new guy," the big detective went on, "he ain't as fast as before, and he's still a kid."

Cashdollar glowered back, then laughed. He picked up the ancient old-fashioned telephone on its third ring and pushed the button. "Homicide! Detective Cashdollar speaking."

"Ahhhh. Is this the Homicide Department?"

"The Homicide Division. That's what I said."

"This is Elmo Naughton."

It took a moment before Donnie Cashdollar connected the name to that scruffy druggie with the wild ponytail, whom he'd been sorry to have known for so many years. Then:

"Elmo Naughton! Last time I saw you, you were pretty messed up." Detective Cashdollar paused and listened. "You still messed up on coke, Elmo? You messed up now? You sound like you got a mouthful of mashed potatoes mixed with some thumbtacks down your throat."

"Oh, no, no, nooo. I'm never going there again. I learned my lesson."

"Good. That's . . . good. So, Elmo: what can we do you out of?"

"I got someone who wants to hire a hit man."

"Well, what you calling us for, son?" Cashdollar winked at Derrigan Slaughter, who knew how to follow a one-sided conversation. "We got no hit men here." And he smiled at his own joke.

Elmo Naughton obviously didn't get it. He coughed.

"Okay, Elmo, back up." Cashdollar's voice was matter-of-fact, now. "Tell us the facts. How'd this happen?"

"I got this friend. Excuse me, acquaintance. Brianna Edwards. She called me up and flat-out asked, 'Do you know how to get someone that can break somebody's legs?' And it turned out, she didn't want someone to break anybody's legs. She had someone she wanted dead. Killed. Whacked out. She wanted . . . curtains for this guy. Checkout time. The big sleep . . . ."

"Okay, Elmo, I got it. Do you know who the lucky fellow is? The intended vic?"

"Ahhhhh . . . excuse me?"

"Who is it, this Brianna wants to kill?" Across the little beat-up metal desk with the plastic top, Derrigan Slaughter shook his head.

"Some guy named Alan Anderson Blackburn. Lives somewhere in Ohio, but he comes to Houston all the time on business. I guess she wants the hit to be done there, in that suburb, you know, Sugar Land, where she lives."

"Okay. Murder in Sugar Land." Donnie Cashdollar was writing. "Well, we gotta call up this Alan Anderson Blackburn and tell him."

Elmo Naughton coughed again. "I can't imagine why Brianna called me about this."

"No, I can't imagine either," Detective Cashdollar deadpanned, and with effort, he managed not to laugh out loud, which is what Detective Slaughter was doing. Cashdollar put his hand over the phone.

"Say, what do I get for this?" Elmo's voice suddenly was bright and enthusiastic. "I've got a get-out-of-jail card now, don't I?"

"Well, a lot of steps got to happen before anything like that." Detective Cashdollar shook his head. "Tell you what. If all this pans out, and if you testify, I'll see if we can get some kinda good-conduct medal for a fine citizen like you."

"So," he went on, "it all depends on what happens next, about this . . . this Murder in Sugar Land."

*　　*　　*

Across town, at Delmar Stadium, it was almost halftime. Robert Herrick had seats in the bleachers, near the midfield line. It was the Lamar Redskins—the soccer team—against the Bellaire Cardinals.

"I've made it to most of the games where Robby has played," Robert said to Maria Melendes, speaking about his son, Robby. "I've missed a couple of these soccer games recently because of that case against Jimmy Coleman, the case for Mr. Escondido, who lost his one good lung. You know how that one was. But I wouldn't miss this particular game. Lamar High School against Bellaire High School; it's the battle of the century, almost."

Maria smiled. And he felt his stomach flutter, the way he always did when she smiled, even after all this time together with her. And laughing, she said, "Robert, do you have to exaggerate everything? How can it be the game of the century, when these two teams play soccer against each other every year, without fail, at the same time every year?"

He laughed. One of the wonderful things about Maria was how often she made him laugh. "Well, but Maria . . . I'm not in front of a court right now, or on the witness stand, you know. It's only the game of the year, I guess, and so I . . . *stand . . . corrected.* By you, of course, my Cuban wife. Cubans are very exacting. Very precise. Very bossy, too. Like you, my beautiful wife. But rhetorically, you've got to admit it's right, what I said; because every year, it *seems* like the soccer game of the century."

"Okay. I'll let you off the hook." And she laughed again. "Remember, I come from a family where getting a B instead of an A—which ought to be considered pretty good, right?—but getting a B meant having to give my father what he called 'a complete explanation' of why it wasn't an A. He would say, in Spanish, 'I've worked too hard all my life to have you acting lazy.' And then he would repeat it in English. Because of the way I was raised, I tend to be pretty precise about things. Even about minor exaggerations during soccer games, I guess."

Robert thought about that for an instant—and nodded. Maria had come to the United States from Cuba at the age of twelve. Her father was Dr. Jorge Melendes, who had been the respected Director-General of the hospital at Miramar, until he got crosswise of the Communists' national health administration. As soon as he could bribe his way out of Castro's jails, Dr. Melendes had gotten his wife and children out of Cuba. And using a vessel that was only one step up from an inner-tube contraption, they had floated to the shores of Florida. In a strange world, without being able to speak a word of English, Maria had made a new life.

"Look!" she said suddenly. "Robby has the ball. He's playing . . . what was the position? You told me, Robert. He's playing the position of . . . the right wing?"

"Yes. The right wing."

And they watched while Robert Herrick Junior handled the ball. And passed it to a midfielder.

"He's going to pull off what looks like it might be a pretty good give-and-go." Now, Robert was excited too, at seeing this.

Having given the ball to the midfielder, Robby did his next part of the give-and-go: the "go" part. He raced as fast as he could, down the right sideline, past the midfield defender, and deep into Bellaire territory—the other team's part of the field.

His own midfielder passed him the ball.

Robby dribbled three times and managed to pass around another defender. Here he was, alone in the right corner next to the opposing goal. He turned the ball and crossed it, kicking it in front of the goal.

One of his strikers was there . . . and muscled the ball, hard, toward the goal. The Bellaire goalie was there, and he blocked it. But it bounced out, and another kick by the striker put it into the corner of the goal.

Robby threw his arms into the air and ran toward the goal, toward his striker.

But something was wrong. The linesman was signaling.

The public address system crackled, and a loud voice boomed, "Offside!" The voice repeated, "The linesman has signaled, *offside*." And the announcer gave the number of the offending striker, the one who allegedly had gotten too far downfield.

"I didn't think so, at all," Robert said quickly. He turned to Maria, who didn't know the game, and explained: "What *'offside'* means is, nobody on the offensive team can get closer to the goal than the last defensive player, unless the ball is in front of him. But I was watching that, and the Lamar players didn't get offside."

The big screen showed the replay. It was hard to see, and it was hard to be sure, but Robert was certain; there was no offside, and it was a goal.

The crowd saw it too, and roared its disapproval. Or at least, the Lamar High School fans roared *their* disapproval.

And Robert Herrick found himself yelling at the linesman: "You blind son of a bitch!"

Maria laughed at him, again. "Come on, Robert! It's just a game. Robby's playing wonderfully, Lamar is ahead by two goals, and they'll have many more chances."

"I just don't like it."

"You don't like what you see as injustice." She smiled at him. "You never accept injustice, and you always feel you have to charge off and challenge what you see as something even slightly wrong. And you're always sure of it, even with little injustices, like a close call by a sports judge."

Seeing her smile, below her almond eyes and with her face framed by her red hair in soft curls, he did what he always did under the circumstances. He stared in appreciation, and he felt the butterflies in his stomach. She was beautiful, and more than that, she always made him look for a sense of proportion. I need that, he told himself.

*　　*　　*

An hour later, the game was over. Bellaire had made it close, but Lamar had pulled out the victory, by three goals to two.

"It's a school night, Robby. You've got to come home."

He was sullen. "I've got nothing important at school tomorrow." He wanted to celebrate the victory some more, with his friends and teammates.

"Yes, but it's going to be near midnight when we get home. And that's late enough for a Thursday evening."

Maria laughed again, maybe for the hundredth time tonight. "Robby doesn't agree, Robert. To him, this is an injustice, and he's got the same attitude about injustice that you do."

And all three of them laughed, at that. Robby didn't at first, but Maria's example proved irresistible.

14
THE HIT MAN

As far as I'm concerned, it's a good thing we called Elmo about Alan." Brianna's hands were shaking. "I want the guy dead, now, after reading what he wrote. Dead, for real."

"I know what you mean." Delia was angry too. "I remember getting that letter from Anderson. Or should I say, from Alan. I loved it. I didn't know that he had said the same sweet, loving, wonderful things to you, Brianna."

"Heck, neither of us realized he even knew the other one of us, much less that he wrote the same love letters to both of us."

"Or slept with both of us."

"Delia, maybe you can handle it. I can't." At that, she broke out in sobs. "I loved . . . that horrible guy . . . so much."

"I know, Baby." Delia looked almost as downcast as Brianna, now. "I wish there was something I could do that would make this all go away."

"Figure out . . . how to put him out of his misery. And out of mine."

"So . . . for you, you're saying . . . it's getting to where it's no longer a prank, this idea we had about hiring someone to . . . get him?"

"Well, he made a fool out of me. Out of us. And I'm hurt, beyond words. How could he do this? How could anyone do this?"

*   *   *

Suddenly, the telephone rang. It echoed, like a noise from far, far away: an otherworldly kind of interruption. It was a trivial intervention by an irrelevant reality that tried to overshadow the moment, but couldn't.

After the ring, there was a pause. Then, the ring blared at them again. It seemed louder now, and more insistent.

Brianna moved mechanically, composing herself. She felt almost grateful for the distraction, as she picked up the phone. "Hello?"

"Is this Brianna Edwards?"

"Speaking."

Detective Cashdollar put on his best hit-man voice. "This is Ramey Berger. I heard from Elmo Naughton that I oughta call you."

There was a long pause. Then, a muffled sound, as though Ms. Edwards had her hand over the phone. Cashdollar-Berger thought he heard her telling someone else to "pick ____ that other ____, and don't ____ make any noise when you ____ it up." He heard an almost imperceptible click.

Brianna Edwards came back on the line. "This is new to me. I never hired a hit man before."

"That's okay." Cashdollar-Berger put on a casual voice. "You'll get used to it. Now listen: Is there someplace you'd be comfortable meeting? It ought to be someplace in public, but someplace where you don't usually go."

"Why public?"

"I'm thinking about you, Ms. Edwards. Yes, you're inexperienced. You probably want this to be someplace where there's some other folks, so you don't feel like there's danger. And we meet, and then we go to the parking lot and talk way out of earshot of anyone else."

"Oh. I . . . I see. Yes, I suppose that's . . . best."

"So, you're in Sugar Land?"

"Yes."

"Should we meet someplace in City Center there, someplace you don't usually go?"

"I . . . I just don't know."

"All right. Let's say the Blue Marlin. It's just north of Highway 6. It's got a big parking lot. I'll meet you inside, by the bar. I will have a black newsboy-type hat on. Three o'clock tomorrow. It'll be open, the Blue Marlin, but there won't be many people. Start out by saying 'Berger' to me. And I'll walk with you outside to the parking lot and give you my background and terms."

Mercifully, the call ended. Brianna stared at the telephone.

"We've come this far," Delia said. "If we're going to teach that jerk Alan-Anderson a lesson, Brianna, you've got to go meet this guy and get his cooperation. You've got to keep acting."

"I don't really look forward to that. But I want even less to see Alan get away with it. We need to scare him so he stays scared for a while."

"Scare him?"

"Or put him into the ground. At this point, I don't give a damn which one. I wish he would just . . . die."

* * *

Three o'clock. The Blue Marlin. Brianna was there, as worried as a cat in a tree who sees a dog climbing toward her.

"Okay, Brianna," Detective Cashdollar said to her after she called him by his assumed name, standing by the bar. "Let's go on out to the parking lot."

In the parking lot, they moved to a place where there was nobody. "Now, what do we do?" Brianna was so nervous she seemed ready to bounce out of her skin.

"You need more imagination. Okay, so you're inexperienced, but you need to check to see if I'm wearing a wire." Just to be helpful, he moved her hand to all the places where a microphone might be. "I'm an honest criminal." He laughed.

The hit man was wearing the most tastelessly uncoordinated outfit Brianna had ever seen. Gray pants. A maroon Jacket. A green striped shirt, and a blue tie. On top of his head, as promised, a black newsboy's cap leaned at an odd angle.

"Okay, so I don't know how to do this. I'm depending on you to know how to get this guy killed." Brianna's voice was cracking. "Tell me something about who you are. I mean, like . . . your experience or whatever."

Donnie Cashdollar affected a bored sort of voice in his role as Ramey Berger. "Okay. I'm gonna give you a short version of the 'Philosophy of a Hit Man.'" He paused for effect, and then started his rehearsed speech.

"Disgust, I should say, is the reason I kill people. Disgust at their lies. Their thievery. And the whores they surround themselves with." He paused again, to let it sink in.

"It's not something just anybody can make a living at, contract killings," the pretend-hit man continued. "But it earns me some money, and that's also a reason to do it. I won't lie to you. The money is a reason for doing it, too."

Cashdollar-Berger looked hard at Brianna, and he decided there was no reason not to lay it on thick. "It's like this couple of folks I popped a week or so ago in Baytown," he deadpanned. "I tied 'em up and put duct tape all over them. It makes 'em relax. They think if you've gone to that kind of trouble with them, tying them up and spreading a little duct tape, you're not gonna send 'em to the bone orchard. You're not gonna kill them after all, or even hurt them, and they let it out. They tell you the whole deal."

The fake assassin was wound up, now. "And so, I got them to tell me what my customers wanted to know, which was how they'd hidden the money they'd stolen. And the dishonesty of it all, that's what got to me. I don't like dishonesty. Or injustice. You see, it's actually an honorable profession, the profession of a homicidal contractor. There's stuff outside the law, injustice that the law can't deal with. That's when only the professional contractor can make it right, and do it honorably. So, that's what I do."

Brianna was enthralled, even though she was horrified. This hit man was telling her exactly what Robert Herrick had told her: that the law couldn't make justice happen. But the difference was, he had a solution.

"Anyway, my deal included whacking them out, so that's what I did," Cashdollar-Berger said with satisfaction. "That's what I hired on to do."

Brianna shivered in spite of herself, but she was mesmerized. She felt the enthusiasm of the moment, and she wasn't going to chicken out now. "This . . . this guy was dishonest too. This Alan Anderson Blackburn, he . . . practically invented being dishonest. Really dishonest. And what he did was an injustice, and he figured he'd . . . he'd get away with it, because the law just doesn't deal with this kind of thing. A professional . . . a professional contract man ought to be interested in this case, because it's . . . yes, it's disgusting."

Abruptly, Cashdollar-Berger said, "Okay. I can do this for you. For Five Thousand. I ought to get more, but Elmo Naughton told me you're impecunious." He saw her puzzled look. "Impecunious. It means you don't have a lot of money. So, five thousand. Rock bottom, special, fire-sale price."

"I . . . I think we may be able to put that together. Whew. Five thousand. I'll see . . . if we can get it."

$$* \quad * \quad *$$

Across Highway 6, at the top of a six-story parking garage, two police officers in plain clothes held a parabolic dish, trained on the two conspirators, with a long, cylinder-shaped microphone at its center. The third officer held a video camera with a long lens. Earpieces and a viewfinder told them, as Brianna parted company from Donnie Cashdollar, that they had captured it all on sound and film.

In a court of law, there would be no doubt that Brianna Edwards was guilty as sin. Now, they needed to lasso the other co-conspirator, Delia Marchand.

15
GETTING THE MONEY

Brianna, are we doing this or aren't we?" Delia waved her arms. "I go back and forth."

"But when you think about that letter, the one Alan-Anderson wrote me, you know the answer."

"Don't remind me. You don't need to remind me. But you're right. I hate him. I'm really hurt, but . . . I'm beyond being hurt. I hate him."

"I hate him too."

"This all reminds me of *Hamlet*. You know, the play by Shakespeare."

"You've got me, Brianna. I never read that play. Or saw it. *Hamlet?* Truth is, I'm not into Shakespeare. Not so much."

"Well, it's a common kind of story. Prince Hamlet, he can't figure out what to do. He wants revenge. But he goes back and forth and can't decide. At one point, he even plans on suicide as a solution to the pain he feels. That's the speech he makes about *'To be, or not to be.'"*

"Okay." Delia half-smiled. "I've heard about that speech. Thank you, Miss English-Literature Expert."

"And I've thought about it, too. Killing myself, I mean. With pills, but I don't know what kind. It hurts so much, what Alan did. It hurts that much."

"No, Brianna. I don't want you to do that. Think positive."

"No, I agree. I wouldn't actually do it. Thinking about isn't the same as doing it, and the thought passed by pretty fast. And I'll tell you what: I am thinking positive. Damn positive, in fact."

"Positive, about what?"

"Well, Prince Hamlet finally gets beyond delaying. And he acts. And when he acts, he acts explosively."

"What does that mean?"

"It means, five thousand dollars. We need to get the money together. We need to get that five thousand dollars."

"Which means . . . ."

"That's right. It means that you've got to go to the bank, Delia. We need the five thousand dollars that guy wants. That Ramey Berger. You owe me a couple of thousand dollars, and you've got it in your account. And more."

"Ahhh . . . Well . . . I don't know. I still can't quite believe we're doing this."

Brianna smiled. At first, she couldn't quite understand why she was smiling, but then, she explained it. "Right now, it's the first time I've felt this good in a long, long time."

*   *   *

Sitting at the same cheap metal desk in the Homicide Division, Detective Derrigan Slaughter lifted the telephone. Across the ugly squares of green linoleum on the floor, with yellow and white splotches on them, Detective Donnie Cashdollar sat and witnessed the scene. Slaughter looked elegant in a perfectly cut blue suit and a blue-and-red tie. His partner, fresh from playing the part of a hit man in his undercover capacity, looked disheveled in his trademark uncoordinated outfit: gray pants, a maroon jacket, a green striped shirt, and a blue tie. He still sported his black newsboy's cap.

A voice at the other end of the line answered Detective Slaughter's call. "Hello. Alan Blackburn speaking."

"This is Alan Anderson Blackburn?" To ask was redundant, but Slaughter knew that it was important to get the right person—and only the right person.

"Yes. I said that. Just like I said, I'm Alan Blackburn. My full name is Alan Anderson Blackburn."

"This be Detective Derrigan Slaughter, Houston PO-leece Depa'tment, Homicide Division."

Predictably, there was a sharp intake of breath at the other end of the line. "Homicide what?"

"Listen, Mr. Blackburn, don't panic, 'cause you ain't in trouble. Not with us, at least, you ain't in trouble. There do be a problem, but we ain't calling you about nothing illegal that you might have done. That ain't the purpose, at all."

A pause. Then: "Well, what *is* the purpose? What can I . . . do for you, Detective?"

"I'll just come right out, here, and say it. We done uncovered the fact that someone wants to kill you."

Silence.

"And it's our job to call you up and tell you about it," Detective Slaughter went on. "I repeat, you ain't done nothing illegal. And we done made ourselves get on top of it. And we done made ourselves pretty sure that we got it stopped."

Silence. Then: "Who . . . what . . . what's it all about?"

Quickly, Slaughter sketched the events leading up to the undercover role in which Donnie Cashdollar had played "Ramey Berger." It had to be told to the intended victim because, if anything else happened—if the person hiring the hit man went on and hired another hit man, for example, and bypassed the man she knew as Ramey Berger—well, then, the hired killing might actually happen. That was why the intended victim, Mr. Alan Anderson Blackburn, had to be told.

Blackburn considered it all. "I guess . . . then . . . I shouldn't be coming to Sugar Land, or to Texas, any time soon."

"Smart on your part," Detective Slaughter answered, firmly. "And I might add, you shouldn't be telling this to *nobody*. If you become a blabbermouth, you probably gonna mess up our getting these folks properly arrested."

"And I guess you guys will . . . give me . . . protection?"

"Ahhh . . . well . . . no, suh. That would be . . . in the movies." The big Detective smiled in spite of himself, and so did Detective Cashdollar. "It just ain't in the budget, I'm afraid. When you see that there show called *Law and Order* on TV, they can give everybody what they call 'protection,' 'cause the TV writers don't have to pay for it, and they don't have to take three shifts of two PO-lice officers offa the street. I mean two for each a' the three shifts. In real life, we just ain't able to do that."

"I . . . I see."

"We gonna be watching, Mr. Blackburn. And we gonna act fast. We think we got this thing nipped in the bud, so to speak. So, like I done said, we gonna act fast, to make the APP–REE–hension."

Donnie Cashdollar smiled at that, because Police officers rarely refer to an arrest as an "apprehension." Usually, they call it something like a "throwdown," or "th'ow-down," as in, for example, proudly explaining, "We done th'ew down on them Bozos, right after they done hoisted that bundle."

But as Detective Cashdollar knew, Derrigan Slaughter was a man of the Deep South, where good verbal usage was a cultural value. Colorful expression and rolling rhetoric were a deeply desired capability, and so this particular arrest became an "APP-REE-hension" in Detective Slaughter's treatment of the subject.

Again, from Alan Anderson Blackburn: "I . . . I see."

Blackburn's voice showed that, naturally, he was struggling with the whole concept. "But . . . what I don't understand is, why would Brianna do something like this?" He sounded anguished. "And Delia. Why would somebody like Delia Marchand . . . *Delia Marchand?* . . . do . . . something like this?"

"Well, I can't say. We ain't no kinda sociologists, here in the Homicide Division." He drew out the word dramatically: "SOSH-ee-O-OLL-o-gists."

Every police officer understands what might be called "the crime victim's ultimate question." The victim of a violent crime always has a fixation: an overwhelming need to ask, "Why?" It is a quest to learn, "What made this happen? Why did this person do this to me and my family? What on earth was the reason?" It's natural; it's the victim's effort to understand what is now an upside-down world, filled with shock and pain. The victim desperately wants to replace this disorientation with a semblance of normality.

But usually, there is no rationality to be found.

Yet even as they know how unanswerable the question is, police officers everywhere understand and sympathize with the terrible depth of the victim's need to know. And so Derrigan Slaughter answered, as gently as he could, "I'm sorry, Mr. Blackburn. Ain't nothing that shoulda happened to you, that's fo' sure. I'm sorry. But they ain't no good reason that I can give you 'bout why it happened, neither."

*   *   *

The Wells Fargo branch bank in Sugar Land is on Highway 6, not far from the parking lot where Brianna Edwards had conspired with Donnie Cashdollar's alter ego. The "hit man" named Ramey Berger.

And now, Delia Marchand emerged from the Wells Fargo branch and saw a large African-American gentleman wearing an elegant pearl gray suit approach her. And approach her. Too closely.

The man was in her face, now. "Delia Marchand?"

She hesitated. Startled, and frightened.

"I'm Detective Derrigan Slaughter. Homicide Division. I got a warrant for yo' arrest."

The inevitable question tumbled out of Delia's mouth. "What . . . for?"

"Solicitation of capital murder."

"What does that mean? What did I actually do, to make it so that there's a 'warrant for my arrest'?

"You gonna have to turn around. That's right. Put yo' hands behind you."

"Ooooof. Do you have to do this? I've got nothing with me. Nothing like a weapon that I could do anything with, to you. Or anyone! And I'm peaceful." Every first-time arrested suspect claims peacefulness—and wants to sit in the patrol car like an ordinary passenger. Derrigan Slaughter avoided answering. The suspect usually realizes, spontaneously, that police policy is to cuff everyone.

"Where's Brianna Edwards?" Slaughter asked.

"Circling the block. She's gonna pick me up."

Derrigan Slaughter was already frisking Delia, ignoring her muffled protests. When he opened her purse, she said out loud, "You can't do that. Not without a warrant."

"Su-PREEM Court says I can, Missy." Derrigan Slaughter's voice was authoritative. "It gonna be called a *'search incident,'* or actually, a *'search incident to an arrest.'* Here's what that mean. When a PO-leece officer th'ow down on you . . . I mean when he arrest you . . . he searches everything within yo' reach. From yo' outstretched left hand to yo' outstretched right hand. 'Wingtip to wingtip,' as they say."

Police officers are experts on some stray parts of criminal procedure, including tidbits of search and seizure. Or at least, they know words and phrases about legalisms that let them do what they would like to do. So now, Derrigan Slaughter's voice carried a tiny note of pride, as he carefully and thoroughly described the 'wingtip' rule that came from the Supreme Court case of *Chimel v. California*:

"A PO-liceman who arrest you, well, the law say that he can search anywhere that the SUS-peck be able to lunge to reach a weapon. That's what the Su-PREEM Court say: where they can 'lunge to reach a weapon.' And that includes yo' purse."

Inside the purse, the big Detective found wads of green paper, tied together in bank wrappers. Hundred-dollar bills. Each bundle about half an inch thick, it seemed. Three bundles, each with ten hundred-dollar bills. Three thousand dollars.

"Okay, Delia. You got the right to remain silent . . . ."

And when he finished reading the *Miranda* warnings from a little blue card, the Detective asked the question that was calculated to get the "SUS-peck" to spill the beans: "Now, Miss Delia. With these rights in mind, are you willing to discuss the charges against you?" Usually, when you say that to the person wearing handcuffs for the first time, she falls all over herself explaining why things aren't what they seem to be. And usually, her chatter creates lots of useful evidence.

Delia looked toward the other side of the street. There was Brianna, in her red BMW, coming around the corner to pick her up. Immediately, uniformed officers from Sugar Land P.D. surrounded the car. They were Detective Slaughter's backup. Usually, they would have arrested Delia themselves, this being in Sugar Land, and they being Sugar Land officers; but Slaughter and Cashdollar were the ones who had broken the case, after all. Letting Slaughter have the first crack at these criminals was merely professional courtesy.

And meanwhile, Delia wisely did what the *Miranda* warnings suggested she perhaps should. . . .

She remained silent.

16
INTERROGATION

Delia Marchand?"

"Yes." The interrogation room in Sugar Land was spiffier than the same rooms in Houston, because Sugar Land is wealthier. But not much larger, because interrogation rooms are designed to be small.

"I'm Donnie Cashdollar." The detective wearing the mismatched outfit leaned back, and his chair hit the wall.

"Pleased to make your acquaintance." Delia's words oozed sarcasm.

Cashdollar's knees knocked against Delia's, here in this cramped space. But for purposes of interrogation, the confinement of the space was ideal. The social psychologists' experiments prove that physical closeness enhances authority. The work of Stanley Milgram and Solomon Asch, for instance, shows that an official-looking guy in a uniform can get ordinary people to do surprising things, just by asserting authority. Close physical confrontation is a factor that strengthens the psychological effect.

And now, Donnie Cashdollar did what veteran detectives know will increase the authority response even further. He reached out and touched Delia's arm. Lightly. Just a touch.

"Delia, are you ready to discuss the charges against you?"

Delia stirred, uncomfortably but defiantly. "I've got the right to remain silent. And I want a lawyer."

At that, Detective Cashdollar did something contrary to expectation. He repeated the *Miranda* warnings, including the right to remain silent and the right to an attorney. Sometimes it works. Starting over sometimes creates an atmosphere of inevitability, of unavoidable interrogation. At the same time, no court is going to fault a detective for repeating the *Miranda* warnings. "Now, with these rights in mind, are you ready to discuss the charges against you?"

Delia looked straight at him. "No," she said. "I want a lawyer."

In spite of what the Supreme Court wrote in the *Miranda* case, and in spite of police officers' repetition after repetition of what the Court wrote about appointing a lawyer for the suspect, Donnie Cashdollar wasn't about to rush out and get a lawyer, just because the suspect asked for one. If they have nothing that looks as though it will persuade the suspect to reconsider, the interrogators just return the suspect to jail. And that is what Donnie Cashdollar did, now, with Delia Marchand.

*   *   *

Meanwhile, Detective Derrigan Slaughter sat with Brianna Edwards in another tiny room. But while Delia Marchand was closemouthed, Brianna wanted to talk. And talk. And talk.

"But . . . all I did was to take my friend to the . . . *bank!*" She sounded anguished. She thought to herself, "Why doesn't this policeman believe me?"

"Well, Brianna, we know that ain't true."

There are manuals that provide strategies for police interrogation. One of the most important techniques, the manuals say, is to confront the suspect immediately if the suspect lies.

"Yo' 'friend,'" Derrigan Slaughter drew the word out to give a sense of irony, "done EE-merged from that bank carrying wads and wads of cash. To pay off a guy you all was gonna hire to kill somebody."

"I had no idea what she was going to the bank for! And we didn't really want to kill anyone. We were just going to pay Ramey Berger to scare him."

Create an impression of omniscience, the manuals advise. The interrogator knows everything. All that remains is for the suspect to confirm what the police department has already determined, with certainty.

And so, Detective Slaughter sighed and said, "Brianna, I gotta tell you again, we know that that ain't true. You met with a guy named 'Ramey Berger.' But he wasn't no Ramey Berger. He was an undercover detective named Donnie Cashdollar, who's gonna testify against you."

Brianna flinched. Then: "But . . . but *Detective!* That was something my friend Elmo Naughton told me to do, to meet with that guy."

"Elmo Naughton gonna testify, too."

"But . . . I had no intention to do anything illegal!"

"Well, that ain't true either. You're on tape, Brianna. The meeting with that hired killer, who ain't no hired killer and who's gonna testify against you, is all on tape. You done made it into the movies, Brianna. On tape, you say you want this guy to, quote, 'kill' this other guy. Come on, Brianna. Stop the lyin'."

The interrogation went on for another forty-five minutes. At the end, it was a good example of the reasons why criminal defense lawyers tell their clients to keep their mouths shut.

Brianna Edwards confirmed meeting with the pretend hit man, "Ramey Berger." She admitted saying she depended on him to know to "kill" Alan Blackburn. "But I didn't really mean it!"

She admitted knowing that Delia was going to withdraw "a lot of money." But she attempted to explain: "We wanted the hit man just to scare him! And we figured we had to pay him to do that." She even seemed to believe it.

And she told a lot of provable lies.

And since this interrogation was also filmed, just like the meeting with the pretended hit man, everything she said in the interrogation room was on tape.

* * *

Fifteen miles to the north, the setting sun peeked softly through the big plantation shutters around Robert Herrick's living room. This was his refuge, this century-old home in River Oaks, which he had gutted and modernized. Maria Melendes sat to his right, in a light blue wing chair. To the left was his daughter Cynthia, known as "Pepper" for so long that her real name was virtually forgotten. And next to Pepper was her new husband, Jonathan.

Robert had his grandson, Robert III, on his lap. "Stand up, Robert the Third!" And grandfather Robert held the little boy's hands.

"Look at him smile!" Maria Melendes smiled too. And Robert ("big" Robert, as he was coming to be called) felt the puddle in his stomach that he always felt, whenever he saw Maria's beautiful smile.

"Babies always love to stand up," said Pepper. She had become almost annoying, with the pretensions she had now about her knowledge of raising children. Robert remembered finding out that she was pregnant during the last week of a major trial that involved a disaster with a propane truck. She and Jonathan had married, too quickly, but . . . knock on wood, Robert thought . . . it seemed to be working out.

"Robert, it's so nice when you don't have a constant stream of days in trial and neither do I." Maria smiled again, and again she made him feel fortunate to have her.

"Well, I suppose we ought to retire." And they both laughed, because that was not on either of their radar screens, at all.

The telephone rang, too loudly. Robert picked it up. "Hello."

The voice was metallic. An automated voice. *"This is a collect call from the County Jail in Fort Bend County, Texas. Will you accept the call?"*

"Who? What?" Robert blurted out. But a call from a jail always began this way, because jails don't pay for their prisoners' telephone calls. Who could it be? Had Tom Kennedy been charged with drunk driving? Had his son, Robby, been incarcerated for some youthful folly? "Yes! Yes, I'll accept it."

"Robert, it's me. Brianna." The voice was muffled and halting. Hyperventilating.

"Brianna! A collect call from you, at . . . the Fort Bend County . . . jail? Brianna, what on earth is going on?"

"I've been . . . arrested, Robert. I need a lawyer. And . . . and I want you."

Her voice sounded bewildered. But no more bewildered than Robert Herrick's. "Brianna, you know I don't do criminal defense. I know nothing about criminal defense. I just can't." And the Famous Lawyer for the Little Guy waved his hand.

But at this point, any further communication became impossible, because at this point, Brianna Edwards started crying hysterically. And shouting, incoherently. "I did . . . nothing. *Nothing! I didn't kill anybody! Or try to! I don't know . . . I can't tell . . . I don't have any idea what's going on! Or why! Or why I'm charged with this, or why all of the policemen and prosecutors in the WORLD hate my guts! I need your . . . help, . . . Robert, . . . pleeeease!"*

He stopped, frozen. Habit took over. An instinct to protect. It overwhelmed him. And then: "Brianna. Brianna! I'm sorry this has happened. I'll get somebody to locate where you are in the Fort Bend County jail. And I'll find out when I can come visit you. I'll be there for you. Soon as I can."

Tom Kennedy is right, he told himself as he put the telephone down. It's my tragic flaw. I tend to charge off and try to help anyone who's in trouble, even if I can't see any way that I can possibly be of any help at all.

17

SOLICITATION OF CAPITAL MURDER

I t was not a welcome delivery. A deputy sheriff brought Brianna's copy of the indictment to her inside the Fort Bend County lockup, near Sugar Land. And he "served" it on her (which, in lawyer talk, just means he handed it to her).

The paper was plain, written in black and white, with the words partly pre-printed and party typed fresh, in language that sounded legalistic, unforgiving, and ugly:

"IN THE NAME AND BY THE AUTHORITY OF THE STATE OF TEXAS:

"The duly organized Grand Jury of Fort Bend County, Texas presents, in the District Court of Fort Bend County, Texas, that in Fort Bend County, Texas,

"one BRIANNA EDWARDS, hereafter styled the Defendant, heretofore did then and there, unlawfully:

"with the intent that a capital felony be committed, namely capital murder, request, command, solicit, and attempt to induce DONNIE CASHDOLLAR, a/k/a RAMEY BERGER, to engage in specific conduct, namely to cause the death of ALAN ANDERSON BLACKBURN, for remuneration and the promise of remuneration, namely, money,

"under circumstances surrounding her conduct, as the defendant believed them to be, as would constitute the capital felony.

"AGAINST THE PEACE AND DIGNITY OF THE STATE.

"[Original signed,]

"Presiding Juror of the Grand Jury."

Brianna stared at the words and tried to understand them. They seemed foggy and unreal. And foreign, like scratchy symbols written in Latin or Sanskrit. The indictment described her in such terribly cold and harsh terminology! There was no sense of proportion in this document: no room for human comprehension, no tolerance, no realization that their so-called "solicitation" of a crime—solicitation of a *crime!*—was merely a . . . well, a silly prank. A joke. A play-act; a fantasy . . . an overblown caper, that . . . certainly . . . wasn't . . . capital murder! Whatever that meant! Not really! Not at all!

As hard as she tried, she could not make out what the words really meant. She couldn't connect them to any reason for her confinement, now, in this awful place, this jail. "Are they trying to say that Delia and I are major criminals? That we wanted to commit a *murder?* That the silly things we did were anything more than a prank?" She didn't say the words out loud, but she thought them; and she thought them so forcefully, that she might as well have shouted them.

*   *   *

The sunlight curled softly through the plantation shutters in the living room of the Herrick home. Maria and Robby had the scrabble board out, and the competition was fierce.

"No, Robby!" Maria laughed. "This is Scrabble, and you have to follow the rules. You can't spell out the word 'VAROOM,' even if it does use your scrabble letters to best advantage. Especially if you spell it this way, the way you have it: '*VARUM*'!"

"What do you mean?" His expression was pained. :You yourself just called it a word! You referred to it as spelling out *the word* 'VAROOM.' And anyway, of course it's a word! Of course it is."

"What does it mean, according to you, this word 'VAROOM'?" She was still laughing.

"It's the sound that a car or a rocket makes when it goes by really fast." Robby looked confident about this. "A really fast thing going by you makes a noise like, 'VAROOM'! Or 'V-A-R-U-M'!"

"And where did you see this word?"

"I can't remember the last time I saw it. I've seen it so many times, I can't remember. It's out there, lots of times. Okay, one time recently I saw it in the comics in the newspaper."

"In what comic strip?"

"I don't remember. It was some adventure comic. Maybe it was *Tom Corbett, Space Cadet.*"

"But Tom Corbett hasn't been in the newspapers for years!" Maria was amused. Robby still looked pained.

Robert came into the room at precisely this anxious moment. "I heard mention of *Tom Corbett, Space Cadet!* That was my favorite comic book, when I was a kid. I don't understand why Tom Corbett has been gone so long. So: what's going on?"

It took them about ten minutes to explain what had taken them less than a minute to discuss, about the word 'VAROOM.' Or 'VARUM.'

"Well," Robert said, "I've got to go visit Brianna in the county jail. I have an appointment to see my client. I don't have time to look it up in the dictionary. Which is what you ought to do, to find out whether a word is a word, when you're playing Scrabble. Why don't you look it up in the dictionary?"

But suddenly, Maria was waving her arms and pointing across the room. "Robert, look at that!"

The television was on, without any sound. The screen carried a tease: *"Two Sugar Land Women Arrested for Hiring Hit Man in Love Triangle!"*

As quickly as he could, Robert turned on the sound. It was clear that the case against Brianna and Delia was going to supply Action News with lip-smacking prose for the four o'clock news, the five o'clock news, the six o'clock news, and as many other o'clocks as it could be stretched to fill.

The anchor's face appeared on the screen. "Good evening, friends. I'm John Moreno, and this . . . is . . . Action News!" Footage of a body outline, drawn in chalk on a wet city street, wrapped around his shoulders before he could go on.

"I've never seen a case with pictures of a chalk outline," Maria said immediately. "The on-scene officers have cameras these days, and they take pictures of the body."

"I know." Robert shook his head. "Let's see what else they mess up."

"Action News has learned that Sugar Land P.D. is holding two young ladies in a murder-for-hire case!" John Moreno managed to say it coherently, but at the same time, to sound breathless. "Brianna Edwards and

Delia Marchand were charged today with . . . *solicitation of capital murder!*"

"Well, that much is true, unfortunately," said Robert.

John Moreno sounded even more excited as he added: "And here's what's different about this case, according to sources close to the investigation! It's a love triangle with two ladies and one man. And the . . . man was the . . . target! Maybe the two ladies were jealous of each other."

"And that much . . . is totally made up," Robert said.

Action News had footage, then, of a bystander outside the bank at the time Delia was arrested. "She had wads of money. You could see it when the officer pulled it out of her purse. Enough to pay a hit man and still have a pile of money that could suffocate a giraffe."

John Moreno wrapped it up. "The first hearing in this case is scheduled for tomorrow morning. Whenever there are developments, you can be sure that . . . Action News will bring them to you right away. And . . . you can be sure that this isn't the last you'll hear of *this* story about the love triangle!"

Robert shook his head. "Well, it's fascinating watching the news, but I've got to go. To meet with Brianna." He smiled at his wife and son. "So, you two can get back to the Scrabble game. Here's what I think. 'VA-ROOM' isn't likely to be a word, and 'VARUM' isn't a word, for sure. But Robby ought to get something for being so ingenious in his justifications. Maybe an honorary law degree."

Maria and Robby both laughed at that. Robert walked to the back door and left the house. He remained deeply uncertain about what might be the outcome of the debate over that non-word, "VARUM." But he fixed his thoughts, finally, on the difficulties facing Brianna Edwards.

18
PROBABLE CAUSE

Early, early morning dawned, here in the Fort Bend County lockup. The deputy shouted it tonelessly: "Okay, buckaroos! Rise and shine, all a you jailbirds. Momma's cookin' is here."

And Brianna slowly climbed out of a restless sleep. It was way, waaay too early for this.

There were floppy pancakes with sloppy sauce that pretended to be syrup but wouldn't be called that by anyone with any sense. And there was some kind of mystery meat shaped like sausages. Then, before she knew it, Brianna found herself part of what inmates call "the line"—a line of prisoners, all chained together, who sleepily boarded a bus.

The trip to the courthouse was a blur. So was the walk to the holdover cell. Brianna waited while other inmates lost their handcuffs and transferred out of the holdover.

Finally, it was her turn. "Okay, Brianna. Lift up your hands and let's get these bracelets off."

"Ooof. These things, these handcuffs . . . they're always too tight. Can't you people come up with something that's a little bit softer?"

The jailer was not overly sympathetic. "It's part of the deal, for folks in jail. Everybody gets treated the same way. Bad, that is; everybody gets treated bad. But that's good, because everybody gets treated the same way. Now, watch this step here, Brianna, where the linoleum is broken, 'cause it steps down. We don't want that you should break your hind end before you even get your pretty self down outta the holdover cell."

"Wow, this light is bright, here in the courtroom. It's blinding." The door pulled back to close, and Brianna shielded her eyes. "Or rather, I guess it's just dark back there in the holdover. . . ."

She stopped. "Hey, look! There's Delia!"

And she sat next to Delia. Until the clerk called her. And the judge found out from her that she didn't have a lawyer, not yet. He told her to sit and wait. "You'll be represented by the public defender."

The probable cause hearings droned on, with the prosecutor softly summarizing the police reports, and the public defender having little to say. "This is what these probable cause hearings are like," the judge announced.

Finally, her name: "Brianna Edwards." The clerk said it in a loud monotone. Brianna stepped up to the ledge below the judge's bench, barely in front of it. "This isn't like on TV," she thought. She could have reached up and touched the judge, if she had jumped.

"Probable cause?" the judge asked, without looking up.

"Your honor, the defendant called an individual named 'Elmo,'" the prosecutor mumbled. "And asked him to recommend a person who could, quote, 'break someone's knees.' And she added, 'Actually, worse.' Elmo Naughton immediately called the Homicide Division, and he will be a witness for the prosecution. Then, this defendant, Brianna Edwards, met with an undercover officer who assumed the role of this person, this hit man, who would kill the person she wanted killed. That conversation was recorded, voice and video, and it will be available for the jury. During that time, this defendant, Brianna Edwards, said, quote, 'I'm depending on you to know how to get this guy killed.' The undercover officer, who of course will testify, even launched into a speech that he told her was, quote, the 'Philosophy of a Hit Man.'" There's not much question that there's probable cause. The charge is solicitation of capital murder, and there's no question there's enough evidence to hold this defendant."

"What says the defense?" asked the judge.

"Your honor, when she talked to this Elmo, Ms. Edwards didn't ask about a murder." The public defender was straining and hesitant. "She just said, 'break his knees.' That's the only specific statement to Elmo. And there's only one offhand reference when she met with the undercover guy posing as a killer. Obviously, he was able to draw out of her some remarks that she wouldn't have made, but for nervousness. She obviously was scared, and you can hear it all over the voice recording."

"But this is just probable cause." The judge made marks with his pen and, once again, also made some taps at his laptop. "Bail remains at two hundred thousand."

Brianna sat down. And next, Delia was up in front of the judge. It sounded as though the prosecutor went through the same speech, a little more smoothly this time, probably because he had rehearsed it, in a manner of speaking, when he had talked about Brianna herself. The main difference was that the prosecutor added some remarks from the later police reports, the ones that explained Delia's arrest outside the bank. "Brianna Edwards was the wheel on that occasion, your honor, and Sugar Land P.D. arrested Brianna Edwards coming around the block, just a few feet away from this defendant. Coming to pick her up, obviously."

The public defender said the same things as he had about Brianna. And he added, as an argument for Delia's release, "Besides, the alleged hit man's fee was supposed to be five thousand dollars, and this defendant, Delia, had only three thousand that she had withdrawn from the bank. It could have been for anything. Maybe she was closing a real estate deal, for all we know."

The judge rolled his eyes. And he said the same thing that he had said so many times today. "But this is just probable cause."

19
LAWYER AND CLIENT

I called Mike Robillard on the way over here." Robert Herrick sat on a metal chair in the Fort Bend County Jail. "He's a solid criminal defense lawyer."

"Well, that's fine," Brianna Edwards replied firmly. "But Robert, I want you to represent me."

"Brianna, it's . . . a difficult case, frankly. It's probably an impossible case. You need a real criminal defense lawyer."

"I want you to help me."

"Well . . . we'll see. Now, tell me what you told the police in this . . . this interrogation."

And as best she could remember, Brianna Edwards told him. Her story didn't make sense, Robert could see. Even her telling him about what she had told the police; that didn't make sense either, because her explanation of how the Detective had accused her of lying was accompanied by nothing that gave rise to any accusations of lying, and Robert knew that wasn't likely.

"That's going to hurt. The tape, I mean. The interview of you is on tape, I'm sure."

"There wasn't any camera."

"It was there, I have no doubt. It wasn't easily visible, no. But they don't have to tell you they're taping it, of course."

"They don't even have to tell me they're taping me?" Brianna's eyes were wide.

"Well, they'll want to try you and Delia together. In one trial. It saves courtroom time, expense, and effort. And they'll be hoping that the two of you get crosswise of each other and point the finger at each other. Your best strategy, for both of you, may be to stick together."

He stopped there. One of the worst things a lawyer can do is to advise his client to "get the story straight" with someone else, when there's no joint defense agreement yet in place.

"And there would be a benefit, if the two of you are tried together. They can't use the video of your interrogation. Your interview, which I strongly suspect would bury you, couldn't be used."

Brianna brightened. "They can't use my statements against me?" It was beginning to dawn on her, finally, that her attempts to "defend" herself in front of Detective Slaughter had only sucked her deeper into the quicksand.

"The Supreme Court says so. I forget the name of the case. But in a joint trial, where one defendant has given a statement, the prosecutors can't use that statement, because the jury might use it against the other defendant. Supreme Court says so."

"That's great!"

"Well, don't celebrate too much, just yet, Brianna. There's a mountain of evidence that they have, that they *can* use. That they *will* use. There's Elmo Naughton. And Ramey Berger, who just happens to be a Detective named Donnie Cashdollar. There's you, on tape, saying how you're counting on Ramey Berger to 'kill' Alan Blackburn. Alan, of course, will be a witness too, and that will show the jury how you and Delia had motive to kill. And then, the icing on the cake. Delia comes out of the bank with a purse full of money, too much to use for anything but hiring a hit man, and you're right there, a few feet away, ready to pick her up."

Brianna hung her head.

"In fact, I can see only one way to get you out of this. Only one way. But it's a long shot." Robert shook his head. "A *really* long shot."

20

A SHARK OUT OF WATER

Judge Winley Waddell smiled as he called out the well-known name. "Mister Herrick?"

"Yes, your honor." Robert stood ramrod straight.

"I've heard your name, of course, Mr. Herrick. But you've never graced this court with your presence, far as I'm aware." Judges often perk up when a lawyer who's a household name appears in front of them. It's a boring job, being a judge. The judge sits there as silent as a predatory cat most of the time, but he's never allowed to pounce. Lawyers with big reputations make the business more entertaining.

And it's even more interesting, when a famous name appears, if the judge thinks the lawyer has some disadvantages. Such as, in this instance, the disadvantages of a difficult case and a type of law with which the famous lawyer has little experience. Like Robert Herrick here. In this situation, the judge is thinking, "I wonder whether he's going to fall on his famous rear end!"

Judge Waddell smiled. "Are you like a fish out of water, Mr. Herrick? Or—since you're a lawyer, and from what I hear you're a good one—should I say, 'a shark out of water'?"

It wasn't very funny, but since it was the judge who said it, everyone laughed. Politely.

Robert Herrick chose his words carefully. "Your honor, I've tried cases right here in Fort Bend County, and I know your honor's reputation for careful decisions and for fairness. But no, I've never had the pleasure of appearing before you."

It was a polite untruth. In fact, he and his co-counsel had commiserated about getting assigned to Winley Waddell, who had a reputation as a prejudiced lightweight. But it never hurts to be nice to the judge. "So anyway, judge," Robert went on, "I'm associated with a lawyer who knows his way around. That's Mr. Robillard, here. Mike Robillard represents the other defendant, Delia Marchand, and I represent Ms. Brianna Edwards, so we'll be a team. And that will make up for my fumbling mistakes."

Mike Robillard stood up, at that. "Mike Robillard, your honor. Good morning!" He was the foil to Robert Herrick, opposite in every way. Short; about five-foot-eight. Balding, with a crown of gray hair. Eyes that were gray and cloudy. A hang-dog sort of expression.

"Mr. Robillard, nice to see you again."

So far everything was friendly. Everything was nice. Let's see whether it stays that way, Robert thought. As we go through these motions I've filed.

"A motion for severance, I suppose?" The judge had his pen poised.

"No, your honor." Robert's voice was firm. "We don't want the two defendants severed. It's a case that Mr. Robillard and I intend to defend vigorously. Together."

The prosecutors looked surprised. But then the lead prosecutor said, "No objection, your honor."

And the judge looked positively delighted. "Okay! We're gonna avoid aggravating the backlog."

"That's right, your honor." Robert smiled.

"All right, let's get down to business." The judge lifted a half-inch pile of paper, stapled together. "First, you've got a motion to suppress. A motion, that is, to throw out the video where your client, Mr. Herrick, talks to the undercover detective to hire him to kill the intended victim. You want me to throw out the videotape of your client committing the crime . . . I mean, the *alleged* crime. And you've got this enormous brief that you've filed."

The judge half-grinned, and he lifted the brief that contained the arguments to support the motion to suppress. Carefully and elaborately, with everyone watching, Judge Winley Waddell rolled the brief into a cylinder. And he put it up to his eye, like a telescope.

"Counsel, I've 'looked through' your brief, now." The judge looked pleased at his little joke. "I've looked through it. Literally." His smile faded. "And there's no doubt that you've got lots of ingenious reasons, and there's no doubt that the reason for the length of the brief is that there's no real merit to the argument. Just a lot of ingeniousness."

The Assistant District Attorney stood, now. "Your honor, Paul Gage, for the State of Texas."

"Yes, Mr. Gage."

"I've read the brief carefully. Cover to cover. Your honor can't possibly read briefs this convoluted in every case without ballooning the docket and exploding your backlog, which already has thousands of indictments. And you couldn't do justice in any of them if you did." Paul Gage was known as the best trial lawyer in the Fort Bend prosecutor's office, and it was beginning to show.

"You got that right," the judge muttered.

"Your honor," the prosecutor went on, "I've read the brief, and here's what it says, in a nutshell. The brief says that this video of Brianna Edwards, which shows her committing the heart of the crime, is an 'illegal search and seizure,' and that it has to be thrown out because, supposedly, it violates the Fourth Amendment to the Constitution. That's wrong, because what this defendant did was done in a public place where the defendant had set up the meeting, and she had no 'expectation of privacy' whatsoever. That's the phrase that appears in all the Supreme Court cases, and Brianna Edwards didn't have any such expectation of privacy."

Paul Gage waited a few seconds to let that sink in. "There's also a second argument in the brief, even more far out, based on the Fifth Amendment, which of course says that no one can be 'compelled'—that's the words of the Constitution—'compelled' to be a witness against himself. And the answer to that, is that the defendant was not in custody, wasn't under arrest, and had set up the meeting by her own initiative. She simply was not compelled, in any sense of the word."

The judge looked at Robert Herrick. "That sounds right to me."

"In Mr. Herrick's defense," Paul Gage volunteered, "it has to be added, that the brief is extremely well written, in the manner of a civil case brief to an appellate court. It puts the cases together in a way that is, just as your honor has said, 'ingenious.' But there's not one case about a defendant actually, voluntarily committing a crime on videotape, where the tape was suppressed.

"I've got to brag on Mr. Herrick." The prosecutor smiled, and he nodded at Robert. "He's created the appearance of unconstitutionality out of thin air."

"Congratulations, Mr. Herrick." The judge was ready to decide. "It's *overruled*. The motion to suppress the movie of the defendant committing the alleged crime is . . . *overruled*."

The judge read the title to the next document. "Also, Herrick and Robillard have filed what we call a '*Brady* Motion.' It's called a 'Motion to Disclose Exculpatory Information, or Information which Could Show Innocence, or Information That Could Impeach Any Witness for the State.' . . . So, Mr. Gage? What about this one?"

"We are very familiar with the prosecution's duty under the Supreme Court's decision in *Brady v. Maryland.*" Paul Gage seemed relaxed and confident. "In fact, it is our intention to provide the defense with everything we've got, every paper, every document, everything that we know of that reports on this case, because we don't think there's any evidence of innocence in it, at all. Mr. Herrick and Mr. Robillard can walk through it barefoot."

"The motion's granted, then." The judge made a check mark on the list of motions. "And next, here's the big motion. A *'Motion for Discovery.'* He paused. 'The defense lawyers want all kinds of stuff to be given to them, Mr. Gage, but most of it seems like stuff they have a right to, so let's get down to it."

The judge held the motion up, to read it. This time, he didn't roll it up and "look through" it, because a mistake, here, could mean that an appellate court would reverse his decision. "First thing, there's a request that the prosecution provide every statement allegedly made by either defendant. Mr. Gage?"

"We will provide all of the reports, as I said."

The judge looked at him. "And the videotape of the meeting with the hit man? I mean, the fake hit man? And the videotape of interrogations of the defendants, because I'm sure there are videotapes?" Robert Herrick perked up, a little, at that. The judge might have a reputation as being difficult to deal with . . . but maybe he wasn't as incompetent as the rumors suggested.

"Well . . . ahhh . . . yes, your honor." Gage knew that the law required him to show the videotape to defense counsel. "We suspect that the reason the defendants want that is to figure out how to 'wire around' what's actually said, by making up stuff, but yes, we'll provide that." The prosecutor's voice was sarcastic and drawn out when he said the words "wire around," but it was weary too. As if he had said, "Okay, I know we're going to get nothing but a pack of lies back from this, but I'll give the videotapes to them."

The Motion for Discovery took another forty-five minutes to plow through. The defense got favorable rulings on almost everything, which was the expected result, because the law entitled the defendants to most of the discovery they asked for. There was a request for the criminal records of any of the State's witnesses. Granted. That meant Elmo Naughton's arrests and convictions would be available on a printout. A request to inspect any physical evidence in the possession of the State. Granted. That meant that Herrick and Robillard would be able to look at the piles of hundred-dollar bills, with their bank wrappers. The Fort Bend Police

Property Room would let them inspect the bills inside their plastic evidence bags, without taking them out, while police property custodians looked on with sharp eyes.

There were a few requests that were denied. A request for a written transcription of all of the video evidence. "You can make that yourself, if you want it," said the judge, after the prosecutors told him they hadn't made one. Request denied. And then, a request to return the three thousand dollars to Delia Marchand, the three thousand dollars she had had in her purse when she left the bank. "Maybe it will let her pay her lawyer, your honor," Mike Robillard suggested hopefully.

"But it's physical evidence of a crime, or an alleged crime, and it's evidence that the jury's entitled to see!" The judge sounded incredulous. "That request *is denied!*"

All told, the hearing took two hours. As he left the courtroom, Robert Herrick was covered with sweat.

Brianna Edwards stared at him. "Robert, I was hoping the judge would throw out all of the videotapes."

"Not me," Robert answered. "I didn't even have any hope of it."

"So, why even file that kind of motion, that motion to suppress the videos? Won't you just make the judge mad?"

"Not if you're careful." Robert shook his head and smiled at his client. He needed her to keep her courage up, as best she could. "That's why we filed that long brief supporting the motion to suppress. That gave us some cover. We were able to file the motion with a straight face and keep it from seeming frivolous."

"But what good is that, if you know the judge is going to disagree with you?"

"It helps us, anyway. First of all, we got a reading of the judge. We know where he likes our case and where he doesn't.

"Second, it helps us with our other motions. If you get the judge to rule against you on something you don't expect to win, but the judge has to think about it . . . well, then, the judge wants to compromise, maybe. To be fair to both sides. And he'll look for something that is correct in your other motions, so that he can rule in your favor. So he can appear to be evenhanded. And we got everything we possibly could have, from the motion for discovery."

He smiled at his client, again. "We got what we need, in the way of information from the prosecutors. Lawyers call it 'discovery.' And it's going to help our strategy. The worst is yet to come—at trial. We've got to listen to the evidence of the prosecution in a jury trial, and that's never any fun. But we've got something, now, that I think we can use."

21
KILLING CASANOVA

Alan Anderson Blackburn, known as "Alan" to Brianna and as "Anderson" to Delia, stood by his rented Mercedes. He stationed himself at the next-to-top floor of the parking garage. There wasn't a good reason for parking on this floor, at least not from a parking point of view, because there was plenty of room on lower floors. But there was a good strategic reason: it was quiet here.

"Come, on guys," Alan said under his breath. He looked at this watch. "They're always making me wait." A few more minutes and he'd have to leave. It just wasn't smart, standing here like this.

As the money man in this transaction, he didn't have anything in his possession that would break the law. Just a paper bag with fifty thousand dollars in cash. Still, you invited questions if you waited a long time: questions from security guards, if nothing else. And it meant that anyone who wanted to set up a surveillance would have an easier time of it. Not that that was easy in a multi-floor parking garage, but still, the possibility bothered him. And if the DEA or local drug cops happened to stop him and look, they'd want some answers. "Why fifty thousand in cash? And why's it tucked away inside this paper bag from the grocery store?"

And now, at last, a noise. A car. Quiet at first. . . . Then louder.

He saw it round the corner. A black Mercedes, just like the one he'd rented, the one beside him now.

The second Mercedes stopped across the way from his. Someone got out of the driver's seat. And then, the passenger door opened, and another man, a big man, got out.

Something seemed wrong, but Alan couldn't quite put his finger on it. Then: that's silly, he told himself. He was always nervous. He felt nervous at the wrong times, he told himself.

Driving the route from Houston up to Cincinnati, and then to Columbus and Cleveland—that's where he ought to be worried, he reminded himself. There were thousands of places where something could happen, with fifty thousand dollars worth of white powder in the trunk. What if he had a wreck? Or got stopped by a too-inquisitive officer? This exchange wasn't something to worry about, the exchange that was about to happen now. It would take only a minute, and it was much safer than the upcoming trip across the country. His nervousness was worry over nothing.

"Hello, Carlos."

"Alan." Carlos looked at him quizzically. With a puzzled, and puzzling, expression. So did the heavyset man next to him.

"I got some bad news for you, my friend." Carlos was matter-of-fact, as always, with no feeling in his voice. "It's time to change our methods."

"What? What does that mean?" Suddenly, Alan was nervous again.

"Relax, Casanova. I realize you been having a good time here with your two girlfriends, and you've pretty much gotten rich from this kinda business. But we got no more stuff to give you."

"What? I still don't understand."

"You will understand, once I tell you. We got a message from Rojo in Cincinnati. Brother, you shouldn't do that."

"Do what?" The hair on Alan's neck was standing up. "You're talking riddles."

"You shorted Rojo. And he's after me."

"I *did no such thing*." Now, Alan was scared, angry, and bewildered, all at the same time.

"We got no goods for you, Casanova. But we'll take the fifty thousand you've got there in your grocery bag. We gonna ship it off to El Rojo, your Ohio connection, to make our business partner feel a little more copacetic. After you shorted him. That wasn't smart."

*   *   *

Ten floors down, in his uncomfortable rent-a-cop uniform, the security guard heard the gunshot. One echoing blast, just a minute or so after that black Mercedes had gone by him, on the way up. And he drew his own revolver. But he wasn't foolhardy. He stationed himself outside of the garage, hidden from view, where he could see without being seen himself.

He watched, now, as the same black Mercedes spun by him, turning with the loudest scream of tires that he'd ever heard here. The shiny dark metal flashed out of the garage and accelerated on the West Loop frontage road, with a roar.

At the angle from which he was watching, he was able to get two of the numbers on the license plate. Just two. But he couldn't tell anyone, later, whether the numbers ran together, or whether they were at the beginning of the number sequence, or whether they were at the end.

*　　*　　*

The next day, Robert Herrick heard the news. He sat at his huge mahogany desk, beneath the greenhouse windows that bordered his office. A hundred geraniums bloomed, in different shades of red and orange. Tom Kennedy faced him, across the desk.

"Paul Gage, he's a decent sort of guy. You know, the prosecutor in Sugar Land."

"How's that?" Kennedy knew Robert's philosophy. Our opponents are just that: opponents. Not enemies. Everyone in this office knew that professional courtesy was a job requirement. Everybody fights hard for our clients, but nobody is allowed to be a jerk.

"Gage called me right away when it happened. Alan Anderson Blackburn has been killed. Murdered. And Gage told me that whoever killed the poor guy was almost certainly unrelated to Brianna and Delia. Blackburn's murder has nothing to do with our ladies, or at least the police and prosecutors don't have any indication."

Tom Kennedy was amazed." It's just some sort of . . . coincidence?"

"Well, you never know for sure. But a coincidence, yes. That's what they think."

"I . . . can hardly believe it." Kennedy shook his head.

"That's what Assistant D.A. Paul Gage says, and he ought to know." Robert fiddled with the knobs on a tape recorder. "I actually have Gage on tape."

"You taped him?"

"Relax, Tom." Robert smiled, in spite of the situation. "I asked him first. He was kind of surprised, Gage was. And I told him, 'Hey, listen, you guys tape everyone. You tape every call that goes through the jail, and a lot of conversations outside. This is important, and I'm just trying to be sure I get it right.' And Paul Gage, poor guy, he acted dumfounded for a few seconds, and finally, he just kind of laughed and said, 'Well, I guess it's all right. Go ahead.'"

"He can afford to do that, in this case," said Tom Kennedy, flatly. "He's got the evidence."

"Well . . . right. But still, it's a classy thing for him to do. He's on the other side from us, but I don't mind saying it. I appreciate his doing right by us. "Robert pushed the button. "Listen." The tape recorder made a gravelly sound. It scraped and whirred. It seemed to take forever, though, before it got to the voices they were interested in hearing.

22
THE STIPULATION

hey sat still for a moment, Robert and Tom, waiting for the tape recorder to reach the conversation. There was a lot of static that seemed to go on forever. And a click. And there were various swishing noises, made by the recorder as it advanced. And finally, here it was.

"*Okay, this is Robert Herrick, speaking by telephone to Paul Gage.*"

A pause. Then: "*I've notified Mr. Gage that this conversation is taped, and he has consented to this taping. Mr. Gage, please confirm.*"

"*That's right.*" Paul Gage had a radio announcer's voice. Friendly and smooth. A voice that undoubtedly was useful in the courtroom.

"*So, Mr. Gage, would you tell me, again, what you just told me? . . . About Mr. Blackburn?*"

"*Alan Anderson Blackburn. Yes. Mr. Blackburn was found shot to death yesterday evening, found by a security guard. It looks like an execution. The Homicide Division tells me that there is a bullet wound of entry in the back of his head, less than an inch to the right of the mid-line, and an exit wound at the occipital lobe, two inches left. There's a lot of what they call 'powder stippling.' You know, powder stippling, . . . which means bloody dots smeared in a circle on his head, from the gunpowder that gets rocketed out from the muzzle. And there's an 'abrasion collar': a blackened ring of burned skin, burned from the heat of the bullet. This means, of course, that the gunshot was a contact or near-contact wound, with the muzzle right at the victim's head, maybe even touching it. This was an execution, pure and simple. The detectives recovered a .38 slug, thought to be fired from a revolver.*"

Robert's voice was even, but hesitant, as he tried to absorb it. *"And aside from the manner and means of death … what is your best knowledge about the perpetrator?"*

"What's important to you, Mr. Herrick, is that we do not know of, and do not suspect, any connection to your client, Brianna Edwards, or to Delia Marchand. Drug Enforcement Intelligence has been aware of Mr. Blackburn's activities for some time now. There was a black Mercedes involved, probably driven by the bad guys, and the security guard thinks he got two of the license numbers, but that hasn't been useful, of course, because you can't trace a vehicle with two numbers when you don't know how they're placed on the license plate, or even whether they're accurate."

Paul Gage's voice dropped an octave. *"But it's not too surprising that our suspects are hard to identify. Mr. Blackburn was known to associate with a Mr. Carlos Leiner, who is a well known character. A big cocaine importer. A dangerous guy, who shepherds drug caravans out of Mexico through Houston and then north. Leiner has been known to favor Mercedes automobiles."*

"He favors them? Then, you mean …. This wasn't Carlos Leiner's usual car?"

"We suspect it was stolen, the car that the killers were using. But as I say, we can't pinpoint the vehicle."

"This is … surprising." Robert Herrick still sounded hesitant. *"And I guess you're saying, it's random?"*

"Not exactly 'random,'" Paul Gage corrected. *"It's almost certainly got something to do with controlled substances. You know, the drug trade. Cocaine, to be exact. But the point is, we think it's unrelated to Brianna Edwards and Delia Marchand. Your two ladies didn't do it. Or at least, we've got nothing that connects them."*

There was a pause. Then, Robert Herrick spoke. *"You realize, Paul, that I'm going to need evidence about this. For the trial."*

"Oh, don't worry, Robert. We're not going to mention it, and we're not even going to try to pin the killing of Mr. Blackburn on your ladies. We couldn't tie it to your clients, anyway, even if we wanted to." Paul Gage sounded dismissive, as though that should take care of it.

"Well, thanks. You've been very professional, and I appreciate your advising me of this so promptly."

Paul Gage's voice was pleasant, but professional. *"You're welcome. It's something we would do as a matter of course. Remember your 'Brady' motion, Robert? The request you made to the judge, to order me to turn over exculpatory evidence? And I've got a duty to do that anyway. This fulfills the duty."*

"I understand. Thanks." Robert drew his words out slowly. "But listen: I need it for the trial. The State of Texas has a lot of evidence. I ought to have a little evidence, right? I mean, that's only fair."

"Okay, Robert." Paul Gage laughed. "I'm slow, I guess, but the light is starting to dawn. You want the jury to know that someone killed Alan Blackburn, and that the 'someone' who did it . . . wasn't connected to Brianna or Delia. And that's going to help you create reasonable doubt about whether they, Brianna and Delia, tried to kill him. Is that it?"

"You've got it. And like I say, it's . . . only fair." Robert's voice was upbeat. "You know, Paul, all of us lawyers appreciate small victories, even in difficult cases, especially if small victories are all we have."

"Okay. I admire your creativity. How about this." Paul Gage's voice drifted into the monotone that accompanies formula-type dictation. ". . . 'It is hereby stipulated and agreed, between the State and counsel for the defense, that the jury may be informed as follows, by defense counsel's reading to them a written version of what follows.' Paragraph. And Quote. 'The individual known as Alan Anderson Blackburn was discovered killed by persons then unknown. The State has no evidence or indication that the killing was perpetrated by or on behalf of Brianna Edwards or Delia Marchand, or by anyone acting together with them or connected with them in any way.'"

The prosecutor paused to take a breath, and then continued dictating. "'The killing was committed by a single gunshot at close range, in the form of a loose contact wound, or a close-to-contact wound. It occurred in a parking garage on the eighth floor, just off the West Loop, Interstate 610, in Houston, Texas, not in Sugar Land. Mr. Blackburn was suspected of engaging in traffic of controlled substances, namely cocaine.'"

"All right." Robert sounded satisfied. "It's possible, I guess, that reading this stipulation to the jury may be enough. I've got to let you know, though, that I may need to introduce actual evidence about parts of the story."

"Oh, I understand. But hold on, Robert. I've got to be careful about this too. It's not just you." Paul Gage's words were pleasant. "I'm not through. So, let me add: 'This agreement and stipulation is binding only if it is agreed to, also, by Mr. Robillard, as counsel for Ms. Marchand, and only if it is written exactly as spoken here, and signed by counsel for all three parties.'" Paul Gage paused for a moment. "And here's the catch, Robert. I've got to add this, too. Quote, 'This agreement and stipulation shall be effective only if the State does not learn of any possible evidence *that, in the State's sole judgment, connects Brianna Edwards or Delia Marchand to the death of Mr. Blackburn. And if any such possible evidence should appear, however slight or circumstantial, this stipulation shall be null and void and of no effect whatsoever, and it shall not be read to the jury.'"*

Robert thought about it, quickly. Then he said, *"You're a prince of a guy, Paul. Even if you do happen to be on the wrong side of this case."*

At that, the prosecutor favored Robert with a friendly laugh. Then, the lawyers exchanged a few pleasantries, and the tape ended.

∗   ∗   ∗

Tom Kennedy stirred in his chair. "I'll get this stipulation typed up. And I'll get Robillard to sign it and forward it to Paul Gage."

"Right." Robert sat back, behind the big desk. "This stipulation gives us proof of some facts that we might have trouble proving, such as that Mr. Blackburn was suspected of participating in the drug trade. Without this stipulation, I can see a judge excluding that fact, by saying it's 'too speculative.' And here's another good thing. The stipulation doesn't tie us down. We can introduce other evidence if we want to. Paul Gage is bending over backward to be fair." He paused. "Mr. Gage can afford to do that, of course—to be very fair, that is—because he's got enough firepower to blow us clean out of the water, as we all know. But still, it's good to know he plays by the rules."

"So far," Kennedy added.

23

THE COMEDIAN

Two radio patrol guys done found the murder vehicle," said Derrigan Slaughter. "They done found that black Mercedes. The car involved in killing Alan Anderson Blackburn."

He and his partner sat at their usual banged-up desk, reading police reports. Detective work is seldom as glamorous as Hollywood pictures it. They turned page after page: reams of paper, or what seemed like reams.

Slaughter frowned. "What I mean is, the license plate on that Mercedes, it's got the same two numbers that the security guard gave us, right at the beginning. It's gotta be the murder car. But they done found it in a substan-chu-ally burned condition. It says here, the bad guys done burned it up and left pretty much nothin."

Detective Cashdollar was philosophical. "That was their intention, of course: to destroy anything that identified them. They stole the car to begin with, then burned it. But hey . . . look at this fingerprint report! Those killers screwed up, and someone, quote, 'left a partial print on the passenger door.'"

"Looks like the guy who burned the car done stood on the driver's side," Slaughter agreed. "And the passenger side didn't get completely erased."

"It's a piece of good luck. But it's only a partial print, and not enough for a real ID. Still . . . it might turn out to be a big help. The fingerprint gurus found five of what they call 'points' in this partial print."

"Gotta remember, a fingerprint expert doesn't just look at the whole print." Slaughter stared at the report. "The examiner's always gonna focus on four kinds of little bitty characteristics, or what they call 'points': that is, ridge endings; forks; dots; and circles."

"Right," said Detective Cashdollar. "And when they find the same eight to ten points on two prints—eight to ten ridge endings, or forks, or dots, or circles—that's when they're able to say that the prints 'match.' . . . But here, they've got only five points."

He flipped a page. "Well, so five points isn't enough for a real ID. But look here! . . . Maybe this partial print is still useful, even with just five points."

"Well, first, we know it ain't the car owner's print. They done printed him, and it ain't him."

"Right. And second, it also isn't this guy Carlos, who was known to associate with our victim, Blackburn. It says here that Carlos's full name is Carlos Leiner, and he's a big-time dope dealer. Normally, he'd be an ideal suspect. But the print guys say it's not Carlos Leiner's print."

"And they can't say for sure who it is." Derrigan Slaughter lifted up a fingerprint page. "But here's somethin, . . . somethin *good*. Somethin that might pay off. The print guys, quote, 'cannot eliminate' this here other SUS-peck, who go by the name of 'Porfilio Garza.'"

"So . . . They ran this five-point partial through the National Crime Information Computer, the NCIC." Detective Cashdollar scanned down the report. "The NCIC can't identify Porfilio Garza. Or at least, the computer can't say it's him for sure, because there's possibly other guys with similar characteristics. The same five points. But the key thing is, this five-point partial is likely to be Porfilio Garza's. That's what they're really saying."

Derrigan Slaughter nodded. "Right. And whatever the print guys might be knowin, you and me, Donnie, . . . we know. We know it's Porfilio. Them dope cops say Porfilio's a regular around here, and yes indeed, he do participate in them drug gangs. He likes the drug smugglin business. This Porfilio, he even got a nickname. They call him 'El Comico': 'The Comedian.' And this five-point partial print is, quote, 'CON-sistent' with . . . Good Old Porfilio, the Comedian."

Cashdollar stared at the mug shot. "He looks like a mean, nasty character. Porfilio probably finds lots of comic relief in killing guys like Mr. Blackburn—our dearly departed."

*   *   *

Very few local people are familiar with the tiny airport known as "Houston West." The access road to that airport is wedged between a water reservoir and the biggest dog park in America. And the dog park has a much bigger, much more visible sign than the little airport does.

But West Airport is there, and on that day, its short runways were perfectly adequate for the six-passenger Cessna Stationair that was landing. Detectives Slaughter and Cashdollar were there to greet the little red and white aircraft. So was a backup team of police officers and DEA agents, all of them well armed.

It made sense for them to be here. The Cessna came from Juarez, Mexico. A hunch told Slaughter and Cashdollar that Porfilio Garza, the drug smuggler known as The Comedian, might be aboard—a hunch, that is, that they checked out with DEA intelligence, which told them that yes, The Comedian was a likely passenger.

Derrigan Slaughter was surrounded by officers with drawn weapons as he approached the Cessna. "Porfilio Garza? We got a warrant for your arrest."

"I not understand," was Garza's response. "Not nothing is on this plane. No drugs, not at all."

"It's not surprising that there are no drugs on board," Donnie Cashdollar said. "This is a visible flight to an established airport. Makes more sense to truck 'em in. But you, Porfilio, wouldn't take that risk, and you'd fly yourself in.

"Anyway, you're under arrest for the murder of Alan Anderson Blackburn," he added. And he read the *Miranda* warnings from a little blue card.

"I have not done it!" said The Comedian immediately. "I not have nothing to do with no murder. It was Carlos. It was only a surprise to me, not expected! I was there, yes, and I can tell what happen. But I did nothing. It was all Carlos."

One of the DEA agents spoke up. "There are three short barreled AR-15 weapons on this aircraft. All modified to be fully automatic. Plus an AK type, also modified to automatic. All illegal. All of them are there in plain sight, right by where you were sitting, Porfilio. You're under arrest for that offense, too."

It is always best to have a backup crime that is fully provable, such as a firearms crime, if you want to be sure you can hold the suspect. And there was no question about it. These officers wanted to be sure, really sure, that they could hold Porfilio Garza, the drug smuggler known as The Comedian.

*   *   *

As things turned out, Porfilio the Comedian didn't act like a tough guy while he was under arrest. When they got to the police station and went into an interrogation room, all he wanted to do was talk.

"I not speak English as good as I want," he said. "If you talk to me fast, I not understand. Talk to me slow, and I understand some of it, but I still not understand all of it."

"Well, we gonna let you talk to us." Detective Slaughter adopted his most friendly tone of voice. "So, tell us. What done happened with that guy, Mister Alan Blackburn?"

"I not know all of the reason that Carlos stayed mad at this guy." Porfilio shrugged his shoulders. "But Carlos say it have something to do with a connection in north part of America with some guy name 'El Rojo.' This guy we meet with, this . . . Mister Blackburn, he cheat El Rojo, Carlos say. So, he say we got to get rid of this guy Blackburn."

"Okay. So, you stole this here Mercedes, you said, and you done drove over to the meeting place with Blackburn. And Carlos is mad at Blackburn because allegedly, he cheated your friend known as El Rojo. And then? . . . What happened then?"

Porfilio put on his best innocent look. "We get out of the car. Blackburn already there, standing there. Carlos talk to him, and I don't remember it all, except he tell him that El Rojo is mad. And he take money from Blackburn to give to El Rojo. And then, I not know what's gonna happen, but he make Mister Blackburn sit down on his legs."

"On his knees?"

"On his knees, yes. And he stand there behind this man. That is, Carlos, he stand there, and he shoot into the back of Mister Blackburn's head. I not know what gonna happen, and it happen just like this, just that fast. To me, . . . was all a surprise. I not know this man, this . . . Blackburn, but Carlos kill him, just like that. And very fast, Carlos say to me, 'Let's go,' and he's the one who drive, and we drive out of there in a hurry. That's all."

"Hmmmm." Both detectives were skeptical. "Okay, it coulda happened that way. I don't know."

"I can go, now?" The Comedian was hopeful.

Derrigan Slaughter shook his head. "I see why they call you The Comedian."

24
CAN A LAWYER HAVE A LIFE?

Across town, Robert Herrick faced Tom Kennedy across the big mahogany desk in his office. Way down below them, cars crawled along Memorial Drive, and Buffalo Bayou slipped lazily toward downtown. The two lawyers knew nothing about Porfilio the Comedian yet, or about Carlos Leiner.

"We've got less than a month until we try the case for Brianna and Delia," Kennedy said. "So, Robert, you're . . . playing baseball tonight?"

"If it doesn't rain." Robert smiled.

"You always tell me that a lawyer's got to have a life, in addition to being a lawyer. I'm sure that's right. But it's hard to do. And there's so much that we have to get done before this trial."

"Can a lawyer ever have a life?" Robert smiled again. "Not unless he makes it happen."

Under the greenhouse windows, dozens of red and pink geraniums bloomed. The afternoon was beautiful—blue sky with wispy clouds—and the crescents, circles, and squares in the huge oriental carpet seemed to shimmer in the bright light.

"Look at it this way," Robert went on. "We try six to eight cases a year. We have lots more set for trial, and we'd try those too, except that a lot of them settle on the courthouse steps, just before trial, because the defendants like to wait to see whether we really can put our witnesses together."

"Well, that's right, of course."

"So, that many times a year, we're preparing for a trial that's coming soon. Sometimes, we get ready for trial a couple dozen times a year. If a lawyer faces that kind of schedule, he'd better make time to do something else, or else he's never going to have a life."

Robert looked out the window, toward the west. "And if you don't have a life, you're no good to anyone. You're no good to the lawyers you work with, or to your family, or—for that matter—to your clients. It's hard, yes, but it's important to make it happen.

"So, yes, I'm going to join my team and play baseball tonight. If it doesn't rain, and if I can keep my mind on it."

* * *

That evening, the first inning didn't go well for Robert's team, the Houston Cardinals. The other team was the menacingly named Colt '45's, and they had jumped on the Cardinals to make it four to nothing, right at the beginning.

"How'd these guys get four runs against us already?" Manuel Diaz was Robert's catcher. "Robert, I don't think your fast ball is working."

"Something's not working. But I don't know what it is. I feel like I'm hitting the spots I'm trying to hit. One pitch on the inside corner, then one on the outside corner. One at the top of the strike zone, then one down low. My pitches seem to be going where we want them to, and we're mixing them up."

"Well, yeah, you're hitting the target I'm giving you. But these guys, these Colt '45's, they're just hitting fools. They're teeing off on you, Robert."

"What should we do?"

Diaz shrugged. "Well, if what you're doin' ain't working, it's always best to try something different."

Robert looked at him. "Okay. That sounds like a piece of baseball wisdom. 'If what you're doin' ain't working, try something different.'"

"That's right. Yes, you got a good fastball. But you got a good curve ball, too, Robert, and you got that change-up. The fastball ain't working. I'm gonna call for those breaking balls. Let's try something different."

Robert repeated it. "If it ain't working, try something different." He liked the sound of it. "I'm always learning stuff on the baseball field that actually is stuff about life, not just about baseball, even if the baseball field is where you learn it."

"What's that?"

"Never mind." I always make things too complicated, he thought to himself. In fact, it happened frequently, and his teammates were fond of kidding him about it. They liked to laugh and say to him, "Come on, Robert. Most everybody here is smart. Nobody went to Harvard except you."

*   *   *

Two and a half hours later, when the game was over, Diaz said, "Congratulations, Robert. You went the distance. The whole game."

"I know, because I feel it. I'm tired." He already had his arm wrapped with ice.

The curve ball and the change-up had done the trick. After the first inning, Robert had thrown only an occasional fastball, just for variety, just when the Colt '45's weren't expecting it.

"Six to four." Diaz shook Robert's hand. "Us Cardinals, we always score at least a few runs, and if we can get the other team out, it's enough to win."

"Well, and as a wise man told me, 'if what you're doing isn't working, it's best to try something else.'"

"Well, ahhh . . . yes." The catcher stared at him. "But Robert, you know. . . . Only you could get stuck in a single thought like that . . . for that many innings."

25
THE EXPERT WITNESS

The next morning, Robert Herrick was occupied with other matters. "As you were saying, Tom, we've got only a matter of weeks before we go to trial. That's why we're going to New Orleans, right now, to meet with this expert witness, Professor Thompson."

Robert kept his G-II aircraft at Bush Intercontinental Airport. At the time he had acquired it, the G-II was one of the world's most luxurious private airplanes, and he still loved it. Right now, they were ten thousand feet over Galveston Bay, and the pilot was telling the engines to climb to altitude.

In the rear seats, Maria sat together with Pepper, Jonathan, and Robert III. "You kids having a good time?" Robert asked.

Maria held up a glass of good champagne and laughed. "This kid is having an *excellent* time."

"Well, Tom and I have to do a little work, right now. So hold the noise down to a dull roar."

Tom Kennedy sat backward, just behind the cockpit, facing Robert across a burled wood table. "I'm not completely up on Brianna's case, you know. I've been keeping all of the rest of the cases alive while you've been working nonstop on Brianna."

"Okay. So, let me explain. Professor Thompson is a professor at Tulane University, in New Orleans. He's the chair of the Psychology Department. But maybe I ought to back up and explain it from the beginning."

"Good idea. Maybe I'll understand it that way."

"We don't have a he-said-she-said case, at least so far as the video evidence is concerned." Robert paused. "Brianna's words are on tape, and they're clear, and they can't be disputed. Oh, there are some parts where the facts are contradictory. Apparently, this Elmo Naughton has told a couple of different stories about what was said to him. We can show that anything said about Brianna's words to Elmo Naughton, when it's reported by Elmo Naughton, isn't believable. But Brianna's voice on tape to the pretend hit man is pretty clear, and it looks incriminating."

"It IS incriminating," Tom Kennedy agreed.

"As far as the words that are spoken, yes. We can't dispute the words. But we can analyze what they mean."

"How's that?"

"Speaking words isn't enough for the crime of ... *soliciting capital murder*. You've got to *intend* that the words will be acted on. That the murder will be carried out. And the intent has to be corroborated. And the prosecution has to prove all of that ... beyond a reasonable doubt. The intent, plus the corroboration."

"Okay. All criminal cases have to be proved beyond a reasonable doubt. We don't ever handle criminal cases, except for this one. But I know, it has to be proved beyond a reasonable doubt. Still: Don't the words prove what Brianna intended?"

"Superficially. Maybe superficially. But listen. You know Brianna. She says it was never intended to be carried out. It was a 'prank,' in her words, and Delia's too. And if it was a prank that they never intended to see through, if they didn't intend to produce an actual murder ... then it isn't solicitation of capital murder. It's foolish, it's careless, it's stupid to do, but it's not a crime without an actual intent to kill."

"Okay. But the jury can listen to the words and decide that these ladies *did* intend it."

"Or, they can decide they *didn't* intend it. They can decide that Brianna said the words, yes, but she never intended for Alan Blackburn to be killed. And remember: if the jurors aren't completely convinced—if they have a reasonable doubt about whether she intended to see him killed—they have to find her not guilty."

Tom was skeptical. "If they have a reasonable doubt about what Brianna meant—if they aren't sure she intended to get Alan killed, and she just was pulling a prank—then they have to acquit Brianna and Delia. They have to find them not guilty. Right. But it sounds far-fetched, after you watch this tape. And Robert ... *that's* your approach to this case?"

"Well ... yes. You see, Tom, no other approach looks like it will work. And here's the point ... if what you've been doing isn't working, then it's best to try something else."

"You sound like a Zen master or something."

"Not exactly. I heard it on the baseball field. But yes, that's my theory: 'She said it, but the prosecutors can't prove she meant it.' And it's the reason for our trip to New Orleans. To try something different."

The G-II lurched and dove down sharply, as if to question Robert's theory of the case. "The flight path from here to New Orleans is right along the coast, where wet, colder air meets air that's warm and dry," he said quickly. "It's always bumpy."

"Right," said Tom. "If what you're doing isn't working, it's best to try something else, and this case is pretty bumpy."

*   *   *

Most of the way to New Orleans, Robert and Tom discussed how a jury might think about Brianna's words. What the words might mean. Finally, the aircraft began to descend.

"We're coming into Louis Armstrong Field—the New Orleans Airport—from the north." Robert pointed down at the large body of water underneath them. "We're over Lake Pontchartrain. I'd better tell you a little more about this trip, and why we're here."

He showed Tom his handwritten notes. "I've arranged to meet with this expert in psychology, this Professor Thompson at Tulane, to talk about the connection between Brianna's words and her intent. Or the lack of that connection. You see, I thought that maybe we could analyze what Brianna said . . . and find some evidence that she *didn't* intend to have a murder carried out. From the pattern of the words, themselves."

They sped over bayou country, far below. There were massive cypress trees, with huge cypress knees sticking out of the water, and with Spanish moss festooning them. Expanses of dark water flashed by, interspersed with grassy mounds and clumps of trees.

Robert tapped a pencil on the legal pad. "I've looked into it, and I have a couple of possible expert witnesses lined up. One of them is what they call a 'forensic linguist.' An expert in 'discourse analysis.' The field is well established, and it's used to assess threats, to figure out which threats are serious and which threats are not serious, by focusing on the words as a way to tell what the intent is, behind them. It's an important field these days for a lot of reasons, including terrorism. Forensic linguists are a major resource when it comes to threat assessment. And our forensic linguist is named Professor Suarez, from Rice University."

"Forensic linguistics," Tom echoed. "Threat assessment. It sounds like something that will baffle the jury, if nothing else."

"But that's not the subject, today. Professor Suarez, the forensic linguist, is for later. I also have talked to this Professor Thompson, whom we're going to visit right now, and he's another potential expert witness. He is knowledgeable about a lot of fields of psychology, including human motivation. And he's an expert in the psychology of detecting motives. I hope he will be able to tell us that there's no clear indication in Brianna's words that she actually intended to have a murder carried out."

"It sounds crazy." Tom shook his head. "Brianna says to the undercover officer, on tape, 'I'm depending on you to know how to kill him.' And the psychologist is going to tell us that her intent wasn't clear?"

The G-II lurched again. It slowed and descended, in preparation for the landing at Louis Armstrong Field.

*   *   *

The renowned psychologist, whose name was Professor Barry Thompson, looked exactly like what he was: a renowned psychologist. Bald on top of his head, with a ring of white hair. Rimless glasses. A short mustache. A grey jacket with leather elbow patches. Dark brown slacks and soft brown earth shoes.

Good, thought Robert Herrick. It helps, if the expert looks the way he's supposed to.

The psychologist smiled. He liked this case. "Superficially, Brianna's words can be read to suggest a motivation to see this individual killed, yes," said Professor Barry Thompson. "But there are many contraindications, too. In my opinion, this is not the speech pattern of a person who intends to kill."

"Please tell us why, Professor." Robert sounded like a student, taking a basic course in motivational psychology.

"I see only one occasion when the subject—by that, I mean Brianna Edwards—referred to killing anyone. Usually, a subject who intends an act and who talks to another person to motivate him . . . that kind of subject will clarify the motivation unmistakably. Your forensic linguist would probably refer to it as 'interlocking.' If the threat is serious, the co-conspirator will repeat himself or herself with interlocking statements. Statements that repeatedly emphasize the intended result."

Robert nodded. "And then, there's what you told me about the equivocal nature of the statement. You said it in our telephone conversation, before I came here to New Orleans. What did you mean by saying that Brianna's words were 'equivocal'?"

The professor laughed. "Are you saying I was equivocal, when I used the word 'equivocal'?"

It wasn't a very good joke, but good enough under these strained circumstances to make everyone chuckle.

"And I suppose, yes, that it's equivocal to call a statement equivocal, without explaining why." The professor was still amused by his own attempt at humor. "But here's what I meant. Usually, if someone has a strong motivation, they're not going to express it in terms of another person's mental state. They won't just say, 'You'll know how to kill him,' the way Brianna did. They'll say, 'I want it.' Or, in this case, 'I want this person dead.' But that's not what Brianna Edwards says. Instead, she says she thinks that the undercover officer will 'know how' to do it. It's equivocal, and it isn't indicative of a strong motivation. In fact, it's contra-indicative."

"Professor, it's always hard to judge future violence, isn't it?" Robert sounded hopeful.

"Oh, of course. One of the things that people always assume that psychologists can do—but we can't— is to judge future dangerousness. We're really poor at that. Including psychologists who've dedicated their careers to it. On the one hand, it would be very, very useful, if we were able to do it. For example, if we have a person convicted of murder, or assault, or robbery, and if that person is up for parole, it would be nice if we could tell accurately whether they'll do it again. But frankly, human beings are terrible at that. Including psychologists. We can only make our best guess."

The psychologist brightened into a smile. "And, of course, the prosecution has to prove that your two ladies intended to kill, and it has to be proved beyond a reasonable doubt. And these words don't prove it, even if they're on tape."

*   *   *

Back at the hotel, Robert said, "Well, we've got an extra day to have a life in this beautiful city. Did I hear about somebody who wanted to go on the Cemetery Tour? And visit all the ghosts in the St. Louis Bone Orchard?"

Maria, Pepper, and Jonathan all spoke at once. "Me!" "Me!" "Me!"

"That leaves you, Robert, to take care of Robert III." Maria laughed. "You're not Cuban, and that's why you don't even believe in ghosts."

"Well, maybe I'll take Robert III and go to Preservation Hall. I'll introduce my grandson to some really good old-time jazz." Robert always loved Preservation Hall, with its faded sign hanging crookedly on the wall: "Traditional requests $1. All others $2. 'The Saints' $5." Of course, inflation meant that Robert would pay $20 today to request his favorites, such as the St. James Infirmary Blues or the Yellow Dog Blues. "I'm going to give the band a fifty-dollar bill and ask them to let me sing the Basin Street Blues."

"Just don't go next door to Pat O'Brien's and order a Hurricane," Pepper deadpanned. "Unless you let Robert III drink one too."

*   *   *

The flight back home was celebratory. "That psychologist, he's going to be an excellent witness." Tom Kennedy lifted a glass of eighteen-year-old Scotch, from the G-II's well-stocked bar.

"I'm happy to have him on our side, yes." Robert smiled. "But let's not get too excited. I've got to put him through a cross-examination. I've deliberately reserved that kind of preparation until later—until a time closer to the trial. There are lots of questions that Paul Gage can ask, to poke holes in Professor Thompson's testimony.

"He can say: 'Professor, what about the fact that Brianna Edwards talked to Elmo Naughton and said she wanted someone to kill this guy?' Or, 'Brianna went out there to the bar at the Blue Marlin, and she used a code word to introduce herself to this hit man, and she went out to the parking lot, and she talked to him there. Doesn't all of that give us some corroboration of her intent?' Or, the best question of all: 'And Delia withdrew a lot of cash, an abnormal amount, and Brianna was there to pick her up, right?'"

"Unfortunately, it's all true."

Robert nodded. "Yes, and Professor Thompson will have to agree that it's all true. We can't change the facts. We want his testimony to be truthful. I just don't want him to get blindsided."

"So in other words, . . . yes, today was a good day," Tom said. "But . . . we've got a long way to go."

"That's right. Still, it's also right, that today was a good day. If what we were doing, before this, wasn't working . . . I'm glad we tried something different."

26
ELMO NAUGHTON

The rain came down in thick clouds of water, blown into curls by a heavy wind. It was weather of a kind that happens in Houston, alternating with hot summer days.

Inside the house, in his living room, Robert Herrick looked out between the big plantation shutters at the downpour. A chain of lightning ripped across the sky, and too quickly, a peal of thunder crashed, to let them know that the storm was centered directly above them.

Maria Melendes laughed. "Look at Boxer. He's shaking all over. It's not nice to laugh at him, I know, but I can't help it."

"That's right." Robert laughed too. "But when you have a dachshund named Boxer who's that afraid of thunder and lightning, it's hard not to laugh at him." He held his arms out and adopted his most soothing voice. "Come here, Boxer." Instantly, the little dog trotted over and jumped up into the sofa and from there into Robert's lap. "Boxer, it's al-l-l-l-l right. We're going to keep you safe."

He turned to Maria. "This isn't a nice night. I hope it's not an omen."

"A what? An omen? An omen . . . of what?"

"Elmo Naughton called the office and talked to my secretary. To Donna deCarlo. You know, Elmo Naughton. He's the one who says Brianna called him and asked him to get her a hit man. Well, it turns out that . . . Elmo Naughton wants to meet with me."

"I'm glad this case is in Sugar Land," said Maria. "I don't know what I'd do if it were here in Harris County, and if you were up against the same district attorney's office that I work for. It's across the border in Fort Bend County, with a different D.A.'s office. But it's bad enough you've got this crazy case in the first place."

"I know," he said gently. "It's not as if I had a lot of choice."

"Robert, silly, you could have said 'No.' It's easy. Look at me. You just open your mouth and say it like this: 'No-o-o-o.'"

"Well, but I just couldn't, with Brianna in trouble."

"I still don't understand why you're doing it. And now, of all things, you're meeting with this . . . Elmo Naughton? This cocaine addict?"

"I know enough about criminal defense to know that you usually want to interview the witnesses against your client, beforehand. And as it happens, Elmo Naughton contacted me. He wants to talk. I have to find out what he's got to say."

"He's coming to your office?"

"No. Apparently, he's not comfortable with that. It's more like . . he wants to meet at . . . his 'office,' in a way. Elmo Naughton wants me to meet him at this place he goes to called 'The Pink Pussycat Lair.' It's some sort of a . . . 'gentlemen's club.'"

"That's the dumbest euphemism I've ever heard, a 'gentlemen's club.'" Maria frowned. "That Pink Pussycat is a topless bar, just west of midtown, and it's a high crime area. There aren't any 'gentlemen' in the Pink Pussycat Club! It's got all kinds of criminal stuff going on, not just around it, but inside too."

"It's not a place I'd normally choose to go. But it's important to listen to this . . . witness, this Elmo Naughton, for whatever it's worth." He looked out at the rain again, between the shutters. "But meanwhile, it's not a nice night. And I hope it's not an omen."

* * *

The Pink Pussycat Lair was every bit as sleazy as Maria had said. It seemed to be one huge room, big enough for a basketball stadium, but that wasn't what was going on. There were three circular stages in different areas. The one nearest the middle had a shiny pole that projected into the ceiling. On all three stages, young women gyrated in different versions of undress. Red, pink, and blue lights shone down on the three sweaty bodies.

It took several minutes for Robert's eyes to adjust to the darkness, so that he could see beyond the brightness of the floodlights and their narrow, targeted beams. Elmo Naughton was supposed to be wearing a red shirt. He would have his long black hair in a ponytail.

Robert finally located him, in a corner opposite from the entrance. Yes, he had a red shirt and an unkempt, scruffy black ponytail. For some unknown reason, he was wearing mirrored, wraparound sunglasses.

"I saved my first drink to have with you, Mister Herrick." Elmo Naughton smirked, and his voice wobbled more than enough to show that his statement wasn't true. A young lady twisted and bumped in front of him. "This is Gladys. At least, that's her dance name. Her real name's probably something boring—Ellen, or something, probably." And Elmo laughed at that, and Gladys-the-couch-dancer laughed with him.

Robert looked away. "What can I do for you, Elmo?"

"Gladys, leave us alone for a minute." Elmo held up the odd-shaped glass that sat in front of him, which had a reddish-brown liquid in it. "Mr. Herrick . . . instead, maybe I can do something for you. And even better, maybe we can do something for each other."

Uh-oh, Robert thought. Now I'm going to hear it. Some sort of extortion, or some other variety of underhanded proposal.

"I feel really bad about Brianna," Elmo Naughton went on. "I had no idea she'd get in so much trouble. I wouldn'ta called the cops on her, if I'd known."

Robert was silent. There wasn't much to say that would be useful, in response to that. He waited.

Elmo lifted the glass again. "My memory isn't what it used to be. I guess I shoulda used a better football helmet, way back in high school. I can't really say for sure what Brianna said to me, that time that she called me about the guy she was mad at. She was mad . . . that much I remember. I couldn't tell you what she was mad about."

"Well," Robert said, patiently, "What do you now claim, that Brianna said to you, that made you call the Homicide Division?"

"That's exactly what I wanted to talk to you about, Mister Herrick. Like I said a minute ago, I hope we can both do something for each other."

Robert just waited.

"Mister Herrick, I'm in trouble." Elmo Naughton's eyes were wide, and he was as white as chalk. "I got arrested for transfer of cocaine to an undercover cop. And I'm on probation. They'll send me up. Meanwhile, the guys who transferred the cocaine to me—they want some money, naturally. That leaves me without the twenty thousand dollars I need, to pay my lawyer to get me out of my cocaine case."

Robert had no doubt, from watching Elmo, that his fear was genuine, especially his fear of what might happen if he didn't pay for the cocaine that had gotten him arrested.

"The truth is, when I talked to Brianna, I don't know if she ever said anything about a hit man or anything like that, or about whether she talked about killing anyone. I can help you."

Elmo Naughton looked confused, for an instant. Then: "Mister Herrick, I'll be glad to testify to that in court. I'll say that the conversation was innocent. As far as I remember now, it's true. She didn't say anything about killing anybody. But listen. Twenty thousand dollars isn't anything to you. It's nothing. I'm hoping you can help me with the twenty grand."

So that's it, Robert thought.

Quickly, Elmo Naughton added: "It's not that I'm asking for a deal. It's not a deal at all. What I'd do, I'd do anyway, with or without your help. I'll tell the truth in court, which is that I don't remember anything she said about killing anyone. I'm just asking for your help, Mister Herrick, completely unconnected from telling the truth. I'm asking for your help because I need it."

Robert stared at this wretched figure. And he decided what he had to do. "Elmo, I . . . just can't do that." He turned his heel, and he walked away. "I just can't do it."

* * *

At the door, Robert reached into his pocket, almost involuntarily. The recorder was there.

"Mister Herrick, you been dead right." Derrigan Slaughter met him in the parking lot.

"We got it all on tape too," said Donnie Cashdollar.

"I wish we were completely on the same side, gentlemen," said Robert. "Like we've been in other cases before. You guys are fine detectives. I remember those other cases very fondly, where we worked together."

He paused just for a minute. "Can you . . . arrest Elmo Naughton, now? It's extortion."

"Well, we gonna check on that. With the D.A.'s office." Slaughter shook his head. "But I don't know. I don't think Elmo Naughton is excessively smart, you understand, but if he intended to extort twenty thousand dollars, he done it in a way that makes it hard to prove it."

"Robert, we know that what Elmo said to you . . . it sounded like extortion." Cashdollar's voice was expressionless. "And it was meant to sound like extortion. But Elmo covered his tracks really well, if extortion was what he meant."

Detective Slaughter nodded. "There's no law that stops him from asking you to give him twenty thousand dollars. He didn't say that what he'd testify to, depended on whether you gave him the money. In fact, he said the opposite. And he said according to his memory now, he didn't remember Brianna Edwards saying anything about killing anyone. He says he'd tell the truth."

"Well, then, at the very least, he's guilty of making a false report to a police officer, when he called you two gentlemen in the Homicide office."

"Which is a crime, yes," Derrigan Slaughter agreed. "But we can't prove no crime in that phone call, because we can't say that Elmo's report to the police, namely to us, was false. Not a-tall. In fact, we believed him at the time, and we believe him now, for sure, after her meeting with Donnie-the-fake-hit-man, here."

"And he remembers it differently, now," Detective Cashdollar said, flatly. "But that's not a crime, either."

"I see." Robert understood it, even though he was disgusted.

"Well, you done the right thing, Robert, by calling us and asking us to be here." Detective Slaughter smiled. "And I don't know exactly what the D.A.'s in Sugar Land gonna do with Elmo Naughton. They almost gotta put him on the witness stand. But they can't, unless they want to tell the jury beforehand that their case be dependin on a witness who's a big-time liar. So, Robert, you done somethin to the prosecution's case, just by visitin the Pink Pussycat tonight. And I guess I'd hafta say, you also done somethin to help the case for your two ladies."

"Yes, you've done 'something,'" Donnie Cashdollar echoed. "But I guess we'll just have to wait, to find out what that . . . 'something' . . . is."

27
CARLOS LEINER

Two days to go. Two days, until the trial was scheduled to start. Lawyers feel the countdown to trial, in pretty much the same way as an astronaut must feel the countdown to a space shuttle launch. Even though the astronaut is doing something much more important, the feeling is the same.

"Tom, get with our audio/visual people." Robert Herrick's nerves were showing, the way they always did on the eve of trial. "Talk to our A/V director—our head guy, Howard Listrom—and talk to whoever else is involved in the Brianna Edwards case."

"Right. I already have."

"That courthouse in Fort Bend County has built-in A/V facilities, and they're absolutely state of the art. Now, that's nice, but it's also cause for concern. Whenever something is 'state of the art,' you can bet there's going to be something else that's not compatible with it."

"Right."

"We've got our own copy of the Brianna Edwards tape. They'll probably play their tape first, the prosecutors will. But we need to be able to play Brianna's words on tape, and freeze it, and back up, and so forth, all easily."

"Right."

"When we have our experts testifying, Professor Thompson from Tulane and Professor Sanchez from Rice, we want to be able to show them any part of the video we might pick out of what Brianna said, or the undercover officer said, immediately, in freeze-frame."

"Robert, you've already told me this."

"And also, be sure to remember that we've got that audiotape from Elmo Naughton. Same thing. We want to be able to play that back, that Elmo Naughton tape. Any part of it, easily.

"Right."

"Audio-visual stuff is really effective, if it plays right. If the technology works. But it's deadly, if the technology doesn't work. You can absolutely lose the jury, when you thought you had them going your way, if your A/V doesn't work, and if everybody just sits there, waiting."

"Right."

"I think the psychology of it is that the jury expects that if you're a good lawyer, your A/V is going to be smooth, like a sitcom on TV. And if it isn't, the jury thinks you aren't a good lawyer. And if you're not a good lawyer, you must not have a good case. And then, you lose."

"Robert, I know. You tell me this before every trial."

"And Howard and I have put together a whole passel of exhibits: charts and lists and suchlike. Better run through those, too. Go out to Fort Bend County, and test it all in the courtroom. Make sure."

"Got it. Robert, this is what we usually do before a trial like this."

Robert finally smiled. "Sorry. I'm in this kind of mood. I'm preparing for battle. . . . And by the way, did I mention, test our A/V in the actual courtroom, and be sure about it?"

*　　*　　*

The arrest of Carlos Leiner was quick and sure. It was almost a non-event.

It happened one evening when Maria Melendes was sitting at the complaint desk in the main Police Station. All of the assistant district attorneys hated complaint desk duty, including Maria. The job consisted, mainly, of telling citizens that they had no valid case against whoever they claimed had allegedly assaulted them, or threatened them, or stolen from them. The complaint desk was a safety valve. People who had talked to multiple police officers, without any officer thinking that there was a provable crime, still had the opportunity to come in and talk to an assistant prosecutor. But in most cases—almost all—the allegations that citizens brought to the complaint desk amounted to nothing that could make a case in court.

There was a second part of the duty that was slightly more interesting. If a police officer stumbled upon a case that was unclear, and he needed some help, a prosecutor was there to give advice. The assistant D.A. on duty might have to put together an affidavit for a search warrant, or an arrest warrant, or a criminal complaint in a complicated case.

The night was still young. Maria had talked to twenty-two citizens and had a perfect record. None had anything to say that justified a criminal charge. A chubby secretary with magenta-dyed hair, whose name was April, had ushered in a citizen a few minutes ago, and he had told her a long, complicated story. Maria's mind had started wandering, the way it always did at the complaint desk.

"No, I can't have this individual arrested," she found herself saying to this citizen, who had lots of tattoos and several body piercings. "Okay, so you're saying, he pulled a gun on you. And pointed it at you. I'll assume you are right, and I'll agree with you and believe you, so far. But you told me that you, quote, 'threatened to beat the hell out of him,' immediately before that. The police officers who refused to arrest him were right, even though you wanted them to arrest him."

"But I thought it was a crime to point a gun at someone!" the citizen practically shouted.

"It can be. There's a crime called 'reckless conduct' that includes pointing a gun at someone. But see, it doesn't apply here, because you were a lot bigger, and you were talking about beating him up. He has a right of self-defense. Usually, it doesn't include a gun, but it can."

"Well, he started it, because he called me a liar."

"I know. You told me that. The problem is, it just isn't a crime, what happened to you here, with a gun pointed at you after you made that kind of threat."

The citizen looked sullen. And then, he looked really angry. Maria was ready to send April to call an officer, quickly. But then, the citizen got up. "I'll just shoot him next time myself." And he stalked out.

April knew what to do now. "Next!" she hollered, at the long line of citizens waiting to get to Maria.

"Wait a minute! I've got to catch my breath." But as soon as Maria said it, the telephone rang, and . . . slowly, she picked it up. "Complaint desk."

"This is Officer Nordstrom. We got a Mister Carlos Leiner. Just arrested. It's for that Blackburn murder."

The ordinary murder in this city is not particularly memorable. It usually involves a wife killing a husband, or vice versa, or a boyfriend and girlfriend, or two hotheads outside a bar. But Carlos Leiner's name had made big news, along with Alan Blackburn. It symbolized an invasion of drug gangs with their brand of commercial violence, and it had happened in an upscale, safe, and in fact, expensive part of town, near the glittering

Galleria, with its long list of merchants to the wealthy. Carlos Leiner and Alan Blackburn had been all over the news.

"We threw down on Carlos at this Holiday Inn out the Katy Freeway, not far from the West Airport," Nordstrom went on. "Got a tip, passed on by DEA. We're bringing him in."

"Good for you. What do you need from me?"

"It's a murder. Maybe a death penalty murder. We need to get you to decide about that. And we need a search warrant. We think the murder weapon may be right there, in that Holiday Inn. We need a warrant."

"From what I recall, it may be a capital case. This Carlos took fifty thousand dollars from Blackburn, right? I can see two ways it's maybe a capital murder. One, it's a murder for 'remuneration.' Remuneration means money. And also, number two, it's a murder in the course of a robbery. As I recall, Blackburn was going to give Carlos the money in exchange for a drug buy, but Carlos just took the money. Isn't that right?"

"Right." Officer Nordstrom sounded very, very happy at that. Officers are always in a good mood after they make an arrest, Maria thought, and the bigger the arrest, the better the mood.

"We know there's a firearm in that hotel room," Nordstrom went on, "because we asked, and Carlos told us. And it's the same caliber as the gun that was used to kill Alan Blackburn. We left two guys there to sit on the scene and guard the room. We figured we probably could have seized the gun legally, but it's better to be safe than sorry, and so we thought we'd get a warrant."

"I'm glad you waited. I can just see a big fight about a Motion to Suppress the murder weapon when this case gets to trial." Maria pulled out the search warrant forms. "You did the right thing.

"So," she said, "let's get Carlos Leiner ready to get charged."

28

THE FIFTH AMENDMENT

Down in Fort Bend County, Robert Herrick and Mike Robillard were meeting with their clients.

"I hate it that you ladies are still inside this jail," said Robert. "The attorney rooms here aren't very elegant, and I'm sure the rest of it is . . . well, unpleasant too."

"You got that right," said Brianna tonelessly.

"It's worse than unpleasant." Delia's voice was sarcastic. "That's a too-pleasant way of describing it."

Mike Robillard was the fourth person present. "Well, we'd better get started. We've got a lot of wood to chop, here, and a short time before the trial starts."

"Right," Robert agreed. "Now, we've discussed this before, but remember that Mike represents you, Delia, and I represent you, Brianna. But we have a joint defense agreement. We're going to hang together. Do you both want that? Do you both want to continue that?"

"Yes," said Delia.

"We've signed that document that you had us sign," Brianna added, "To agree to a joint defense."

"All right. I've told you, already, about the witnesses we think Paul Gage is going to call, for the prosecution. And I've told you about the cross-examinations we've prepared for those witnesses. We have written outlines of possible cross-examinations, now. Mike Robillard and I will divide the witnesses, according to which one of us seems best for each one."

He paused. "And we've told you about the forensic linguist we've hired"—he and Robillard both smiled at that, because it was an unusual approach to a defense—"and about the psychologist we have, from Tulane University."

Delia frowned. "This is expensive."

"Don't worry," said Robert quickly. His adrenalin was flowing, and he wanted to win this case, not to bill his clients for expenses they couldn't pay. "It's on me and Mike. It's on the house."

"So, ladies." Mike Robillard said. "Now we get down to it. The hardest question."

"What's . . . that?" Brianna wanted to know.

"Whether you two ought to testify. Or either one of you."

Like all criminal defendants, Brianna and Delia had assumed they'd tell their story at trial.

"And the answer is, Robert and I are probably going to advise both of you, in the strongest possible terms, to listen to the wisdom that James Madison gave us, when he cranked down the Fifth Amendment. We're probably going to be telling you, don't. Don't testify."

"Why? . . . Why's that?" Brianna looked disappointed.

"Because it would be easy to answer the questions that Robert and I would ask you," Mike Robillard said firmly. "But then, the prosecutors get to ask you questions. Paul Gage gets to ask you all the questions he wants to."

"Oh." Brianna hadn't thought of that.

"And there would be lots of questions you couldn't answer very well. Like, 'What was the money from the bank for?' Or, 'Brianna, you told the undercover officer you figured he'd know how to kill Alan Blackburn, didn't you?' And on and on."

"Listen to your lawyers," Robert said, just as firmly. "We think you probably shouldn't testify."

"You keep saying, 'probably.' Both of you. What do you mean, by 'probably'?" Delia wanted to know.

"You never make this kind of decision until it's time to make it." Mike Robillard shook his head. "It depends on what develops at trial. And so, you've got to be ready to testify, even though you probably won't."

"So get ready, ladies." Robert's voice was sympathetic. "That's what we're here for, today. We're going to simulate the courtroom, right here. And Mike and I are going to take you through what your testimony would be, even though there probably won't be any."

"Including some really mean questions," Mike Robillard added. "To get you ready for what the prosecutors will ask you."

*　　*　　*

Several miles away, in the police station, Maria was meeting with Norbert Salazar, the firearms expert. She held up a plastic sleeve with a tag that had the case number and Carlos Leiner's name on it. "This evidence envelope has the bullet that was recovered from the scene." And delicately, she handed it to Salazar. "This is the bullet that killed Alan Blackburn."

"Good. I've already fired the weapon that they got from the defendant." The firearms examiner pointed to the .38 revolver that the on-scene officers had recovered from Carlos Leiner's hotel room. "It shouldn't take us long to find out whether this is the murder weapon."

He inserted the test-fired bullet, the one he'd fired into the test instrument from the known weapon. That bullet went into a cradle that could rotate it. He clamped it in place. Next, the bullet from the crime scene went into its cradle and was clamped.

"This comparison microscope shows the two bullets, one above the other." Norbert Salazar explained. "In magnified images, of course. It's a brand-new instrument. It gives clearer images than we've ever had before. And better positioning."

"I know the basic method." Maria said. "If the stripes or striations from the barrel are the same on both bullets, then they were fired from the same gun. That's because guns have rifling trails inside their barrels, and usually they make the bullet spin, which makes it more accurate. And the markings on the bullets that result from this . . . they're unique to each gun. Is there anything new?"

"Only the microscope itself," Salazar replied. "You've got the idea. This baby"—he pointed at the scope—"it lets us rotate it around better than before, put the images on top of each other, put them side by side, and do lots of things to move them around. And it takes pictures that are already labeled, for the jury."

He looked into the microscope. Seconds later, he made his pronouncement. "They're the same."

Maria couldn't help having a feeling of victory and a wave of disgust, simultaneously. It was satisfying to catch a really bad guy, and Carlos Leiner was that. But the experience still felt creepy, because one of these bullets had been used to kill a man. To kill Alan Anderson Blackburn.

"You want to see it?" the firearms expert asked.

Hesitantly, she said, "Ah . . . sure." And she bent down toward the eyepiece. Immediately, she saw the two bullets, one above the other. There were three bands of stripes, and then a blank space, and then one stripe, then a blank space, and then two more stripes.

"That's right," agreed Norbert Salazar. "Except that your terminology is strange. What you're calling 'blank spaces,' we refer to as 'lands.' The lands are the part that's not cut into. And what you're calling 'stripes,' we call 'grooves'. That's the part that the gun barrel cuts into."

"Okay. Lands and grooves. They're the same in both bullets, yes. The positioning of the two images in the microscope is perfect, and the grooves from the bottom bullet run right into the other bullet, as if they were continuous. So, yes, call them lands and grooves, or whatever's the correct terminology.

"But Norbert, what matters is, well . . . what matters is that you can testify that Carlos Leiner's gun is the murder weapon."

29
THE DAY OF TRIAL

Sugar Land, Texas, is divided into three parts.

There is the old mill town, near the ancient site where the abandoned sugar mill stands. There are cracker-box houses in one section of the mill town, decaying older homes in another, and well maintained older homes in yet another. All of them are owned by people who are proud to be near the sugar mill, because after all, as everyone knows, . . . that's where Sugar Land got its name. The sugar mill.

Then, there is the country club set, near Sugar Creek Drive. Million-dollar homes, multi-million-dollar homes, and expensive homes costing just under a million, with manicured lawns bordering golf fairways.

And third, since it is located in a county that is always among the fastest-growing areas in America, there are the immigrant communities. A lot of Vietnamese is spoken in Sugar Land. And Chinese. And there are Indian and Pakistani communities. Of course, there are Mexican-Americans and Hispanics, many of whom will be mildly insulted if you mistake one for the other, but they blend into the warp and woof of America that Sugar Land represents, even if they don't always speak English, because most people in Sugar Land know that it's necessary to speak at least a little Spanish.

The old county courthouse is a landmark, and a beautiful one, with its dark center cupola surrounded by four other turrets, and it has its place on the National Register of Historic Places. But the old courthouse is no longer the courthouse. Instead, the brand spanking new county courthouse is called the "Justice Center." And the Justice Center is massive. It is impressive. At the time of its dedication in 2011, members of the press even wrote that the Justice Center was "palatial." But since it's not popular for government buildings to earn such extravagant labels or to be compared to palaces, the city fathers hurried to announce that, by golly, this new courthouse is functional, too. Judge Sandy Bielstein, a Sugar Land Booster and the toastmaster at the dedication, bragged that the Justice Center will "last for generations to come."

Robert Herrick didn't like it. He looked, once again, at the seven heavy stone gates in front of the courthouse. He frowned at the front tower, right in the middle, that offered a soaring, airy entrance inside. And he stared with disapproval at the huge escalators that led up to the Freedom Shrine at the center of the structure, where an enormous eagle sculpture stares at a framed copy of William Barrett Travis's letter from the Alamo.

"What's the matter, Robert?" Tom Kennedy wanted to know. "You look like you swallowed a peck of persimmons."

"This place sends a message that all defendants are guilty," he answered immediately. "I've tried cases in former firehouses, where the air conditioner wheezed. And I've tried cases in humble courthouses and fancy ones. It's a feeling you get, when you walk into a place dominated by eagles and the like. It says to people, your government is well-meaning and good, and it uses its awesome strength only to fight accurate, well-chosen battles for justice, against criminals who are as guilty as sin."

Robert's eyes took in the Freedom Shrine, once more. "The Judge who spoke at the dedication of this place said it best. He said, 'there is a sense of dignity and a sense of justice' in this courthouse. Well, I'm afraid of a too-easy sense of justice, especially in this case that we have now. For Brianna and Delia's case, I'd rather have a humble courtroom, one where the jurors might be just a little more hesitant about the meaning of justice."

*   *   *

Mike Robillard met them at the door to the courtroom. Judge Winley Waddell sat at the bench, hearing motions and pleas in a dozen other cases, seemingly all at once. They watched the judge for a moment, then stepped outside.

"Unfortunately, I'm worried about the message the courtroom sends, just like the building entrance," Robert said quietly. "Heavy wood paneling on the walls. A marble-like floor that is too formal. The audience benches are like church pews. The judge's place is massive and way up high. And the trouble is, it all seems to announce to a jury, 'This is a place of stern justice, where defendants are rightly prosecuted. Because they're *guilty!*'"

Tom laughed. "And that's not all. There are golden eagles on the staffs of the American and Texas flags. Elegant chairs for the jurors. And fancy counsel tables for us. I know, Robert, that you'd like something a little more modest. But one thing we want is audiovisual equipment that is first-class, and it is, in this courtroom. That's at least one good thing."

Mike laughed too. "I guess we'll just have to try this case using our own abilities. We won't have the home field advantage, that's for sure."

And he added, "I've filed our motions. And also, for each of our clients, I've filed an 'Election for the Jury to Assess Sentence,' as we decided to do."

"Let's hope and pray that it's unnecessary to have anyone assess sentence," Robert said, but with something far less than certainty in his voice.

"You can always hope," was Mike Robillard's answer. "If we're lucky, the jury might hang up. Or if we're luckier than lucky, there might be a jury somewhere that would acquit our two ladies. But in this case, we've got to be realistic."

*   *   *

"Good morning, gentlemen." Paul Gage was wearing a light blue suit, very light in color, and he looked friendly and warm-hearted. A defense lawyer can dress in a power suit. A prosecutor does better to look approachable. A light blue suit, or tan, or gray. Paul Gage had even this detail covered.

"Good morning, Paul," the defense lawyers answered. And Mike Robillard added, "Paul, have you given any more thought to how we might be able to move this case along? I mean, how we might avoid a trial."

"Good for you, Mike," Gage replied. "It's always best to see if we can settle it. In fact, I think it's almost malpractice to go to trial, if you can settle the case and get the result that you ought to have."

Good grief, Robert thought. That's the same thing I've said, over and over, to the new lawyers in my law office. But I never thought of it as applying to a criminal case. Immediately, he said to himself, "That's why I'm glad we have Mike Robillard here too, and not just me."

"I've thought it over." Paul Gage was genial. "And I recognize that you did something for your clients, Robert, when you met with that slimy Elmo Naughton. Even though he's my witness, he's pretty slimy. And you got Slaughter and Cashdollar to come along. Good job. Now, don't get me wrong. I still think the evidence in this case is overwhelming."

He looked squarely at the defense lawyers. "This is a serious crime. Punishable by a sentence up to ninety-nine years. Or the jury can give life, if it prefers that word to ninety-nine. Both mean about the same thing."

"Good grief." This time, Robert said it out loud.

Paul Gage and Mike Robillard both laughed at that. "It's strange," the prosecutor added, "how we can be collegial at one moment and fight hard in the next moment. But Robert, welcome to the club. It's got to be this way. Our clients will never understand it . . . how we talk to each other without insults. But imagine what it would be like, if we tried hard to hate each other."

He paused. Then: "I've thought about it. I realize I said I wanted ten years, earlier. Last time we talked about this, I mean—that's what I said: ten years. But we're right here on the edge of a long trial, and there've been new developments that make your position look a little better—such as this meeting with Elmo Naughton. And besides, your clients are clean, with no previous record."

"So, what do you say? Maybe five years' probation?" Mike Robillard asked, hopefully.

"Well . . . no, not exactly. The State of Texas will be willing to recommend a sentence of five years for a plea of guilty. And realize," Paul Gage was entirely serious as he said this, "Realize: on conviction, that's the minimum sentence."

Five years, Robert thought. Five years out of civil society. Five years of . . . well, what would be like a . . . deathlike existence. It made him sick, for Brianna Edwards, to think about it.

"We'll talk to our two ladies about it and let you know," said Mike Robillard noncommittally.

And as much as I dislike it, Robert thought, he's probably right to say that.

*　　*　　*

"Five years in the Texas prison system?" Brianna was incredulous. "I can't do five years."

Mike Robillard found himself forced to act as the voice of reason. "The main exhibit against you is you yourself on tape, Brianna. And it's a tough, tough case for us, facing the kind of evidence we're facing. The jury can give you ninety-nine years."

He paused to let that sink in. "I once knew a judge who sentenced a defendant to twenty years. The defendant immediately said exactly what you just said, Brianna. He said, 'I can't do twenty years!' The judge wasn't fazed at all, and he had a quick answer. He came back with, 'Well, son, just get up to that prison in Huntsville, please . . . and do the best you can!'"

He let that sink in, too. "I can see a judge pleasantly saying to you, 'Okay, Brianna. The jury gave you ninety-nine years. Get up there to Huntsville, and serve it in good health.'"

"Mike's right," Robert said slowly. "It's not fair, but the prosecutors have all the evidence. It's a rare thing, when it's all shown in a movie that can be played to the jury. But that's what this case is like."

"But . . . but . . . the problem is, we didn't mean to kill anyone." Delia's jaw was set. "You've told us that there's no crime if we didn't intend it. And we didn't."

"You ought to consider the five years," Robert said firmly. "This may be the last chance at that." A defense lawyer is ethically bound to tell his client about every plea bargain offer, he said to himself. Even if the defense lawyer thinks the offer is ridiculous. He's got to tell his client, even if it's an offer that the lawyer might reject, or tell his client to reject, or even laugh at.

But this wasn't even that kind of offer. If I were in Brianna's shoes, he realized, I'd . . . probably . . . take the five years, rather than gamble on getting ninety-nine.

"I'm with Delia." Brianna's eyes were wet, and she began to cry, quietly. "I'm not guilty, and I can't do five years in prison."

There was a long pause. Mike Robillard finally broke the silence. "Well, Delia and Brianna, you're telling us that you want to try this case. Robert and I, . . . both, . . . we think you ought to consider what Paul Gage has offered, because . . . well, unless we're incredibly lucky, you're going to be looking at a whole lot more years than five."

"But we're on your side," Robert said, with his best effort at confidence. "We'll get in that courtroom and do the dead level best we can for you."

The lawyers rose up, said their goodbyes, and walked away slowly.

*　　*　　*

Meanwhile, a few miles away, two old friends were getting together. Two political friends.

"What an office, Senator!" The District Attorney was impressed.

"Thanks." The Senator laughed. "For Sugar Land, it's really high up. Eight floors above Town Square. But you can see everything, out to the horizon."

"But it's too bad you can't see all the way out to the edge of your original House-of-Representatives district." The district was long and narrow, gerrymandered like a snake, and it took in parts of the ship channel to the east, NASA engineers' homes to the southwest, and the old sugar city to the south.

The Senator laughed again. "I still think of it as my district, in spite of retiring. This is home."

"Well, it's only right that you should think of it as your district! It's because of you that this city is always one of America's fastest growing. Roadways, airport, professional baseball team—all of it traces back to you."

"The press would say I had my claws into everything."

"But what do they know?"

"There's a lot the press doesn't know, that's true. And a lot of that, they should know. But every once in a while, they know something. And . . . That's what I wanted to talk to you about."

"Yeah?"

"Yes. We've been friends for a long time."

The District Attorney waited. He looked out of the floor-to-ceiling window down at Sugar Land City Hall. Plenty of money, here, and it's the most elegant city hall anyone's ever seen, complete with a fountain that has a cowboys-on-horseback sculpture worthy of Frederick Remington, wading in an enormous fountain. And still, the District Attorney waited.

The Senator spoke, finally. "The press thinks there's too much crime in Sugar Land."

"So do I," the District Attorney echoed. He was an independently elected official, not especially beholden to the Senator except by the broadest ties, and those ties were mutual. He could say what he wanted. But he knew the Senator, and he knew that this politician, even retired, had a closer reading of the electorate than anyone else within the long, long view from the windows of this office.

"Election's coming up." The Senator folded down the bar, which covered twenty feet of bar space with magnificent walnut, glass, and bottles. Twenty kinds of Scotch, from Talisker and Macallan to Laphroaig. He got down two glasses. "I'm not exactly worried, but I want to see you keep doing the magnificent job the voters know you're doing."

They both laughed, at that. The voters know almost nothing about whether a district attorney is doing a good job.

"District Attorneys lose in three ways," the Senator went on. "Number one, is scandal. Racist emails, or funny things with money. Stuff like that. No problem with you there, unless there's something really hidden that I don't know about." He put ice in the glasses with a set of silver tongs. "Number two," he continued, "is a mass exodus of seasoned prosecutors who leave the office and then lambaste their former chief and say he's an incompetent, or a lush, or he's corrupt."

"I don't expect any of that."

"Neither do I. But here's the third way for a district attorney to lose. The district attorney loses if the people think the district attorney isn't tough enough on crime. Which usually happens due to no fault of the district attorney, but because crime increases."

Once again, the District Attorney just waited.

"Crime in Sugar Land is increasing by leaps and bounds," the Senator said. "Oh, of course, I know it's just in proportion to the growth of the city, which has exploded. But the newspapers don't seem to know that growth of the city is the natural reason. And I just sense it. They're on the verge of editorializing about how bad the crime in this city has become, under this District Attorney. We didn't have barroom murders until recently. It's Sugar Land, and that just didn't happen, but it's happening now."

"I know."

"And we even have home invasion robberies. The kind that turn into murders too often."

The District Attorney nodded. "What are you getting at? I can see where it's going, but I know enough to know you can't really know until you ask."

"You need to get tough on crime. Find high profile cases and prosecute them really hard. With lots of visibility. Have a press conference on the ones that are bad enough. For instance . . . what's this case involving these two girls who hired the hit man? Only he wasn't a hit man, and it sounds like you've got the goods on them."

"The Edwards-Marchand case."

"Maybe that's it."

"After hearing this from you, I'm glad I put my best guy on it. Paul Gage."

The Senator poured two fingers into each glass, over ice. "And be sure the press knows he's your best prosecutor. And let them see that you're charging ahead on it. Loaded for bear. Hell bent for leather, as we used to say back in high school on the football field. And be sure the press knows you're determined to get those two criminals. We've got too much of that kind of crime. Too much murder in Sugar Land."

30
THE JURY PANEL

J udge Winley Waddell stepped down from the bench. "All the lawyers in the Edwards and Marchand cases, meet me in chambers."

When they were assembled there, the Judge got straight to the point. "Have you guys tried to settle this case? It would take a long trial, and this court has plenty, plenty of other business."

"Yes, your honor," said the lawyers in chorus.

"Paul, have you made him your best offer?"

"Yes, your honor."

"Okay, make him a better one."

Everyone laughed at that. It was understandable, though. A judge has to be disposition-minded. A judge has to encourage plea bargaining, which sounds bad, even though it's the same process as settlement in civil lawsuits. But whether the judge has civil cases or criminal ones, the judge has absolutely got to get lawyers to settle, or else the judge is going to end up presiding over so many cases that he can't do justice in any of them.

"Yes, your honor," said Paul Gage. "I'll see what kind of deal we can make that's better."

The judge smiled, but his words were serious. "I know you, Paul. You're a fine lawyer, but sometimes you overvalue your cases."

He turned to the defense lawyers. "Mike, have you talked to your client in a deep and serious way? Have you had the talk that will make her get religion?"

"I've never heard it put that way, but yes, your honor. We both have talked to our clients and advised them to consider what Paul has said. I can't go into detail—"

"Of course not. I'm not asking you to give up client confidences. I'm just asking whether you've taken it seriously. Because the jury can give these two defendants ninety-nine years for this crime."

"We know. They know. Your honor, you yourself have advised them of that."

"I'll confer again with Mike and Robert." Paul Gage was still amused by the judge's directness, but his words were serious. "We'll see what we can do."

*   *   *

"Well, Mike," The prosecutor said to Mike Robillard, and he grinned. "This is an unusual case, but I'll tell you this: we've got a lot of evidence on our side. And if guilt were electricity, your clients would be a power-house."

Robert's face fell. "Our clients are 'powerhouses' of guilt?"

But not Mike's. "You know, Paul, I always enjoy trying a case with you, because whether there's any evidence or not, you've always got the bragging part down. You can do that bragging part really well."

And both of them laughed.

"Don't worry, Robert," Mike said. "He's just hoo-rawing us."

"I'm just having a good time with you before we get serious," said Paul. "And there's a lot for your ladies to be serious about. They ought to be looking for a deal."

"What do you have in mind?" Mike asked.

*   *   *

"Okay, ladies." A few minutes later, Mike Robillard was putting on the voice of a salesman. "The judge has gotten involved. And after he said what he said, Paul Gage has come up with a better offer still."

"In exchange for a plea of guilty, he will abandon the capital murder allegations in the indictment." Robert added. "It will be just, simply, solicitation of murder."

"Which has a minimum of two years," said Mike. "Two years. The minimum. The judge told Gage to come up with his best offer, and I think he has."

"Two years . . . in the state prison system?" Brianna was aghast, still.

Delia said, "For me, I appreciate what you've done, Mike, and you too, Robert. But . . . I'm not guilty of solicitation of 'just plain murder,' either."

Mike Robillard's face was hard. "You ought to take it, ladies. It's a lottery, if we go to trial. A roll of the dice. It's likely to mean a sentence much longer than this."

Robert had to agree. He'd been in civil cases, time after time, when his clients had stars in their eyes, and his job—the job of any competent lawyer—was to advise settlement in the strongest possible way. "Mike's right. You ought to take it. It's just romantic, hoping for something that's not going to happen, to think that your chances in a trial are any better than this."

Delia looked downcast. Discouraged. "I can't . . . do what the prosecutor wants."

"Neither can I," said Brianna.

But neither Delia nor Brianna looked nearly as discouraged as both lawyers. "O-o-o-kay," Mike Robillard whispered. "We'll tell the judge to bring in the jury. And we'll do the best we can for you."

*   *   *

The gallery was full. Members of the press, television and newspapers, were most of the audience. But there also were members of the public who were just curious about this case.

When Judge Winley Waddell announced, "Mr. Bailiff, bring in the jury panel!," a loud swell of anticipation erupted from the crowd.

The long line of citizens walked in slowly, guided by a jury shepherd. It was an old joke around the courthouse: it didn't matter whether the potential jurors were smart or dumb, short or tall, open-minded or biased, as long as they were like sheep. As long as they followed the shepherd, and stayed in line, in the proper order.

"It's a terrible jury panel for us," Tom Kennedy whispered.

Robert had to agree. They'd had a study done. Paradoxically, women were worse for the defense than men—the opposite from their usual role, in which women were more acquittal-prone. "Women sometimes are harder on women, and this is that kind of case," their pollster had said. This panel had more women than men.

Also, recent immigrants with new citizenship were bad for the defense. "They believe in the American government, and that means they believe in the prosecutor." This panel was full of people who wore their new citizenship on their sleeves.

And the men on the panel were managerial and professional types. Bad. Middle aged people, mostly. Bad. The jury panel looked like the kind of group that the poll said was worst for Brianna and Delia.

The judge, being an elected official, looked out over all of these citizens—and saw a group of voters. "Good morning, ladies and gentlemen of the jury panel." He smiled broadly.

The judge's speech went on too long. He introduced the attorneys, talked about the courthouse, and even veered into English history with a mention of "the Great Charter, Magna Carta, that is part of our heritage, signed by King John at Runnymede, which says that the 'law of the land' is the guide for all criminal cases." And on and on.

Finally, the judge turned to the prosecutor, who would be the first to address the panel. "Mr. Gage?"

"Thank you, your honor!" And Robert heard the radio announcer's voice, Paul Gage's pleasant voice. "Let me also say good morning, ladies and gentlemen of the jury panel. I am Paul Gage, and I am an assistant to your elected Criminal District Attorney, Mr. William McKee."

The practiced way that Gage said "*elected* Criminal District Attorney" made Robert feel even worse. It was as if he had said, "I'm part of the leadership that you've chosen, through the great American way."

"The *Grand Jury's indictment*"—Gage lingered over those words, as though the indictment were proof of guilt and the Grand Jury became a kind of superior advisor to this jury—"the Grand Jury's indictment charges these two defendants, Brianna Edwards and Delia Marchand, with solicitation of capital murder."

He turned to the citizen at the far right side of the first row. "Mister Andrews, you're the number one juror. Some people would call you the 'guinea pig' juror, because you get the first questions." Everyone on the jury panel laughed pleasantly at that, because even if it wasn't uproariously funny, they were nervous in a courtroom and welcomed any break from the atmosphere. "So, Mr. Andrews, solicitation of capital murder means that these two defendants are charged with attempting to hire a hit man to kill another person."

The prosecutor paused for dramatic effect. "Mr. Andrews, if you were *the elected* Criminal District Attorney of this county, would you be satisfied with a person such as yourself on this jury? Can you be fair to the people of the State of Texas?"

Mr. Andrews smiled. "Yes, I think so."

"And I assume, of course, that you could be fair to the defendant."

"Yes, I think so."

It's useless information, Robert said to himself, because virtually everyone thinks he or she is "fair." But it was good diplomacy. The best lawyer for examining jurors would be a game-show host: someone who was like the faces of Wheel of Fortune or Jeopardy. Someone who knew how to make a show-business presentation. Paul Gage was good at it.

The potential juror, Mr. Andrews, was the manager of a country club. Middle aged. A good juror for the prosecution. But . . . bad for Delia and Brianna.

Paul Gage covered the elements of the crime, by reading them from the indictment. "These are the points that the prosecution must prove, and you will hear them proved."

He talked about the burden of proof beyond a reasonable doubt. "That does not mean beyond all doubt. It means a reasonable proof. It's a burden I gladly accept, and you will hear that kind of proof today."

He even talked about the defendants' right to remain silent. "If they don't testify, you can't consider that. I ask you, not to consider it." Then, his eyes clouded. "But if the defendants do testify, and they don't tell the truth—then, it's your job to hold it against them."

It seemed like an eternity, but it was really only about forty-five minutes, before Paul Gage enthusiastically said, "Thank you, ladies and gentlemen!" And sat down.

31
THE DEFENSE

Mike Robillard spoke to the jury next. His style was different. His delivery was halting, quiet, and slow—but sincere. Different lawyers have different styles, and Robert saw that Mike, too, was effective.

And now it was Robert's turn.

"Good morning, ladies and gentlemen!" His voice was as enthusiastic as Paul Gage's. "The judge told you that I am Robert Herrick, and I am, and he told you that I represent Brianna Edwards, and he's right, I do." The jurors smiled at that unusual turn of phrase. Courtroom humor doesn't need to be very funny.

"Mr. Andrews, I listened while the prosecutor asked you questions, and I have no doubt you're right. You could be fair. And so could everyone else here."

"Thank you," said Mr. Andrews happily.

"It's important to remember that a criminal case is . . . well, different. For one thing, we have a presumption of innocence. As Brianna and Delia sit here, they are innocent. The law says so. Can you follow the law, and believe in the presumption of innocence?"

"Of course!"

"Let's test that out." Robert moved to the other end of the row, to signal that he was going to change the tone. "Imagine that you had to vote right now, Mr. Andrews, on whether Brianna and Delia are innocent or guilty. How . . . would . . . you . . . have to vote?"

"Well, I couldn't decide, yet. I haven't heard any of the evidence."

"Let's think that through." Robert smiled a broad smile. "You haven't heard any evidence yet, and that's the point. What's the right verdict, if there's no evidence of guilt, and only the presumption of innocence?"

The light dawned on Mr. Andrews. "I see what you're getting at."

"Right. Good for you, Mr. Andrews. You'd have to vote not guilty. Not guilty, because there's no evidence yet, and Brianna and Delia are presumed innocent."

"Well, I guess you got me." But the juror's smile showed that he had enjoyed making the point.

It was an old strategy, and a risky one. Sometimes the guinea pig juror sees it as a trick. Sometimes he even gets angry. But this wasn't the kind of case that could be won without taking risks. And Mr. Andrews was happy. So were the other potential jurors. Everyone likes a little puzzle once in a while, a small intellectual challenge, including citizens who report for jury duty.

Robert used the presumption of innocence, then, to emphasize the prosecution's burden of proof. "The lawyers for the state can't just carry the ball to the fifty-one yard line. They have to lug it all the way over the goal line and score a touchdown, because we don't guess a person into the penitentiary."

And he used his favorite metaphor. "The burden of proof beyond a reasonable doubt means something like this. . . . *If the state's case were an airplane with engine trouble, and you were an aircraft mechanic, . . . would you let it fly?*"

The jurors looked at him as he went on. "Let's say that there's a good chance that the state's airplane won't crash. It probably won't crash. It would be easy to say, 'let it fly.' Just like, it would be easy to say, 'find them guilty.' But if you were the aircraft mechanic, 'probably' wouldn't be good enough. You'd want to be certain, before risking people's lives.

"And this is the same situation. Proof beyond a reasonable doubt, when Delia's and Brianna's lives are at stake, means that you have to act just like that aircraft mechanic . . . and you have to say, not guilty . . . unless you're really, really sure."

Thirty minutes later, with sweat running down his back, Robert sat down. "That's a good job," said Mike Robillard.

"But now we have to get our jury and try this case." Robert shook his head. "And that isn't going to be easy."

*   *   *

It's called "picking a jury," but nobody actually gets to pick the jury. Instead, each side gets to remove some people, the ones they dislike the most. And now, Robert and Mike were huddled with Brianna and Delia, to do just that.

"The first one we should strike is the first juror, Mr. Andrews." Mike held the jury list, with a pen poised over it.

"But I liked Mr. Andrews!" Brianna protested.

"Me too," said Delia. "He answered all the questions directly."

"Well, Mike's right." Robert's voice was firm. "The last people we want are people who are sure about things. People who answer decisively. Those are the people that will find you guilty beyond a reasonable doubt. We want people who are slow and indecisive."

Mike drew a line through Mr. Andrews's name on the list. A few minutes later, in this way, they had decided on all of their strikes.

They turned the jury list in, with the names scratched out that they wanted to remove. Paul Gage did the same thing with his list. "He's the prosecutor, and he's getting rid of the ones we want the most," Robert explained to Brianna.

The final twelve—the jury—was made up of eight women and four men. "Eight jurors that our poll says are unfavorable," Robert groaned. There were five jurors in professional and managerial positions. That was bad, too. "We got off the ones we thought were worst," Robert said glumly. "But we still ended up with a jury full of the kind of people the pollsters say will be against us."

*   *   *

With that, the trial ended for the day. But in a way, it continued. It was the subject of a well-attended press conference later that afternoon.

The elected District Attorney pulled a big gooseneck microphone toward himself. The podium said, "District Attorney of Fort Bend County," in six-inch letters. Right above the magnificent circular seal of Fort Bend County. As he started this press conference, the District Attorney thought about the Senator's advice, because after all, a District Attorney is a politician too.

"The prosecution of Brianna Edwards and Delia Marchand is well under way," he announced in a deep baritone. "We intend to vigorously prosecute this case. Many of you in the press have reported on it already. I can't go into the evidence, as I'm sure you understand, because the trial is ongoing. But I want you all to know how strong the tradition of law enforcement is in my office. Let me recite some recent history to show how we prosecute crime in Fort Bend County.

"Last week, we obtained a verdict of life in prison in the Shepherd murder case. Before that, the jury sentenced Carl Manion for murder to sixty years. We asked for life, and the jury gave sixty years, but I never criticize a jury verdict."

The District Attorney named a half dozen other cases that had ended in long sentences. He omitted one case, a celebrated case, in which the defendant had been convicted only of misdemeanor assault in spite of an indictment that charged him with attempted murder, and he had received probation from the jury. After all, jury trials are unpredictable, as lawyers know, and this D.A.'s record really did show a long line of successful prosecutions.

"At my right side is Assistant District Attorney Paul Gage," the District Attorney concluded. "A public servant for nearly twenty years. Veteran of more than twenty-five murder cases. I sometimes tease him about the one case he lost, which he didn't really lose, but the jury reduced it to manslaughter, and Paul, maybe I should have given you a pay cut."

Paul Gage laughed, and so did the members of the press, in a dignified way.

"As usual, with a press conference about an ongoing case, there will be no questions, because I can't discuss the evidence. But with Paul Gage doing it, you can be sure that the case against Brianna Edwards and Delia Marchand will be professionally presented to the jury. And vigorously prosecuted, I guarantee."

32
A GAME OF CHESS

The Alpha Dorrance Memorial Chess Tournament draws masters, grandmasters, and those way below the master level. Tonight, they crowded across the Great Room at the fancy St. Regis Hotel. They hunched over their tables and stared at tiny fields of battle. There was the constant sound of players clicking their time clocks, to beat the limit of three minutes per move.

The Dorrance Tournament insisted on colorful chess pieces and boards. The black chessmen were standard black, but the white pieces were a strange off-white. The "black" squares weren't black; instead they were a dark buff-brown color, and the "white" squares were actually a pale green. During her lifetime, Alpha Dorrance insisted that this color combination was "pure." You could visualize chessmen better across the entire board with these colors.

Now, Elmo Naughton's hand moved with assurance as he advanced his bishop's pawn, his third-from-leftmost pawn, just one space. He touched the top of his clock to stop it.

His opponent laughed. The guy was a middle-aged man from Indiana with heavy horn-rimmed glasses, and evidently, he thought Elmo's move was silly. "I guess cocaine slows down the chess brain. Right, Elmo?"

Elmo, playing as White, recognized this remark by Black for what it was: a distraction. An effort to "push his buttons," or to bring out his emotions. Chess is a mean, cruel game, because it's a game of wits, meaning that a brilliant win can give a player a self-satisfied high, but an unanticipated loss will break his ego. And Elmo Naughton knew the difference.

"But I don't have to worry about a brain slowdown to beat you, Bubba," Elmo said immediately.

His opponent, Black, slapped the chess clock a little harder than usual. Good, Elmo thought.

Chess isn't a game of moves. It's a game of constantly changing strategies. Chess masters know hundreds of tactical sequences, with all of their variations. Their names are wonderfully romantic and medieval-sounding. There's the "Four Knights Game." The "Queen's Indian Defense." The "Sicilian Defense." And it goes on and on.

Elmo Naughton had begun the game with what is called the "Italian Opening." But he had disguised it as the "King's Gambit Opening," and the disguise had been effective, because his opponent didn't seem to recognize the Italian strategy. After five unremarkable moves, Elmo eased into the "Evans Gambit." This aggressive style of play would let him win control of the center of the board and relentlessly attack the black king. And it was likely to bring out the worst in the player across the board. To respond, Black needs to avoid trying to defend his pawns and concentrate on bringing out his big guns—his knights, bishops, rooks, and queen—but that takes patience, and Black, by now, was short on patience.

Suddenly, Elmo's phone vibrated. He looked at the number. "I've got to take this." His opponent shook his head. The chess clock was counting down his three minutes.

Paul Gage's voice came through, from the other end of the line. "Elmo, we've got to have you here. Right now. Remember the deal we've got." The prosecutor's voice was calm, but firm.

"I'll be on the way in fifteen minutes."

His opponent, Black, looked up sharply, at the arrogance of that.

The Italian Opening—the strategy that Elmo had played—is also known as the "Giuoco Piano," which is Italian for "the quiet game." It is deceptive. The "Evans Gambit," into which Elmo had shifted, is the opposite. It suddenly makes the black king difficult to defend, unless Black sacrifices pieces in a way that seems unnatural.

After nine more moves, Elmo checkmated the middle-aged man from Indiana. He called the doorman for his beat-up 1999 Chevy and headed toward Sugar Land. "I'm glad I'm mostly free from cocaine tonight," he told himself. He'd had to clear his mind for the tournament. "I guess I'm even . . . ready to meet with these hard-ass prosecutors."

*   *   *

The District Attorney's office in Fort Bend County is as magnificent as Justice itself. Paul Gage's office overlooked an expansive greenbelt with knots of trees, and it was unusually well appointed for the office of a public servant. One wall was covered by certificates, all attesting to the prowess and civic-mindedness of this assistant district attorney.

"Elmo, make yourself comfortable. We've got this evening to game-plan your testimony. These next few days in this trial are going to be like a game of chess."

Elmo smiled at that.

"To begin with, we've got to tell the defense lawyers about the deal we have with you, Elmo. Our agreement to move for dismissal of that cocaine possession case that's pending against you, in exchange for your testifying."

"Why? Why would you be silly enough to tell about that?"

"Because it's part of the rules, Elmo. And because I don't want to be in a position where I've broken the rules, and after breaking them, I'm dependent on a gentleman who can tell everyone about it, which would be you. Even assuming I'd break that kind of rule, anyway, which I wouldn't."

"Okay." Elmo's voice was sullen. He hated Robert Herrick, and he didn't want him to know anything.

"And also, I've got to have you testify about that deal, early in your testimony." The prosecutor looked at Elmo with a stare that promised not to tolerate any nonsense. "As I said, it's going to be like a game of chess. We're better off telling about this deal ourselves, instead of letting our opponents bring it out with lots of big drama, and imply that we've been covering it up."

"Now," the prosecutor went on, "I need to prepare you for your testimony, step by step."

Two hours later, they finished. The night was pitch dark, and Elmo Naughton was white-hot angry.

"In other words, this guy Robert Herrick taped me without telling me, and he had the cops listening in. And now, he's gonna know about the charges against me, and the agreement for my testimony. He'll probably be in a position to block me from getting out of that cocaine case. It pisses me off, and I'd like to bury his ass."

"Careful, Elmo. The rules are strict. I'm probably going to have to tell the defense lawyers what you just said, about burying his ass. You'd better just keep your thoughts to yourself."

Elmo stalked out. Even though this wasn't the kind of chess game he was good at, he understood the message that silence was the wiser course.

*   *   *

Murders are contagious. You can't have just one. Other people see it, and they get the idea; and by now, Elmo Naughton had gotten the idea.

A short while later, he felt better. He was wide awake, fully engaged, and optimistic. The magic was working. The snow, the powder, the candy. It always made the world brighter, made colors pop out, made excitement. Excitement and optimism about getting even with Robert Herrick.

He trotted to the closet and pulled out his shotgun. A sawed-off version, just over a foot long. He had been given this prize by a customer in need, in exchange for a bag of snow. The guy had begged him to take it: "You can carry this thing under your coat and go anywhere there's not a metal detector." But the customer had advised him, unnecessarily, that "this thing is as illegal as hell."

He put the shotgun in the trunk of his car. Something told him he wouldn't find Robert Herrick very easily tonight, though, and after arming his dilapidated vehicle with this made-for-murder weapon, he went back inside and resumed his cocaine reverie.

33
THE HIT MAN TESTIFIES

Paul Gage's opening statement was smooth, short, accurate, and convincing.

And for Robert Herrick, it was painful to hear.

When the prosecutor raised his voice to finish, all of the jurors gave him their attention. "In the end, the two defendants were arrested together. There was Brianna Edwards, driving the getaway car, ready to pick up Delia Marchand. And there was Delia Marchand, coming out of the bank, carrying wads of crisp new hundred dollar bills. The money to hire a hit man was right there, in her purse!"

Paul Gage marched across the courtroom and swung his arm to point. "Ladies and gentlemen, we don't usually use words like 'caught red-handed.' But if anyone was ever caught red-handed," and he pumped his arm twice with his index finger extended, "it was these two defendants! They did it, and you need to find them guilty!"

Robert knew that the prosecutor usually points at the defendant, but he hadn't expected anything this theatrical. Gage's finger was only a couple of feet from Brianna's nose, and he stared at her, and then at Delia, for an instant. It was a complete, official, and convincing condemnation, symbolizing the prosecutor's absolute certainty of the defendants' guilt. Then, Gage turned on his heel and walked briskly back to his place at counsel table, as if to rid himself of the sight of these two evil spirits.

The courtroom was silent. Then, Judge Waddell spoke.

"Mr. Herrick? Your opening statement?"

"Thank you, your honor!" He deliberately kept his voice firm and upbeat. "Brianna and Delia will reserve their opening statements until the beginning of the case for the defense."

Paul Gage looked surprised. So did the judge. It was permissible for the defense to delay opening, but it was an unusual strategy.

Robert looked directly at the jurors. "We ask you, ladies and gentlemen, to do something really important: to reserve judgment. We will make opening statements for Delia and Brianna after the prosecutor rests. We will have plenty to say at that time, but until then, we beg you: please wait, before deciding."

Mike Robillard had opposed this strategy, at first. "As a defense lawyer, I usually want to tell my story early in the case, right after the prosecutor's opening. Otherwise, jury attitudes can only follow the direction that the prosecutor has set."

"But this case is different," Robert had said, and eventually, his co-counsel had agreed.

"We really don't have a different version of the facts, just a different interpretation," Mike had said finally. "We've already told the jurors, over and over during the jury examination, about our defense, which is that Delia and Brianna never intended for any murder to be carried out. And the key thing is, we have good experts: our psychologist and our forensic linguist, who will tell the jury that our clients never intended to kill anyone."

Mike wrestled with this risky strategy, but finally he came to Robert's position. ". . . And . . . I guess . . . it's probably best not to let Paul Gage know what we're going to do, because then he'd develop his evidence to try to overcome our experts."

Now, Robert sweated through his shirt and hoped that the strategy was a good risk. But as he finished his plea for the jury's patience, he saw that while he was talking to them, the jurors were looking at the prosecutor, and not at him. That was a bad sign.

*   *   *

"Call your first witness," said Judge Winley Waddell to Paul Gage, in the mechanical voice of a man who has said these words many times.

"Ladies and gentlemen of the jury, the State calls Detective Donnie Cashdollar." The prosecutor announced the witness's name as if he were introducing the President of the United States.

The lanky detective walked silently to the witness stand, wearing a blue jacket, red shirt, green tie, and black pants. A few of the jurors' faces betrayed their immediate judgment, which was that the man was not a sharp dresser.

"Introduce yourself to the members of the jury, please."

"Detective Donnie Cashdollar."

"And how are you employed, Detective Cashdollar?"

"I am a detective with the Houston Police Department, Homicide Division."

Any veteran police officer develops enough courtroom experience to become an excellent witness. Robert winced at the word "Homicide," almost as though it were a verdict of guilty. Donnie Cashdollar's testimony sounded like, "These sleazy defendants got our attention in the *Homicide* Division, because they're . . . *homicidal!*"

The prosecutor had Detective Cashdollar tell about his Bachelor's Degree in Criminal Justice and his seventeen years' experience in police work. He had "worked too many homicide cases to count them" and had done plenty of continuing education, "just to stay on top of things." And then, Paul Gage asked about the telephone call from Elmo Naughton. Yes, Detective Cashdollar knew Elmo Naughton; yes, he knew that he was a habitual user of cocaine who also dealt in the stuff; and yes, he was surprised to hear from Elmo.

And then, the prosecutor asked the next question the wrong way. "So, Detective Cashdollar, what did Elmo Naughton tell you?"

It sounded innocent enough. And in most places it would be a proper thing to ask. But not in a courtroom. The Rules of Evidence that govern trials are complicated, and sometimes they make it difficult to tell the story.

Robert Herrick sensed an opening. He stood up, immediately. "Objection, your honor. That question is improper, because it obviously calls for hearsay."

"Sus-TAINED!" The judge's ruling was immediate and definite.

Across the courtroom, Robert saw the prosecutor thinking. And rethinking. His question had raised a red flag. If he had gone about it another way, he could have brought the story out, but by now, it was clear. Anything he asked Detective Cashdollar about what Elmo had said would be hearsay. It would be asking what someone else had said, about the case facts.

"Based on the conversation with Elmo Naughton, did you have occasion to open an investigation that involved one of these defendants?"

Robert stood up quickly. "Objection. That's improper too. It's asking indirectly about what Elmo Naughton may have said."

"Sus-TAINED!"

Sometimes, jurors see objections as obstructions. But Robert had tagged the prosecutor with "improper" questions twice, and by now, Paul Gage had decided to cut his losses.

"Is Elmo Naughton available, to your knowledge, Detective Cashdollar?"

"Yes, of course."

"Is he under subpoena to testify to what he knows of this, if anything?"

"Yes, he is."

And with that, the prosecutor dropped the subject and turned to another line of questioning. Yes, Detective Cashdollar had placed a telephone call after hearing from Elmo Naughton. Yes, he had placed that call to a Ms. Brianna Edwards, in Sugar Land. Yes, when he mentioned the name of Elmo Naughton, Ms. Edwards seemed to know who Elmo was. Yes, Brianna Edwards had asked about a hit man, even if not in those exact words. And the Detective knew it was Brianna Edwards who answered the telephone, because he had arranged to meet with her at a restaurant in Sugar Land in the same conversation.

The judge interrupted. "Since you mentioned a restaurant, that reminds me that it's lunchtime," he announced. "Ladies and gentlemen of the jury, please remember all the admonitions I've given you." He pronounced the word slowly and deliberately—"AD-mun-NISH-uns"—and Robert wondered why he didn't just use a word that all the jurors might recognize, such as "all my orders."

The judge went on: "And do not discuss this case among yourselves or with anyone else, including your wife or husband, just as I've told you before in my other AD-mun-NISH-uns."

*   *   *

"It's as good as we could have hoped for," Mike Robillard told Delia and Brianna. "Robert's got the assistant D.A. stopped in his line of questioning, and he's got the jurors thinking that the assistant D.A. is confused."

"Won't that just make them curious about Elmo Naughton?" Delia wanted to know.

"Maybe." Robert was thoughtful. "It's not an exact science, trying to second-guess jurors. What they sometimes think, though, is 'This assistant D.A. isn't very good at what he's doing, and since he isn't very good at it, he probably doesn't have a very good case.'"

"That's what we're hoping," Mike said. "And twice, the judge has agreed with Robert after he's said that the questions were improper. We can also hope . . . maybe . . . that they'll think the prosecutor is sneaky, since he asked questions that were improper. And they can't trust him."

Brianna and Delia went back to the holdover cell for lunch. Robert and Mike went to the Justice Center cafeteria.

"When it's all said and done," Mike said matter-of-factly, "I wonder if there's any way to stop Paul Gage from making his points, like we're hoping."

"Well, we can always hope," Robert agreed. "But actually, what I most hope is that it doesn't backfire, with the jurors thinking that we're trying to hide the truth from them."

*   *   *

In the afternoon, Paul Gage set up the video of Brianna and Donnie Cashdollar in the parking lot at the Blue Marlin. There was much less testimony that Robert could object to or keep out, and the video was devastating.

The prosecutor froze the frame, and he pointed at Brianna and the fake hit man standing together. "And that's you on the right, Detective Cashdollar? And Brianna Edwards on the left side?"

"Yes, sir."

The prosecutor pushed a button on his remote, and the video went forward. Then, when Brianna asked about the hit man's experience, he stopped it again.

"Detective, what was that we just saw? Did there come a time when the defendant, Brianna Edwards, asked about your experience as a hit man?"

"Yes, sir." Donnie Cashdollar smiled slightly, at the foolishness of it all.

"What so-called 'experience' did you actually have as a hit man, if any?"

"Absolutely none, of course."

"And will the next part of the video show you telling Brianna Edwards a bunch of stories about your so-called 'experience?'"

"Yes, sir." Detective Cashdollar's smile grew wider.

"Why did you tell her that?"

"We had an intended murder victim." Suddenly, now, Cashdollar was deathly serious. "We knew that if we didn't act, Brianna Edwards would keep trying to pay someone to kill Alan Blackburn. And the only way to prevent that was to get her to say it, in a perfectly lawful way, by going undercover. And when you go undercover, you play a role. That's what I had to do, to prevent a murder. And I told her about my fictitious 'experience,' because that would either get her to stop this murder, if she was going to, or say she wanted it done, if she did."

"Did you ever suggest to her that she have Mr. Blackburn murdered, or urge her to, or tell her to, or use any means whatsoever to try to persuade her to have Mr. Blackburn killed?"

"No, sir. Absolutely not."

The prosecutor touched the remote again. And the video showed the undercover officer saying, "Disgust, I should say, is the reason I kill people." Robert cringed. His stomach felt wobbly as the tape moved forward, while the image of Detective Cashdollar explained, on videotape, how he had secured his victims with duct tape before killing them.

The video stopped again. "And Detective, did there come a time when this defendant, Brianna Edwards, said that she assumed you would know how to kill Alan Blackburn?"

"Yes, sir."

"Did her statement to you include the actual word 'kill,' when she said she figured you would *know how* to kill him?"

"Yes, sir. She specifically mentioned 'killing' him, and she used that word, 'kill.'"

The assistant D.A. pushed the remote again, and the jurors were treated to Brianna's image right there on the videotape, saying that she was depending on Cashdollar to know how to kill Alan Blackburn. Then, he pushed the remote one more time again, and the jurors saw and heard Brianna's words a second time, with Cashdollar answering questions about the details of the scene. In all, Paul Gage played the "kill" sequence four times, before deciding that once more would be too much.

Robert had thought the first time was too much. Just once was enough to bury my client, he thought to himself.

34
CROSS-EXAMINING THE DETECTIVE

The rest of the videotape was an anticlimax. Brianna and Detective Cashdollar negotiated the price of five thousand dollars, or at least that was what the videotape appeared to show. They parted ways. And a short time later, after having Cashdollar give the jury a brief sketch of the arrest of Brianna and Delia, the Assistant D.A. said, mercifully, "Pass the witness."

Robert paused for a moment as he reordered his notes. He knew most of what he was going to ask, but the order and the details had to be arranged right now.

"Good afternoon, Detective Cashdollar."

"Good afternoon, Mr. Herrick."

"You and I have known each other a long time, and we've worked on a number of cases together, haven't we?"

"Yes, we have." Donnie Cashdollar smiled.

Robert smiled too, because the two combatants did know and like each other, in spite of the situation. "And Detective, I've never misled you about any case, have I?"

But the Detective was an old hand at courtroom etiquette, and he wasn't going to fall for this. His smile widened. "Wel-l-l-l . . . there's a first time for everything, Mr. Herrick. And I don't know whether you intend to mislead me . . . or the jury . . . right now!"

Suddenly, everyone in the courtroom was having a good time. The jurors laughed. Robert, for his part, knew that Cashdollar had gotten the better of him, but he made a point of not showing it.

"And, Detective, I've got the same concerns about you." He said it with a smile. A trial lawyer has to roll with the punches.

Then: "Now, I have a number of serious questions for you, Detective Cashdollar. First of all, the one statement that the prosecutor played four times, that's the one time, and the *only* time, that Brianna said anything about killing anyone. Isn't that right?"

"Honestly, I didn't count."

"Well, if I told you it was the only time she used the word 'kill,' you wouldn't disagree, would you?"

"No, sir, I guess not."

"And she never said that *she* wanted anyone killed, isn't that right?"

"Well, that's the way I understood what she said."

"Detective, I assume you're not a psychologist. Or a magician with a crystal ball, to determine the exact meaning of someone's words. That's right, isn't it?"

"Well, yes, I'm not a magician. Or a psychologist. I did get a degree in criminology, though."

"Which didn't include a course in psychoanalyzing people's thoughts, I assume."

"No, sir."

"In terms of her words, Brianna Edwards never said she *'wanted'* to have Alan Blackburn killed, did she?"

"Not in those exact words, no."

"Instead, she referred to you, as knowing how."

"How to kill, yes."

Now, Robert told himself, it was time to ask some risky questions, because he'd never win this case without taking risks. "And Detective Cashdollar, since you yourself are not a psychologist, you'd have to depend on a psychologist if you wanted to know the psychological meanings of Brianna's words, isn't that right?"

Paul Gage stood up. "I've been patient, but I think this question calls for speculation that's way beyond what's admissible in evidence."

"Not at all, your honor." Robert's answer was quick. "The detective has testified about his interpretation of the contents of Brianna's mind. All I'm asking him is, to tell us about whatever expertise he might claim about doing that kind of interpretation, compared to a psychologist."

The judge nodded. "The objection is overruled. But Mr. Herrick, keep both feet on the ground, and don't drift off into Cloud-Cuckoo Land."

"Yes, your honor," Robert replied immediately. "So, Detective, you may answer the question. Your psychological analysis of Brianna's intent wouldn't be as well-grounded as a psychological analysis by a real psychologist, would it?"

"I don't know." Cashdollar shrugged. "I've seen some psychologists who I wouldn't trust, even to say what day of the week it was."

That evasive answer, Robert knew, was the best he was going to get. But now, he needed to tie it to the case at hand. "And Detective, if we call a psychologist to testify in Brianna's defense, and the psychologist says that Brianna never had the intent to have any murder carried out, he'd have a better basis for saying it than you do, right?"

"I object," said Paul Gage.

"Sustained," said Judge Winley Waddell. But he was listening intently, and so were the jurors. The question didn't need an answer to make its point.

"And Detective, do you know what a *'forensic linguist'* is?"

Cashdollar's eyes bugged out. "Ahhh ... no, sir. I never heard of ... whatever you called it: a forensic ... whatever."

"Do you know what *'discourse analysis'* is?"

Paul Gage looked as though he wanted to object, but he also looked as though he couldn't think of any reason to claim that the question was improper, because he didn't know what it meant either.

So Detective Cashdollar answered. "Nossir. Never heard of ... discourse ... analysis."

"And Detective, that means, that later, when a forensic linguist testifies for Brianna, that through the use of discourse analysis, he can tell that Brianna never intended for any murder to take place, he'd know more than you about the subject, wouldn't he?"

"Objection, your honor," said Paul Gage quickly.

"Ahhh ... sustained." But the judge's voice showed that he thought the jurors had a right to be curious about forensic linguists and discourse analysis ... and about what on earth they might have to do with this case. Because he, the judge, was curious too.

At the defense table, everyone was pleased. Later, when Professor Sanchez testified as a forensic linguist, his superiority at discourse analysis would have been already established. Even Brianna and Delia managed to smile. Mike Robillard grinned, and Robert could barely keep himself from jumping up and down.

*   *   *

But Robert's exuberance was short-lived. Paul Gage took the witness on redirect examination. And it took only a few questions to poke holes into the impression that Robert had built, so carefully.

"Detective Cashdollar, were you present when Brianna Edwards and Delia Marchand were arrested?"

"Yes, sir."

"And was anything found in Delia Marchand's purse that relates to this case?"

"Yes, sir, absolutely. She had just withdrawn a whole bunch of money, all in bundles of hundred dollar bills, brand-new bills, enough to pay a hit man."

An hour later, at the end of the court day, Robert and Mike went back to Robert's office to work on the case overnight. But what Robert did was to drink a quantity of very good Scotch whiskey from the cabinet he kept in the corner, and he didn't really do a lot of work on the case.

35
ELMO'S STORY

The morning was bright and beautiful, with a few fluffy clouds and plenty of clear blue sky. The fields around the Justice Center were deep green, and the wind just lightly brushed the trees to make them fuller. It was the kind of day that you see frequently in Texas in late August, and all of the hurrying people entering the Justice Center had a spring to their steps. Even the lawyers.

The press was here, in force. Today, Elmo Naughton was scheduled to testify.

The top headline on Sugar Land's local newspaper reported about yesterday's courtroom drama. In three-inch letters, it announced to the world, VIDEO SHOWS DEFENDANTS HIRING HITMAN. Robert shook his head. "I hope that's not everyone's impression of what yesterday's evidence was about."

"Especially not the jury," Mike Robillard agreed.

"Maybe today will be better for us, with Elmo Naughton on the witness stand. Paul Gage has to get him to testify, because he's an essential part of the story, and he's going to be a terrible witness."

But an hour later, unfortunately, Elmo seemed to have found his voice. His long mass of rough black hair was ugly, but it made him seem real and genuine, while he testified in a soft, self-assured voice.

You never can tell how witnesses are going to come across, Robert thought to himself. No matter how much you prepare, a trial develops unpredictably. And that includes witnesses who you think won't be credible. Elmo Naughton, a good witness for the prosecution? It seemed impossible. But that's what was happening.

Paul Gage guided Elmo skillfully through testimony about his friendship with Brianna Edwards. Elmo told the jury that he liked Brianna, and in fact she had helped him when he was in trouble, more than once. Now, the prosecutor eased into the real subject: Brianna's call. The conversation in which she had talked about hiring a killer.

"Elmo, exactly what did Brianna Edwards say about that?"

"Brianna said she needed to 'break somebody's knees.' That's how she put it, in those exact words. I remember, because from what I know about Brianna, it wasn't like her. And then, she added, 'Actually, worse.' Meaning, she wanted something *worse* than breaking somebody's knees! And she thought . . . she said she thought, that I . . . would know people who can do that kind of thing."

"And what did you say, to that?"

"I asked her, flat out, did she mean she wanted to hire . . . a hit man? And I said it didn't sound like her. Because it didn't."

"And what did she say back to you, after that? After you used the words, '*hit man*'?"

"She said she knew it didn't sound like her. And she asked, 'How much does it cost?' I told her it depended. The fact is, I didn't really know about hit men."

"Elmo, just so that the jury can know, have you ever been involved in hiring a hit man?"

His eyes widened. "Never! No! No!"

"Okay, Elmo, relax. Now: did you ask Brianna Edwards whether she really wanted to . . . *kill* someone?"

"Yeah. I said, 'You've got to be really sure.' And then, I asked, flat out, 'You want to kill this guy?' And she got real quiet for a second, and then she said . . . 'Yes.'"

"Your honor, I pass the witness," said Paul Gage immediately.

There's a simple rule: when you get the testimony you need, quit asking. Don't ask the one question too many—the kind of question, here, that might tempt a witness like Elmo Naughton to say something that destroys his own credibility.

Paul Gage had done it well. He had stopped at the right time.

Robert looked at the jurors. They were fascinated. All of them were staring at the witness. All of them believed him. Elmo Naughton shouldn't have been given any credibility whatsoever, but he had all of the jurors believing him.

Worse yet, Judge Winley Waddell immediately said, "It's lunchtime." Inwardly, Robert groaned. The jurors would have an hour and a half to let Elmo's story settle in. And the defense wouldn't have the opportunity to cross-examine Elmo until the jurors had full stomachs. In early afternoon, when everyone would be ready for a nap.

*　*　*

Robert didn't eat much for lunch. His head was churning with contradictory thoughts, the way a lawyer's plans always do, before the cross-examination of an important witness.

Should the first step be to play the audiotape of Elmo Naughton at the Pink Pussycat Lair? The tape would show Elmo saying that Brianna had never asked about a hit man. It would confront Elmo with some statements he'd have a hard time denying, statements that contradicted his testimony here. Or should the first step, instead, be to take apart what Elmo had just now said about the call from Brianna? Elmo would have to admit that Brianna hadn't used the word "kill," herself. Later, Robert could play the Pink Pussycat tape, which would emphasize this point again. Or should he have Elmo describe Brianna's hesitation, her uncertainty, to show that she never intended for a murder to take place?

Start out with what can be agreed to, he told himself. That's the usual rule for cross-examination. And be sure to end with something strong.

But with Elmo Naughton, it was all so uncertain.

*　*　*

"Good afternoon, Mr. Naughton." Robert kept his voice friendly, but firm.

"Ahhhh . . . yeah." Elmo was hostile. Good, Robert thought.

"You now claim that you asked Brianna something like, 'You want to kill this guy?'" Robert raised his voice, slightly. "But actually, it was you, Mr. Naughton, who used the word 'kill.' She never used the word, 'kill.' Isn't that right?"

"Ahhhh . . . yeah. But I knew what she meant."

"I'm asking you what she said. You were the only one who used the word, 'kill,' Mr. Naughton, and Brianna Edwards never said the word 'kill.' Isn't that right?"

"Well . . . yeah. I guess so."

"And you now claim that, before that, you used the words, 'hit man.' But you were the only one who said the words, 'hit man.' Brianna never used those words, did she?"

"I knew what she meant."

"Brianna never used those words, 'hit man,' and you were the only one who used the words, 'hit man,' right?"

". . . I guess." Elmo Naughton was evasive, and he looked evasive. Good.

"Let's be clear." Robert shifted his position, to emphasize the point. "Let's be clear: Brianna was angry. Angry at this fake boyfriend, Alan Blackburn. Anyone would have been angry, after being taken advantage of the way Brianna was. Wouldn't they?"

"I have no idea."

"But even though she was mad, and even though she showed a lot of anger, Brianna herself never used words about killing anyone, or about a hit man. You, Elmo Naughton, were the one who brought up killing or hit men. Isn't that right?"

"I . . . guess so."

"You didn't think Brianna was serious about killing anyone, and you even had to ask her about that, by saying, 'You need to be sure.' Isn't that right?"

"I guess." Elmo was nonchalant, with an attitude that seemed to say, who cares? Good, Robert thought

"And in fact, Brianna was hesitant, and she kept stopping what she was saying?"

"She acted silly. She acted like she didn't have her mind made up, yeah."

For the first hour with Elmo Naughton, Robert asked simple questions, all leading questions, all about a single subject. Elmo was the ideal uncooperative witness: so uncooperative, that anyone on the jury could see it. And then:

"Fact is, Brianna just didn't sound like she *intended* to have anyone killed, did she?"

"No, she didn't. She was silly, like I say."

The point was well made, and Robert knew he needed to drop the subject, rather than give Elmo a chance to help the prosecution. So he went on to another subject. "Mr. Naughton, you asked me to meet you at a place called The Pink Pussycat, didn't you?"

"Well . . . I, . . . well, yeah."

"And at the Pink Pussycat, where you told me to meet you, you asked me to pay you a *bribe,* didn't you?" Robert had chosen the word "bribe" on purpose, hoping that the term was harsh enough so that Elmo would deny it. The jurors all looked up, sharply.

"What? No, I didn't ask anyone for any kinda bribe. You got the wrong case."

"And at the Pink Pussycat Club, where you wanted to meet me, you said, and I quote, 'The conversation was innocent. Brianna never said anything about killing anybody.' You said that, didn't you?"

"I don't remember that."

After that, it was almost an anticlimax when Robert asked Elmo Naughton to identify his own voice on tape. And it was almost an anticlimax, too, when he played the tape and stopped it when Elmo said, "I'm hoping you can help me with the twenty grand." ". . . That was you asking for a bribe, wasn't it, Elmo?" And it was like an anticlimax when Robert played the part of the tape that said that the conversation with Brianna was "innocent," stopping it with each sentence, and asking Elmo whether that was his voice. Whether that was what he had said.

The jurors seemed to expect all of this. Good, thought Robert. Mike seemed pleased.

* * *

But their optimism didn't last long.

Paul Gage's redirect examination of Elmo Naughton was short but effective. "Mr. Naughton, how did you get involved in this case? Who contacted you first? Who was it, who chose to deal with you?"

"Brianna Edwards contacted me."

"It wasn't the police, or me, who chose to do business with you? It was Brianna Edwards, right?"

"Yeah. That's right."

"And after the call from Brianna Edwards, did you call the police? Like a good citizen?"

"Yeah. I thought I was doing the right thing. Mr. Herrick wants to make me look bad, but I did the right thing."

"And is it true that Brianna Edwards went to a specially arranged meeting, later, for the specific purpose of hiring a hit man?"

"Yeah. It was obvious by now what she intended to do."

"And at that meeting with the hit man, did Brianna Edwards say she was depending on him to, quote, 'get this guy killed'? And she used the word, 'killed'? And it's on tape?"

"Yeah."

"And she negotiated the price, on tape, and then, she was there to pick up Delia Marchand at the bank, with the hit-man money?"

"Yeah."

Paul Gage put on his best look of complete disgust. "That's all the questions I have for this . . . *witness.*"

By now, Elmo Naughton was staring at Robert Herrick with a look of white-hot hatred. It was a look that seemed to say, . . . "I'd like to kill you, right now." But that wasn't Robert's biggest concern. He was watching the jurors, who were nodding with agreement throughout all of Elmo's answers to Paul Gage. "We're going to lose this case," he whispered, to no one in particular.

36
THE WORDS OF THE LAW

The next day, Maria said, "Robert, it's Saturday."

"Yes. And I've got to go to the office. Brianna's case isn't going right. I need to get ready for Monday."

"No." She said it in a firm voice: a voice that wouldn't tolerate any nonsense. "No, Robert. You need to pay attention to me. Your wife."

"Ahhhh . . . okay. Can't I do both? Be attentive to you, and also, go to my office?"

"No. You promised to take me to the Museum of Fine Arts."

He remembered. "Oh, no. It's that Jules Olitski exhibit. The blob artist."

"One of the finest modern artists in the world. Those blobs are good blobs, according to me." She frowned at him. "And you promised to take me."

He sighed. It wasn't an invitation, it was an order—and he knew he had to do it.

*   *   *

"The Olitski paintings are upstairs." The museum guide pointed. "Lots of people want to see that."

"Not me," Robert murmured under his breath. She frowned at him.

The first painting was called *Frame Extension*. Robert stared. "It looks like nothing! The left side's white, the right side's gray, and there's a cloudy area where the white and the gray mix, between the two. That's all there is!"

She frowned, again.

The second painting had a more intriguing name: *Key of Aegenor.* "But . . . it's the same thing as the other one! Only this one's got the gray cloud spreading diagonally through the middle. It looks like he just used spray paint!"

"Listen, Robert, it *IS* spray paint." This time, he didn't have to look, to know she was frowning. "Olitski used spray paint on these, you . . . you genius of an art critic."

"Okay. I apologize."

"You don't have to apologize."

"Yes, I do." He put on his best ironic look. "Years ago, a wise man told me his secret to a long and happy marriage. I said spray paint, and it is. I was right, when I guessed about the spray paint. I was right, which is wrong in a marriage. And the wise man told me, 'If you ever discover that you're right about something in your marriage . . . then hurry, as quick as you can, and apologize for being right.'"

She laughed. "You're like a Neanderthal, here. But it's okay. You're taking me to the art museum, and that's good enough."

Olitski's paintings got a little better, he thought, with one called *Turquoise in the Embrace.* A blob of navy blue floated over a mixture of red and yellow blobs, all in a black background, all framed by turquoise slashes on each side. "It's an unusual color combination, and yet, it works," he admitted. And then, there was *Anastasia, Green and Blue:* a close-up of a larger-than-life woman's figure painted in greenish-yellow, reclining on a blue bed, in a red-and-purple room. "Not great, but much better than the spray-painted ones."

"Okay. You're excused to go to the office." She smiled. "The office . . . that's BOR-ing, on a Saturday. But you can go, now that you've done your duty."

"You know," she added, "I can help you. I once had a case that involved the same law that's involved in Brianna's case. The solicitation-of-murder law. There's a part of this law that makes it hard for the prosecutor ever to win one of these cases, unless there's lots of independent evidence, in addition to the solicitation."

He waited. And listened.

"There's a section (a) to the solicitation law—the solicitation statute—but there's also a section (b). And the key to it is section (b)."

"I know. I read it."

"But the point is, part (b) really challenges the prosecutor. It's hard to understand what it really means, until you've tried a case with it. I probably shouldn't give away prosecution secrets, but you're my handsome guy, and you finally brought me to the art museum. So, let me tell you: It doesn't matter that the defendant is on tape, trying to hire a hit man. That's not enough. And it's hard for the prosecutors to supply enough proof, ever . . . in a solicitation-of-murder case. Because of that section (b)."

"I'll go back and look at the law again." He was thinking, hard, about what she had to say.

* * *

"Okay." Tom Kennedy held the book open. "Here's section 15.03 of the Penal Code. "Criminal Solicitation," it's called. . . . This is the solicitation statute."

"And here's part (a) of that law, which is simple, and it's just like what's in the indictment." Robert pointed. "But what we really want to look at, is section (b). And here's section (b)."

"This is going to be pretty technical."

They both read section (b). The words swam together, like gibberish:

> *"A person may not be convicted under this section on the uncorroborated testimony of the person allegedly solicited and unless the solicitation is made under circumstances strongly corroborative of both the solicitation and the actor's intent that the other person act on the solicitation."*

They stared at the words, but they knew they still didn't see everything. There was more in this law than anyone could see at a glance.

Then . . . slowly . . . the light began to dawn. "Look here," said Robert. "let's underline some of the key words." He singled out three phrases. After he had marked it, part (b) looked like this:

> "**A person may not be convicted** under this section on the uncorroborated testimony of the person allegedly solicited and **unless the solicitation is made under circumstances strongly corroborative of** both the solicitation and **the actor's intent that the other person act on the solicitation.**"

Robert stared at the result. Then: "Let's read the important parts out loud."

> "**A person may not be convicted . . . unless (there are) . . . circumstances strongly corroborative of the actor's intent that the other person act on the solicitation.**"

Robert started making a list on a legal pad. "So, there's a lot more to this statute than you can ever have on a videotape. Paul Gage has a lot of requirements to prove."

He felt a rising excitement, and he could tell that Tom did too. This was the game that lawyers play—the game that everyone learns in law school. Lawyers love to read something in a book and see how it can be used for someone, or against someone, because of the precise words of the law, which sometimes are awkwardly written. Lawyers are experts at chopping a law into its tiniest parts.

He held up his index finger. "The solicitation of murder—that's issue number one. But a solicitation isn't enough, even if it's proved way beyond a reasonable doubt. Even if it's on a video."

Tom Kennedy nodded. "First, there's got to be a solicitation of murder—someone has to ask someone else to kill someone. And if the person doing the solicitation is on videotape, maybe that's proved. But that's only the beginning of what Paul Gage has to prove."

Robert marked, *"1. The solicitation itself,"* on his list. "Right. That's only the first thing. . . . The second thing is, the person who does the solicitation—Brianna, here—has to intend for the other person to act. To complete the murder." Robert marked, *"2. Brianna's intent to complete the murder."*

"In other words, Brianna's not guilty unless she actually *intended* for Detective Cashdollar to kill Alan Blackburn. Paul Gage has to prove it beyond a reasonable doubt—that it wasn't a prank, and that Brianna intended for Cashdollar to actually go through with the murder. And, of course, proof of her intent is in her head, not just on the tape."

"And we're still at the beginning." Next, Robert marked: *"3. corroboration of Brianna's intent to complete murder."*

Tom nodded, again. "The third requirement is that, even aside from the words on tape, there has to be 'corroboration' of the fact that Brianna intended a murder."

"In other words, . . . even if the solicitation is proved, and the intent is proved, that's *still* not enough. There have to be *extra* circumstances proving the intent."

And finally, Robert wrote *"4."* on the legal pad. "We're still not through. The fourth thing is, just plain 'corroboration' isn't enough. It isn't enough for Paul Gage to provide just *some* extra circumstances of proof. The law says the extra proof has to be *'strongly'* corroborative. The corroboration has to be strong." He wrote, *"4. Strong corroboration,"* and he underlined the word "strong."

A rising enthusiasm infected both of them. The two lawyers were staring at the list and smiling.

Then another thought dawned on them. A negative realization.

"Well, but . . . Paul Gage isn't going to let himself be beaten that easily." Suddenly, Robert sounded subdued. "There's some other evidence he can point to, as corroboration. The money in Delia's purse, for instance."

"Ahhh . . . yes. Paul Gage will say, 'Withdrawing the money to pay the hit man isn't just corroboration.' He'll say, 'It's *strong* corroboration.'"

Silence. Then, finally, Robert spoke.

"Oh, well. Nothing's ever easy, in a courtroom. Our corroboration defense is worth a shot, at least." He corrected himself, by saying, "Our *strong* corroboration defense." But his voice wavered.

37
ELMO'S REVENGE

Robert and Tom sat there, thinking and wondering how to make the best argument they could, with the defense they had just developed: the defense based on part (b) of the solicitation law, which they began to call the "strong-corroboration-isn't-there" defense. Midnight was approaching, but neither lawyer felt it. Both of them had scribbled lists and phrases and scraps of ideas on legal pads, using number two pencils, worn down, by now, to the wood.

"We can move for dismissal when Paul Gage rests his case," Robert said. "You know what I mean. Technically, it's not a dismissal, but you know what I mean."

"Technically, it's called a 'Motion for Directed Verdict' in a criminal case," Tom corrected. "Or, a 'Motion for Acquittal.'"

"All right." Robert smiled. "We'll file a motion called a *'Motion for Dismissal, and for Directed Verdict, and for Acquittal.'* We can call it by all three names. That ought to cover it."

"I guess that'll cover it. But making the motion, . . . that's the easy part. How do we structure our argument—our explanation to the judge—so that it's not just going through the motions with a lot of nonsense? How do we present it to the judge so there's at least some kind of possibility . . . that the judge might just *grant* it?"

"Ummm, yes. That is the real question, isn't it? We want for this defense to work."

Suddenly, a loud bang-crash noise interrupted them, followed by a series of three quick bangs. Robert jumped. Tom jumped. "It sounded as if it came from the hall, outside," Robert said quickly.

A security guard was among the more-than-a-hundred employees of Robert Herrick and Associates. In fact, there were five security guards, to cover the office around the clock: three to fill three eight-hour shifts, plus two additional guards to cover when the others weren't there. Obviously, these noises had something to do with the security guard.

They hurried out of Robert's office. Around the secretarial bay where Donna deCarlo usually sat. Down the long hallway. Around the corner to the side hallway. And they peered around the edge.

The security guard had the front door open. The huge, floor-to-ceiling glass door stood ajar. One side of it was shattered, and the guard was outside, together with another person who lay on the floor of the external hall in front of the elevators. The wounded man who lay there had long, unkempt black hair tied in a thick, surly ponytail. The two lawyers took the scene in quickly. They saw that the front wall behind the glass door had a tight pattern of gouges, of shotgun pellets, slashing through it, and they saw Elmo Naughton's sawed-off shotgun lying on the floor next to his body.

The security guard was calling 9-1-1. He had dropped his .45, with which he had shot Elmo Naughton at least twice, after Elmo's wild shot through the glass door. There was a great deal of blood, as anyone would expect from a wound inflicted by a .45.

"I think he'll stay alive if you get here quickly!" the security guard yelled into his phone.

Seeing that the danger was under control, Robert approached closer. "What can we do, Elmo?"

"Just stay away from me." The wounded man's hatred was blacker, stronger, and more palpable than ever.

From somewhere, Robert found a blanket and a pillow. The security guard frisked Elmo—was there another weapon?—and, finding nothing, put the pillow beneath Elmo's legs and covered him with the blanket. Within five minutes, a team of paramedics rushed out of the elevator. They wrapped the wounded man's shoulder and his leg, and they got the bleeding stopped. The lead paramedic searched for a vein for what seemed forever—and finally, he got an intravenous feed established. Two minutes later, the paramedics were gone, pushing Elmo on a stretcher.

"I've called HPD," said the security guard. "The police department. They'll be here, but I told them it's non-emergency at this point." He looked at Robert. "I'm glad you went to twenty-four hours on the security."

"I know. It's expensive, but you guys are worth it."

The security guard smiled. "I was on the force in Atlanta, and then the FBI, before I retired. I couldn't stay retired, and I figured this kind of job would be interesting, but not too busy. Man, I was wrong. I never saw anyone with a sawed-off before. And I never had to shoot my weapon, much less shoot anybody and actually hit them."

He and Robert looked at each other. They both knew what it meant. A justifiable shooting—even one that's completely necessary, like this one—can leave a police officer or security guard with serious mental health issues. The effect is unpredictable; sometimes it happens, and sometimes it doesn't. Robert finally spoke up. "You'll have to stay here. You, yourself, know only too well, that you've got to stay, because you'll have to talk to the radio patrol officers who show up, now. Otherwise, I'd send you home and get backup for you. But when you finish here, take some time off, and we'll cover for you."

"You're right. I may need it. Thanks for understanding."

*　　*　　*

The next morning was Sunday. At six o'clock, the telephone rang—and rang and rang, insistently. Robert answered it out of a deep sleep, a sleep made dreary by the happenings of the night before, a sleep that had begun less than two hours earlier.

"This . . . is Robert Herrick. . . . Hello?"

"Attorney Herrick . . . this is Professor Suarez."

". . . Who?"

"Professor Antonio Suarez. You know, from Rice University."

Silence.

"I'm Professor Suarez. You know, the forensic linguist. You've engaged my services for this trial involving your client, Brianna Edwards."

"Okay. . . . You've got my attention. Hi, Professor Suarez. Sorry. I'm waking up."

"It's me who ought to say, I'm sorry. I'm calling, now, at six in the morning on Sunday. It's early, I realize."

"That's . . . all right. Forgive me for being sort of, well, disorganized. A guy tried to break into my office last night, a guy with a shotgun."

"Oh! Well, I'm even more sorry about calling so early, then. I . . . should have waited until a more decent hour. It's just . . . I've been worry-ing about this problem all night, and worrying since Friday, actually, and . . . it's just . . . I had to call you about it. I couldn't wait any longer."

"What is it, Professor Suarez?" He stood up.

"It's my wife. The doctor says she's got breast . . . cancer. Serious. I don't want to go into the details, but it's serious, and they say they need to operate quickly. This coming Thursday."

"I'm so sorry."

"And after that, I plan to be with her. All the time."

The professor's voice caught. "And that means, I can't testify unless there's some kind of television feed. Or unless I can testify right away, now. Monday or Tuesday, like."

Robert's answer was immediate. "I understand." He saw an image of his first wife Patricia, in her hospital bed, almost like a picture on a screen. "Believe me, Professor, I understand." But now, he couldn't focus on the professor's problem very well, because his mind flooded with memories of Patricia in her pain at the end, which was as ever-present as the opiates that were supposed to silence it. "I understand."

"So, you can take care of it?'

"Professor Suarez, I . . . I just don't know."

The professor's voice was panicky, now. "I'm not leaving her. Somebody's got to take care of this."

"It's . . . well . . . the prosecution is still putting on witnesses. We don't get our chance until later. Nobody knows exactly when."

"Can it be done by television?"

"I . . . don't know. But I'd sure like to avoid that. It really reduces the impact of your testimony."

"I understand. Can it be done in the next couple of days? Can I testify Monday or Tuesday?"

"I . . . I . . . well, the prosecution is still putting on witnesses. . . . Well, I don't know. The judge *can* allow it." Robert saw Patricia's image again, close enough to touch, as he grasped for an answer. "The judge can let us put on a witness out of order. It's really unusual, and I don't know whether he will let us do it. Or not."

They talked, this way, for another twenty minutes, repeating what they both had said, several times, because there really was no good answer. Professor Suarez showed a strain, a sound of pain, that only increased as the conversation endured. Robert felt it too.

"Professor, I'll try," he said. "I'll try to get the judge to let us have you testify early. I'll try, early on Monday morning."

Maria walked into the bedroom carrying coffee. "What's going on?"

"When it rains, it pours, just like the old saying goes." His eyes were fixed in the unseeing stare of exhaustion.

38

THE FORENSIC LINGUIST

Monday morning, it rained. And rained. A solid wall of rain. There were flash flood warnings, and flash flood watches, and flash floods that materialized in fact, on streets passable by canoe. But the Justice Center was open, and the courtroom stayed in operation.

"I just hope it's not a signal of doom, this rain," Robert said to Tom. "I've absolutely got to get Judge Waddell to let me put on Professor Suarez out of order."

Once inside the courtroom, he walked up to the bar. "Your honor, may we approach the bench?"

Conferences at the bench were always a crowded affair. There would be at least three lawyers from the prosecution side, three from the defense, and a court reporter, and sometimes a bailiff. And sometimes, a witness too.

"Your honor, I have a witness who will be unavailable soon. He is here in the courtroom. Respectfully, I beg the court's indulgence, to allow us to put this witness on the witness stand early, during the prosecution's case." And he sketched for the judge the situation of Professor Suarez, whose wife had been diagnosed with breast cancer.

The judge looked puzzled. "I don't know." He rearranged some unrelated papers on his desk. "Mr. Gage has witnesses, too, who have schedules. And he's probably prepared his testimony in a certain way. Mr. Herrick, you're asking me to let you put on part of the defense case in the middle of the prosecution's case, and that's a real problem."

"Your honor, I object to Mr. Herrick's motion," the assistant D.A. agreed. "I'm ready to go forward. My evidence won't hang together, and it won't tell the jury the full story, if I get interrupted now. And my witnesses are here, waiting."

There was strain in Robert's voice. "Professor Suarez can tell you, better than I can, how much he needs this. And for my part, I can only say, he is crucial to the defense. The Professor is here, in the courtroom, right now, and I'd like to have him tell you, your honor."

The bailiff brought Professor Suarez to join the throng in front of the judge. And Judge Winley Waddell took over the questioning. "Tell me, Professor Suarez, what your situation is."

"My beautiful wife . . . thirty-two years . . . may leave me, later this week. I mean, she may . . . leave this earth." The Professor's eyes were shining, and his voice broke. "On Thursday, I'm not going to be available. Nothing can keep me away from . . . my wife. And after that, I'll be with her, and nothing can pry me away from her. If I'm going to do this, your honor . . . it's got to be . . . now."

The judge fiddled with papers on top of the bench. He obviously understood the depth of the problem, and so did Paul Gage, who suddenly stood silent. Finally, in a quiet, somber voice, the judge asked: "Mr. Herrick, how long will this testimony take?"

Robert's response was quick. "An hour or so, from me. That depends on Mr. Gage's objections, if he makes them, but an hour of testimony. And I don't know how long Mr. Gage will cross-examine, but I expect that it can be done this morning."

"I don't know." The judge still looked down at his papers, which everyone knew had nothing to do with this question.

At last, he said: "Less than one hour, Mr. Herrick. You're on the clock. Less than one hour, and you will turn into a pumpkin and disappear if you are not through at that time." His face was stern, again. "Do we understand each other?"

"Yes, sir! When do you want me to proceed, your honor?"

"Right now. And don't dilly-dally."

*　*　*

It took ten minutes for the court reporter, bailiff, and other court hangers-on to settle down. And for the bailiff to bring the jury in, and for Professor Suarez to swear the oath and take the witness stand.

He was an impressive witness, by appearance. He didn't look at all like a bookish professor. His navy pinstriped suit was perfectly cut. His silver tie was dotted with tiny blue diamonds. His black wingtip shoes were lustrous, and he wore a white button-down shirt. With his salt-and-pepper hair and tanned skin, he looked like a Fortune 500 executive rather than a professor.

"Your education, please, Professor Suarez? And your current employment?"

"A bachelor's degree in Chinese from Harvard College. A Ph.D. in linguistics from Stanford University. I'm a professor of linguistics at Rice University."

"Isn't Rice sometimes called 'the Harvard of the Southwest,' just to explain what an outstanding University it is?"

"Well, yes." The professor managed a wry smile. "But I'd say, that's a misnomer. The correct phrase would be, 'Harvard is the Rice of the Northeast.'"

The jury liked that. Regional pride is everywhere, and so is regional prejudice—in this case, against pointy-headed Northeasterners, such as those know-nothings at Harvard. Here, everybody knew Rice, and they knew that it was better than someplace far away, like Harvard. Professor Suarez still had to prove himself to this jury, but he had made a good start.

"How many languages do you speak, Professor, and what are they?"

"Seven. Spanish, Chinese, Arabic, German, French, and Japanese."

"That's six. Don't you have one more language?"

A pause. "Oh, of course. English." The jurors laughed.

"Professor, what is linguistics? And what is 'forensic linguistics,' which I understand is your specialty?"

"Linguistics is the study of languages. It's the broad field, not meaning studying single languages like Spanish or Chinese, but studying how languages work. The patterns of languages. Then, 'forensic linguistics' is the use of language patterns to analyze their precise meaning. The meanings of speakers, behind the meaning of their language."

"Tell us more about forensic linguistics. Is it used in a particular way in the United States? Have you done work for the United States and other clients?"

The professor turned to look at the jury. "One important way that forensic linguistics is used, today, is in threat assessment. To evaluate the seriousness of terrorist threats, for example. I have worked for the CIA, which is the Central Intelligence Agency, and also the DIA, which is the Defense Intelligence Agency, to try to prioritize the response to terroristic communications."

He looked back at the lawyers. "And I've worked for numerous international corporations, on problems that range from deciphering regulations put out by foreign governments, to interpreting their competitors' public communications."

And again, Professor Suarez turned to the jury. "I'm sure that everyone in the courtroom will understand that I can't be more detailed, because it would break the law. It's national security, and that includes my corporate work."

"Professor Suarez, can 'forensic linguistics' help us to evaluate the intent of a person who makes a statement?"

"Yes. That's a big part of what it's about. We determine the speaker's real meaning, through what we call 'discourse analysis.' And by 'discourse analysis,' what we mean is the language patterns. To take an obvious example, if someone says, 'I guess so,' that's less affirmative, more uncertain, than if the speaker had said, 'Yes, absolutely,' instead. But discourse analysis is a whole lot more complicated than that, of course. We usually have to look at patterns: whether the statements reinforce, repeat, or interlock—that sort of thing."

"Professor, you've seen the videotape of Detective Donnie Cashdollar impersonating a hit man with Brianna Edwards. Do you have an opinion, based upon your field of expertise and on the videotape, about whether Brianna Edwards really intended for the murder of Alan Blackburn to happen?"

The jurors seemed fascinated, and Paul Gage had had enough. "Your honor, I object. Mr. Herrick hasn't laid the predicate for this question. My objection is based on the *Daubert-Kelly* line of cases. Those cases say that the opinion has to be shown to be reliable before it can be considered as evidence."

The prosecutor shook his head. "And Mr. Herrick hasn't shown that the Professor's alleged opinions are reliable." He emphasized the word "alleged": "the professor's *alleged* opinions."

The jurors looked disappointed. This objection had broken the rhythm, and they wanted to hear the witness. Good, Robert thought. They're impressed with Professor Suarez.

Besides, he was ready for this objection. "Your honor, we'll establish the reliability of the testimony, to show that it's admissible under the *Daubert-Kelly* line of cases." This was a good thing, actually; he had been counting on the prosecutor to object, so that he could get Professor Suarez to promote the reliability of his testimony.

"Professor Suarez, has discourse analysis been tested, and is it reliable?"

"Absolutely." The witness looked professional, competent, and certain. "There have been hundreds of experiments, conducted by linguists and also by psychologists. The experiments show that discourse analysis can determine intentions correctly, if it's properly used."

"Has discourse analysis been written about in scientific publications? Does it have a small error rate, and is it a generally accepted science?"

"Yes, to all those questions. There are many scientific publications. I can't keep up with them all, although I read the two biggest ones from cover to cover. We don't have a specific error rate, but the experiments show that it's much more accurate than meteorological predictions. More accurate than the weather forecasts you see on TV, I mean." He smiled at the jurors, and they laughed. "And discourse analysis is certainly well enough accepted, since it's an important tool for the CIA."

"I'll overrule the objection." Judge Waddell leaned forward across the bench. He wanted to hear this testimony as much as the jury did.

"All right, then, Professor Suarez. Please tell us. What is your professional opinion about Brianna's intent, or lack of intent?"

"She did not intend for a murder to take place. In my professional opinion, analysis of her discourse shows that Brianna Edwards did not—repeat, did not—intend for anyone actually to be murdered."

The jurors sat back. So did the judge. It was downhill from there, and much less exciting, as Robert led the witness through his explanation of his expert opinion.

The witness told the jury about the phenomenon of interlocking statements, about sentence level and discourse-level syntax, and about structures of relevance. And at one point, Professor Suarez even gave the jury this incomprehensible jewel: "The formal equivalence relations within a coherent discourse can become explicit when a transformational grammar converts the text into a canonical arrangement." In fact, there were dozens of other technical concepts that were unfamiliar to anyone in the courtroom but Professor Suarez. And all of them had to be explained, laboriously, in lay terms.

The standard advice with expert witnesses is that the lawyer should get the opinion out first and explain it later. The jury hears the opinion best if it's given first, and jurors who care about the explanation can follow it better if they know where the explanation is going.

Robert was glad he had done it in this order. By the time the learned Professor finished his technicalities, several of the jurors looked as though they were about to nod off to sleep.

And that didn't bother Robert at all. "There are two things that show when you've got a good expert," he told Tom Kennedy ironically. "First, he's certain about the main point, and second, his explanation bores everybody's pants off."

*   *   *

Paul Gage found himself in a difficult situation. The defense lawyers don't have to tell the prosecutor about the testimony they plan to offer. And now, this prosecutor looked blank for a minute. He'd been blindsided.

But Paul Gage had plenty of experience with expert witnesses, and his professionalism took over.

"Professor," he said, "I'm interested in the limits of your assignment. In other words, I want to ask you what you *weren't* asked to do." He looked straight at the witness. "Did Mr. Herrick ask you to consider what happened at Brianna Edwards's arrest, when she was picking up Delia Marchand with money to pay a hit man?"

"No. That wasn't part of my assignment."

The jurors looked up sharply. Had the defense lawyer pulled a fast one? Was Robert Herrick hiding the truth from them?

Paul Gage was up to full speed, by now. "And Professor, you've learned, of course, that Brianna Edwards was interrogated by the arresting officers. But your assignment didn't include finding out about that, or about any interlocking statements in the interrogation, did it?"

"No." Robert cast a sideways look at the jurors. Some of the jurors had unfriendly looks, after hearing this.

"How much have you been paid, by the hour, for your testimony here, Professor?"

"Three hundred and fifty dollars an hour."

"Which might be a hundred times what you earn as a Professor, I imagine?"

"Not a hundred times, no."

"Now, Professor, I remember that whenever I went to the chemistry lab in high school, I always tried to make my experiments turn out the way they were supposed to." The jurors smiled at that, with long-range memories of spilled chemicals, accidental fires, and impossible results, from messy laboratory failures many years ago. "And so, Professor, I imagine you probably meant for your answers, here, to turn out the way Mr. Herrick wanted them to, especially since he was paying three-hundred-fifty an hour for them."

"What? No. No, not at all." The professor was adamant.

"There's a lot of judgment that goes into what you call 'discourse analysis,' isn't there, Professor?"

"There is judgment. And it has to be applied carefully."

"And when you make a judgment about unclear things such as whether two statements interlock or not, then, just a little nudge, just a little push one way or the other, can make a big difference, can't it, Professor?"

"I . . . suppose so."

Paul Gage smiled, at that. "I think I'm getting the hang of it, Professor. I think I'm starting to understand this mumbo-jumbo you call discourse analysis. Your answer to me is, 'I suppose so.' And that's different in meaning from your answers to Mr. Herrick, where you used the word, 'absolutely.' It means you're ready to agree with Mr. Herrick but not with me, doesn't it?"

"I . . . I suppose so." The professor didn't seem happy, now.

"And if we're talking about doing an analysis at this kind of level, or-dinary people who aren't Ph.D.'s can do it perfectly well. These people on the jury can tell that the words, "I guess so," have a different meaning from, *"Yes! Absolutely!"* Isn't that right?"

"Well, but the science of forensic linguistics can help." The witness's voice sounded lame.

Every experienced trial lawyer knows that direct examination is more difficult than it looks. The examination of your own witnesses is the hardest part. Even a careful direct examination can be destroyed during cross-examination, by one well-placed question. Paul Gage spent only about fifteen minutes with Professor Suarez, and none of his cross-examination involved any of the technical concepts that the witness had so carefully explained.

But the prosecutor's cross-examination was effective. Very effective, Robert thought ruefully. He wondered: are we better off with this witness, or were we better off before he testified?

39

STRONG CORROBORATION

Carlos Leiner wasn't used to being in jail. Whenever he'd needed to get out, he'd always been able to buy his way out. He'd been arrested before, but only in Mexico, and he'd never stayed in for more than a few hours.

Now, it was stretching past a month. Not a month in prison—that would be bad enough—but a month in the county jail, where most of the inmates were being held for trial. Where everyone stayed only temporarily, and where the accommodations were much worse than in the state prison system.

He had a lawyer, and from what his people told him, the lawyer was a good one. But Carlos was frustrated, because the lawyer didn't seem to be able to get him out. He recalled their last conversation with a degree of puzzlement. The lawyer had explained, "They don't usually grant bail to a defendant charged with murder, who has no local residence, who has no history of gainful employment anywhere, and who has the kinds of drug connections you do."

"If I can just get out for even a short while," Carlos had said, "I can vanish completely. Not just across the border. Across the border, and hidden where not even people who know my country can find me."

"That's exactly why it's difficult to get you bail," the lawyer had responded.

Carlos was confused by that kind of logic. Things ought to be set up so that a big shot, like me, could get out and disappear. That was his impression of the right way for the world to run.

Now, he was being herded back inside after a half hour on the asphalt courtyard, outside. Herded, like an animal in a big bunch of sheep. The area outside was just a big flat slab, with a chain-link fence around it.

There were basketball courts, but Carlos didn't play basketball; he'd rather ride one of his horses or compete at fencing. They didn't have those particular sports inside the county jail.

The herd split. He found himself going in an unfamiliar direction. This didn't feel right. It didn't feel good.

For one thing, the tattoos were, well, unfriendly. Not that there ever were "friendly" tattoos in Carlos's judgment, but these were . . . not familiar. There was one, here, with two capital S's and a flock of lightning bolts. The same guy had swastikas and gothic eagles. "Already Dead," was written in strange text, in blue and red. Suddenly, Carlos began to realize. There were all kinds of guys here with markings saying, "Aryan Brotherhood."

He yelled at the guard. "I'm in the wrong place!"

"What? You mean you're misclassified?"

"Yes! I shouldn't be here!"

The guard waded through the sea of humanity to come closer, and he wrote down Carlos's inmate number.

"That's not what I mean! I shouldn't be here!" But the guard already was gone.

One of the Aryan Brotherhood inmates had caught his eye. "What're you looking at, you silly spic pussy?"

"I beg your pardon." Carlos was offended by that.

"You really are a pussy, you pussy." There was laughter.

"Nobody talks to me like that."

"I do."

The shank that stuck between his ribs was so quick that he didn't see it. Carlos was a soft target, completely unused to anything like jail, or hand-to-hand combat, or racist gangs who hated Hispanics. He fell on his back, and he stayed there, still and unmoving, until the paramedics arrived.

*   *   *

Meanwhile, for Robert Herrick, the day of judgment was coming on fast. Brianna and Delia's case was nearing its end.

Paul Gage had only a couple of witnesses to go. He had finished with Detective Derrigan Slaughter, whose testimony was short, anyway. Slaughter had told about the arrest. Not much to it.

Robert's cross-examination had been short, too. "Detective, from what you're saying, Delia Marchand had only three thousand dollars. Not five thousand dollars."

"That would be right." The big detective in the pearl gray suit had nodded.

"Three thousand, not five thousand, and so it wasn't the amount that the fake hit man had wanted, right?"

"Well, that'd be right. Maybe these defendants was thinkin in terms of a down payment. I don't know."

"Well, Detective, as far as you knew, Delia Marchand may have been involved in a real estate transaction. Or hiring a lawyer. You know, a lot of lawyers won't take anything but cash as payment, because you can't trust a check from a lot of your clients. Detective Slaughter, you had no way to be sure Delia wasn't going to use three thousand dollars for something like that?"

"I s'pose anything could be possible."

"Now, Brianna Edwards wasn't there with Delia, was she?"

"No. Sugar Land officers done arrested her, down the block."

"And you didn't find anything incriminating on Brianna, did you? Not the missing two thousand dollars? Or any money, beyond pocket change? No weapons or implements of murder?"

"No. No implements of nothin."

And that was it. The rest of the prosecution's witnesses, the ones Paul Gage had yet to call, were officers who had been on top of the parking lot during the meeting between Brianna and the fake hit man, operating the video and the long-range microphone. Their testimony was strong and incriminating, but it would be short. Robert's cross-examination would be short, too: limited to pointing out, once again, that Brianna had never expressed any wish for anyone to be murdered.

Tomorrow would be the day to move for dismissal. He would need to be very persuasive.

*   *   *

For a lawyer, being in trial is a marathon, close to a twenty-four-hour-a-day grind. All day in the courtroom. All night, or most of the night, preparing for what is to come.

Tomorrow, the prosecution probably would rest. That would bring on three serious challenges for the defense. First, the defendants' opening statements. Second, the defendant's first witnesses.

And third, for this case, the *Motion to Dismiss, for Acquittal, or for a Directed Verdict*. Finally, Robert would make his motion based on part (b) of the solicitation law. The motion that the lawyers had come to call, "Our 'there's-not-any-strong-corroboration' Motion."

Tom Kennedy had written a beginning draft long ago, and Robert had tweaked it. In fact, he had repeatedly rewritten it. If you took away the formal beginning and ending that always encircled a motion for the courtroom, the business parts of this motion, now, were surprisingly simple:

"1. The law sets out specific requirements in a solicitation-of-murder case. The requirements are contained in section 15.03(b) of the state Penal Code. These requirements are not met in this case.

"2. Specifically, the relevant language in section 15.03(b) reads as follows: *'A person may not be convicted ... unless [there are] circumstances strongly corroborative of the actor's intent that the other person act on the solicitation.'*

"3. This language means that it is not enough for the prosecution to prove that the defendant said the words of solicitation. It is not enough, even if the words are on videotape. There must, in addition, be an intent on the defendant's part to complete the murder. And there must be *'strong corroboration'* of that intent.

"4. In this case, the required 'strong corroboration' is completely absent. There is no corroboration of the alleged intent, much less 'strong' corroboration.

"5. As is shown by the brief that accompanies this motion, the purpose of the 'strong corroboration' requirement is clear. People use words carelessly sometimes. In enacting the solicitation law, our legislature intended to protect against the conviction of someone who did not really, truly intend for the crime to be carried out.

"FOR THESE REASONS, the defendants move the court to dismiss this prosecution, or to acquit the defendants, or to order a directed verdict of not guilty."

Robert read over the brief again, and then, the motion. For the first time, he read them without making any changes.

"Well, it's one thing for us to file this motion. That's the easy part."

Tom Kennedy nodded. "The other thing—and the harder thing—is going to be for you to get the judge to grant this motion."

"I know that. Only too well."

40
THE MOTION TO DISMISS

I t was a beautiful day, Monday was. It also was a day of reckoning.

"We've got to be ready to put on evidence, unless we get lucky and the judge grants the motion to dismiss," Tom Kennedy said.

"Which we can assume won't happen." Robert shook his head. "And since the judge isn't likely to acquit us, we start by calling Professor Thompson to the witness stand—you know, the psychologist from Tulane, the one we went to see in New Orleans, on the plane—and then see whether we want to put on anyone else."

"Professor Thompson is ready to go. We've had him here for two days, getting prepared."

"And he's been over the proposed direct testimony. And so have I— I've gone over it in detail, several times—so we're as ready as we can possibly be."

Tom went to the clerk's office to file the motion to dismiss, the brief, and the proposed order of dismissal, and to give copies to the other side. But when they reached the courtroom, all their plans seemed inadequate.

"Paul Gage expected our motion to dismiss, of course," Tom told Robert. "He asked me flat out, with a smile, 'Doesn't the money that Delia withdrew from the bank qualify as corroboration?' And then, he said, 'But I understand, you've got to represent your client, and I can't fault you for filing this kind of motion.'"

"He knows it's just a formality. He thinks the judge will overrule it without paying any attention." Robert shook his head. "And he's right."

The judge was occupied right now, hearing a plea of guilty in a burglary case. The court's usual business went on, in spite of the trial. But he interrupted the proceedings to ask, "Mr. Gage, how long are you going to be today, putting on the last of your evidence?"

"I'm through, your honor."

"Good." The judge smiled. "I'm always happy to hear from you, Paul, but I'd like to put some time into the rest of this enormous backlog I've got."

"Your honor, I know you always like hearing from me, as long as it's short." And there was laughter across the courtroom, including from the judge.

Fifteen minutes later, the jury was in the box, and the court reporter sat at the ready. "Mr. Gage, you're ready to announce that you're resting your case?"

"The state rests, your honor."

"What says the defense?"

And Robert felt his adrenalin surge, as a murmur went up from the spectators and press. The reporters were thinking that this case hadn't produced any news that was very exciting in the last few days, and now, at least, there was a promise of something different, with the defense taking over.

"Your honor, this morning we filed what we called our *Motion to Dismiss, to Acquit, and for a Directed Verdict.*"

"Oh, sure." The judge seemed bored, by that. "I should have anticipated that kind of motion, in a case like this."

"And, your honor, we filed a brief. Let me emphasize—it's a *short* brief, containing mostly case authorities. And the text of the statute."

"Well, twist my Kimono," said the judge, and he twisted the arm on his robe to show that he did, in fact, have a sort of Kimono. "I guess it's possible for lawyers to learn something, after all."

"I'm a quick study, your honor. This brief is definitely ... *short.*" Again, there was laughter.

"I've seen this kind of case before," said the judge. "Not frequently, because it's not a frequent charge. Which is a good thing, of course. But I know the basic requirement, which is that the evidence has to include 'strong' corroboration."

"Well then, your honor, you know most of what's in our brief."

"True. I've been over it while you've been talking. Yes, this is a short brief. That's a good thing. You probably want to add to it, though, is that right? I never knew a lawyer who didn't also want to make a speech."

"Actually, your honor, Mr. Robillard is going to speak to you first. My co-counsel, Mike Robillard. We've sometimes forgotten that there are two defendants here, and the evidence in the two cases is different. Mr. Robillard will urge the court to acquit Delia Marchand, who is his client."

"All right. Mr. Robillard?"

"Your honor, the corroboration requirement just isn't anywhere close to being met with respect to my client, Delia Marchand." Mike Robillard's voice was quieter than Robert's, but in this case, it was insistent. He and Robert had agreed that Mike would argue Delia's case first, because she had a better shot at acquittal. The hope was, if Delia could be acquitted, the judge might be ready to acquit Brianna too.

"The only evidence that mentions Delia," Mike went on, "is that she went to the bank. And as she exited the bank, she had three thousand dollars with her. That isn't evidence of a crime, at all. The law, as your honor knows, requires 'strong corroboration,' as you said just a moment ago. In Delia's case, there's not just an absence of evidence that makes out any corroboration of any intent on her part to see a murder committed. In fact, there's no evidence to prove a crime at all."

The judge nodded. "I've been assuming that the jury would decide this case, but I'd have to say, Mr. Robillard, you have a point. Isn't that right, Mr. Gage? I mean, you and the other prosecutors might believe that Delia Marchand had a heart full of violence and murder, but even if she did, there's no evidence of it, is there?"

"I see the case completely differently, your honor." Paul Gage stood up.

"I thought you might." The judge smiled.

"Brianna Edwards was right there to pick up Delia Marchand. It's an unusual amount of money to withdraw in cash. The jury would be able to infer a conspiracy from the physical closeness of the two defendants at that moment, and from the possession of a large amount of cash. Since that is the case, the evidence against Brianna Edwards is evidence against Delia Marchand, too. And therefore, the evidence against Delia Marchand includes the videotaped effort to hire a murder."

"Mr. Robillard, I suppose you might have a different view of the matter." Judges like to hear good lawyers argue a case well, and Judge Waddell had a smile on his face.

"I do, your honor. The withdrawal of three thousand dollars is not a suspicious circumstance at all. In the first place, the only mention of money in the videotape was about a *different amount* of money. The undercover officer had insisted on *five* thousand dollars. Delia Marchand had *three* thousand. If that's what anyone could call 'strong' corroboration, then they can call Assistant District Attorney Paul Gage a *space alien,* just as easily."

"He might be." The judge saw the lawyers getting worked up. This was fun.

"He might be, your honor, that's right—Mr. Gage is an alien from the star system Polaris—but it doesn't change the fact that not only is the three thousand dollars not 'strong' corroboration, it also isn't even evidence of a crime at all. Having three thousand dollars isn't unusual. It's been mentioned in this case, that paying that amount in cash is common, when someone hires an attorney. Lawyers know that a certain percentage of their clients aren't reliable when it comes to writing checks, so they insist on cash. Often, amounts much bigger than three thousand dollars. Also, people withdraw that kind of money to travel abroad. There are lots of reasons for Delia to have three thousand dollars, and again, it doesn't fit the five thousand dollars that the undercover officer demanded."

"Mr. Gage?" The judge had his pen poised, ready to write.

"My argument is short, your honor. We think the money, close after Brianna Edward's performance on videotape, and close physically to Brianna Edwards, creates evidence of the crime, and together with the other evidence, it contains more than enough corroboration."

The judge looked up at the clock. "It's . . . about time to break for lunch. . . . Let me think about this one. I never figured this case would end with me directing a verdict and dismissing the case, but I've got to consider it. I'll let you know my decision when we get back, at 1:30."

Wow, Robert thought. The judge's rulings weren't always predictable. But one thing was certain. This judge always knew when it was lunchtime, precisely and unmistakably.

*   *   *

Meanwhile, twenty miles to the north, an unusual meeting was taking place. An introduction, inside the county jail.

How do you introduce yourself to the guy in the next cell, if you're an inmate and you're in what they call "administrative segregation?" Elmo Naughton did it by just asking, "Hey, man, who are you?"

"My name? My name's Carlos Leiner."

"I'm Elmo Naughton. In here for what they call attempted murder."

"Me, Carlos Leiner, they charged me with murder." But Carlos was confused by his surroundings. "What's this thing they call 'administrative segregation'? They told me I'm in administrative segregation."

"Also known as 'admin seg,' for short. It just means you're not with the other prisoners. Could be you're dangerous. I think that's what they think about me. Or, maybe you're likely to be assaulted or killed if you're put with other people."

Carlos didn't say anything, at that. He'd been inside long enough to know it was better to seem dangerous than to seem like a victim.

These two gentlemen, of course, had plenty of time. There was a great deal of discussion about how each of them was going to get out of this place pretty soon, even though most of it was fantasy. And there was discussion of the loose ends that both of them felt in their lives, mostly having to do with revenge against acquaintances whom they blamed for their respective predicaments. The predicaments, actually, would properly have been blamed on their own actions, but that wasn't part of their conversation.

"I imagine you have plenty of people on the outside who could get rid of this guy I want dead. This guy, Robert Herrick," Elmo Naughton said.

"You imagine right," Carlos Leiner answered. "I just wish I could get rid of Porfilio Garza. They've got him in some kind of protective custody. But the guy you want, this Robert, he's on the outside. It can be done. But it'll cost you some money."

"No problem," Elmo replied.

*   *   *

"Well, I promised you an answer," said the judge after lunch. "This case is harder than I thought. But I've arrived at the conclusion that I must grant a directed verdict in favor of Delia Marchand. Under the law, I have to dismiss the case against her."

He paused. "There aren't a lot of rulings in the courts of appeals about solicitation crimes. But it turns out, a high percentage of the cases end up with the defendant being acquitted, even when the jury convicts them. This requirement of strong corroboration—not just corroborating the words of solicitation, but also the intent to carry out the murder—is a real obstacle to convicting anyone for this crime."

Paul Gage still had an argument to make. "Your honor, the careful thing to do would be to let the jury decide. If the jury were to acquit Delia Marchand, that would answer the question. I don't expect that, but it would give an authoritative end to the case against her. On the other hand, if the jury were to convict Delia Marchand, then a court of appeals would have the authoritative answer. That court might think that there is sufficient corroboration, just as I do."

"Well, but I have to do what's right." The judge sounded weary. "My own judgment is that Ms. Marchand cannot be convicted on this evidence. And that means, keeping her under accusation would do violence to her rights. If I'm correct—and I can only go by what seems right to me—then keeping her in custody would be a continuing wrong, and it might last for years, before an appellate court acted. And while she's in jail, the cost to the people of this state would be enormous: possibly hundreds of thousands of dollars."

He paused again. "As to Delia Marchand, the motion is granted. She is acquitted."

And then, immediately, Judge Waddell looked at Robert Herrick. "But that leaves Brianna Edwards's motion still outstanding. And the evidence is different against her."

Robert Herrick felt the adrenalin rush that always accompanies this moment—the moment when a lawyer stands up to make a difficult argument, and an important one. He also felt the perspiration trickling down his back.

"Your honor, is the evidence really different? Yes and no. The evidence against Brianna Edwards includes a videotape, and it contains foolish words, unwise words, words that she shouldn't have said. So yes, the evidence is different, so far as the words Brianna spoke are concerned. But no, the evidence really isn't different, when you ask about corroboration of her supposed intent. There isn't any, and the evidence, there, is the same as the evidence about Delia. In fact, it's weaker."

The judge looked puzzled. "How so?"

"All there is, against Brianna, is the videotape, really. The money in Delia's hand was only that—money in Delia's hand. It was never connected to Brianna. And it didn't fit the alleged solicitation at all, which was for five thousand dollars, and this was three. There simply isn't any corroboration of any intent on Brianna's part to have a murder actually committed."

"Mr. Gage? What say you about that?" The judge was wrestling with it. Good, Robert thought.

"Again, your honor, the evidence shows that Brianna Edwards was present with Delia Marchand when she withdrew the money to pay the hit man. She drove Delia to the bank. She was circling the block to pick up Delia, when she was arrested."

"Your honor," Robert said immediately, "our brief cites the case of *Ganesan v. State*. In that case—the *Ganesan* case—the defendant had withdrawn not just three thousand dollars, but *one hundred thousand* dollars—$100,000. The court of appeals held that Ganesan should have been acquitted in spite of that. The $100,000 wasn't connected to the alleged solicitation in *Ganesan*, by any evidence at all. And it's not connected to Brianna, here, either."

He put on his best imitation of having been offended. "And I was shocked—shocked—when Mr. Gage claimed that there was evidence that Delia withdrew the money, quote, 'to pay a hit man'! The only evidence that it had anything to do with a hit man was Mr. Gage's bald, unnecessary, unadulterated speculation. The only witness who said anything like that was Mr. Gage, just now, and unfortunately, he's not a witness."

"Oh, well." The judge didn't take the bait. "I understood what he meant. That was his interpretation of the evidence."

"Elmo Naughton is a witness, too," said Paul Gage promptly. "His testimony quoted the words that Brianna Edwards used. He said that she told him she wanted someone's legs broken—'or worse,' as she put it. And when he asked whether she was serious, whether she wanted someone killed, Brianna Edwards answered, 'Yeah.'"

"Your honor," Robert attempted, now, to look exasperated, "Elmo Naughton can't tell you any more than what he claims she said: the alleged solicitation. He can't supply anything showing that she intended to go through with any murder. In the second place, Elmo Naughton is a thoroughly discredited witness. He contradicted himself on tape, and he even attempted to get a bribe for saying the opposite.

"In the third place, every statement that anyone has said that Brianna has said, was equivocal. She was hesitant. She was unsure. And also, your honor, you've heard from Professor Suarez. The forensic linguist, who explained the science of discourse analysis, and who is an expert in threat assessment, working for the CIA and the DIA. And his expert testimony is, No, Brianna had no intent—none—to see any murder actually committed."

"But . . . I keep coming back to . . . the fact that she's on tape hiring a hit man . . . ." The judge seemed puzzled by the sense of Robert's argument, and he was trying to compare it to his intuitive view of a solicitation of murder that was right there, visible, on videotape.

"Your honor, have you ever been to a football game and heard someone yell, *'Kill 'em'*? Or even, *'Let's murder the other side'*? By that reasoning you've just given us, those people are guilty of solicitation of murder. Of course, that's wrong, because there's no intent to carry out an actual murder. But here, it's the same thing. There's no evidence that Brianna had any intent to commit a murder. There's nothing, outside of the words themselves. It's just like the football game example. And our legislature was aware of this problem when it passed this law. The legislature had no desire to see people get convicted and sentenced to life in prison, for yelling, 'Kill 'em!' at a football game."

"This isn't about someone yelling 'Kill 'em' at a football game," said Paul Gage, firmly.

"No, it's not," the judge agreed. "But it's hard to point to any actual . . . *evidence* of an intent to kill, outside of the words Brianna Edwards spoke. That's what Mr. Herrick is arguing, and that's what matters. Outside of the words, there's no evidence of Brianna's intent to cause a murder. No corroboration. Elmo Naughton can't supply it, even assuming Elmo Naughton could supply anything worthwhile. The money that Delia Marchand had, that sounds more incriminating at first, but when you get down to it, the money's not connected to Brianna, and it doesn't corroborate Brianna's intent, if she had any."

"Your honor, our best case authority isn't really the usual kind of case." Robert held up a reprint of a news magazine, with the headline THE SINS OF JUSTICE YARBROUGH. He pointed at the headline. "Several years ago, we had a Texas Supreme Court Justice who acted like a criminal. Don Yarbrough got elected because his name sounded like Senator Ralph Yarborough. Incredibly, Supreme Court Justice Don Yarbrough tried to hire a hit man to kill a political opponent. The hit man wasn't a real hit man, though; he was an undercover witness. The solicitation of murder was taped, and it was clear.

"But this news story explains that the District Attorney's office in that case refused to prosecute this rogue supreme court justice, because there was no corroboration. We cited this news story in our brief. It's an unusual way to cite an authority, but it's a persuasive case, because it's similar."

"I recall that incident." The judge nodded. "The solicitation law wouldn't have kept Don Yarbrough from being impeached and removed, thank goodness, so he resigned."

"Yes, your honor. If there ever was a situation calling for vigorous prosecution, this was it: a supreme court justice plotting a murder. But this corroboration requirement kept him from being convicted of a crime. Which is the correct result in this case, too."

"You're saying there wasn't any corroboration in the news case about Justice Don Yarbrough." The judge nodded. "And . . . you're saying, there's not any here."

"But, your honor, the cases say that you should look to the totality of the evidence." Paul Gage was firm. "Elmo Naughton. The money. The relationship between the two defendants. The jury ought to decide about all of that."

"Well, I'm looking at all of the evidence." The judge was still puzzled. "And . . . I don't see anything in any of it that proves Brianna Edwards's ultimate intent, or even loosely corroborates it, other than the statements themselves. Which aren't enough."

Robert felt his hopes rising. It was almost a physical surge within his body. The news reporters were poised on the edges of their seats, ready to run outside and splash the shocking headlines on pulp paper. Or run their teases on TV.

"I just can't see it, though," the judge said. "Dismissal, acquittal, a directed verdict . . . on *this* kind of evidence?" The news reporters sat back and relaxed.

And then, Judge Waddell did what he usually did when a difficult ruling was coming up. "Let's take a break."

41
JUDGE AND JURY

Fifteen minutes stretched out to twenty. Which stretched out to thirty. Judge Winley Waddell still wasn't back. "I wonder if he's going to the books. Looking up cases," said Tom Kennedy.

"I hope not." Robert shook his head. "Our argument is clear and simple. The cases are complicated."

"Isn't that always the way it is?"

Robert contented himself with going into the hall and meeting once again with the psychologist. He was anxious to be ready to put on evidence for the defense, because he expected Judge Waddell to refuse to dismiss. "Professor Thompson, the key point is going to come early in your testimony. I'll ask for your professional conclusion."

"And I'm well-rehearsed on what to say." The professor smiled. "My line is, 'She had no intent to see any murder carried out.' It's a good thing that this is actually, in fact, my professional conclusion, so I can tell the truth, right? Robert, if I didn't know better, I'd diagnose you as having obsessive compulsive personality disorder."

Robert laughed. "You'd be just like everybody else, then."

After forty-five minutes, a buzz arose from the spectators in the courtroom, and a flurry of activity told them that the judge had returned. Robert got back to counsel table just as Winley Waddell was sitting at the bench.

"Mr. Bailiff, please bring in the jury panel." Oh, no, Robert thought. We're going to be left to the tender mercies of the jury, a jury who has seen my client on videotape committing a crime. He watched, along with everyone else, as the jurors filed into the box, slowly.

"Ladies and gentlemen of the jury. Counsel on both sides. Ms. Edwards and Ms. Marchand. Ladies and gentlemen of the press." Winley

Waddell was nervous; Robert had never heard a judge address a court-room assembly this way. The judge concluded now with, "Ladies and gentlemen of this city and county, and from elsewhere."

The judge's voice was excessively formal, and so were his words. "No judge wishes to see a serious crime go unaddressed. No judge likes making rulings that set guilty people free. On the other hand, no judge ever desires to have his rulings contradict the essential rights of a citizen. And the difficulty is, and here I speak especially to you jurors, it often is not easy to be sure about either of those two outcomes. If a judge knew unerringly each time that a crime was proved, and if the same judge recognized with equal certainty every occasion on which it was his duty to protect the defendant, the world would furnish an easy pedestal from which to hold this office, the office of a judge. But it is not easy. Not at all, because every case is different, and every situation is a variation from what has gone before."

Good grief, Robert thought. I've never heard a speech like this from a district judge. Is he going to convict Brianna himself, without even asking the jury?

"Of course, I'm not answering the essential question, by saying those words." The judge looked down. "They are only background. So let me just come out with it. The law requires me to say that Brianna Edwards is acquitted, just as Delia Marchand is acquitted. The cases against both defendants are dismissed."

"What?" whispered Brianna to her lawyers. "What does that mean?"

"Just listen for a minute." Robert wasn't sure he'd heard it right, himself.

"The defense lawyers have made a motion for this, and they are right," the judge went on. "A crime of solicitation is made up of words. And sometimes people are careless with words. Our law is wisely written so that it prevents anyone from being convicted on mere careless words. And that includes words captured on tape, when there is no intent to carry out the meaning of the words."

He rubbed his hands together. He's still nervous, Robert thought; but maybe that's good. "Ladies and gentlemen of the jury," the judge went on, "there have been parts of this trial that you haven't been able to hear. The law prevents it. And I've heard from the lawyers—frequently, as you know; maybe too frequently." The jurors smiled and nodded, at that.

"Sometimes it's the judge's job to decide the case by himself, all by himself. And yet, you see, you—the jury—are an essential part of that. Here's why. We never know ahead of time when this is going to happen, when this awful, awesome, enormous responsibility settles down on me, alone. The judge and the jury *both* have to hear all of the evidence first. So, we have to have you here, and me here too, and we all have to wait until the end."

He rubbed his hands harder. "You ladies and gentlemen of the jury— you've heard that the crime of solicitation has to be 'corroborated.' Not just as to the words, the careless words or even the intentional words, that were said by the defendant. For instance, imagine that a spectator yells, 'Kill 'em!' at a football game." Here, Judge Waddell nodded at Robert. "That person isn't guilty of solicitation of murder. The words were said, but that's not enough to convict someone. Because in that situation, there's no intent to actually commit a murder, and there's no corroboration outside the words themselves.

"Now, this case is different from yelling, 'Kill 'em!' at a football game. But the same principle applies. There's no showing, by evidence, that the defendants in this case intended . . . *intended* . . . to have anybody murdered. Not outside of the words themselves, and the law says that the words are not enough. And that is when the responsibility settles down on me—the awesome responsibility—to say, 'This case is dismissed. There is no sufficient evidence for the jury to decide the case. The defendants have to be acquitted.' And so that is what I must do."

At counsel table, Brianna hugged Robert. It was clear, finally, and she understood.

"Mr. Gage." The judge smiled, and the prosecutor stood up. "You may not have achieved a conviction in this case. But you did your duty skillfully and well." The judge looked back again at the jurors. "Some cases need to be tried, even though the outcome is in doubt. Some cases need to be tried, even if at the end the ruling is not favorable to the District Attorney. Ladies and gentlemen of the jury, Mr. Gage has represented you, as citizens, extremely capably. He has done his job in this case, and so has your elected District Attorney."

The judge turned now to the defense side of the courtroom. "Ms. Marchand, you are free to go. You are acquitted. Ms. Edwards, you are free to go. You are acquitted. Of course, even as I say that, I have to give the order to the clerk, who gives it to the sheriff, who holds your belongings, and you have to be processed out from the jail. So you have to go back there to the jail momentarily, but it will not take long."

The judge looked thoughtful for a moment, as if he had something more to say. Finally, he said it. "Brianna. Delia. Your actions in this case didn't amount to a crime, but they came close enough to it so that the District Attorney's office was fully justified in vigorously prosecuting this case. Please, Brianna, and please, Delia, take this as a teachable moment.

Be more careful in the future, both about who you associate with and what you do. Please, ladies . . . learn from this experience."

* * *

Paul Gage was not happy. "A wise professor in law school told us, 'Whenever, if ever, you lose a jury trial, walk across the courtroom and shake hands with that guy on the other side, who you are convinced is a sleazebag."

Robert had to laugh, at that. "I understand it. The other guy isn't just an opponent, in that instant, when you've had a bad outcome. The outcome, itself, guarantees that you're always going to think that the other side did something underhanded. Something wrong. Something sleazy. But in the end, there aren't any enemies; there are only opponents. And so, the basic idea is, even if the guy is a sleazebag in your mind, shake his hand."

"I don't agree with the judge's ruling, at all. Or with the football-game analogy. But yes, Robert, you've got the basic idea."

"And there are many people who'd tell you that, yes, for sure, I'm a sleazebag." They shook hands. "Paul, you were a class act in this case. As well as a fine lawyer. I hope I never meet you in court again."

* * *

Together with Tom and his clients, Robert finally relaxed. "The judge felt he had to make that kind of speech, I'm sure," he said.

"To make the prosecutor feel better?" Brianna wanted to know. "And to make himself feel better?" Like most defendants, she thought anything said in addition to, "You're free to go," was unnecessary.

"Not exactly. To a judge, jurors are more than jurors. They're voters. In fact, to a judge, the most important thing about jurors is, they are *voters*. People who show up for jury duty are also the most likely to show up to vote. And as voters, they are the ones who know best what the judge is like."

Robert paused. "And if the judge just sends them on their merry way without letting them decide the case, after sacrificing their time and attention and hearing all the evidence, the likelihood is, they'll think the judge is unfair. Or incompetent, or worse. So, Judge Waddell wanted to make that speech. To explain himself to the voters."

"Well, I just wanted to get out of there." Brianna was firm, and Delia nodded.

"Which brings up another point. The press will want to interview you, Brianna. And you, Delia. I've talked to the major news outlets, and there's a way to minimize the intrusion into your lives. I've proposed a press conference. If you meet with them now, they're much less likely to harass you later. It's up to you, of course, but I'd do it if I were you."

Brianna was willing. "Of course." She liked to talk, as she had demonstrated throughout this case. Delia was more reluctant, but she agreed too: ". . . All right."

*   *   *

The local newspaper asked the first question. "Brianna, the judge asked you to take this as a learning experience. Have you learned anything from it?"

"Absolutely." Brianna's expression was pained. "We've paid for this, even though it wasn't a crime. We've spent most of a year in jail, first of all. We've had all of our friends, all of our family, gossiping like mad over this thing that wasn't a crime. And this thing that wasn't a crime . . . it was an indictment for *solicitation of capital murder*, for goodness sake! In other words, we've got to live down a reputation for being a pair of serial killers. And you never really get your reputation back."

"We were in jail for what seemed forever," Delia agreed. "Have you ever been in jail, even overnight? You think you're never going to get out. And in fact, we were threatened with life imprisonment."

"We had to sit through that trial," Brianna went on. "And listen to Elmo Naughton. And I had to see myself acting stupid on videotape, at the same time that the whole world saw it. And that's without even bringing up the fact that we lost all of what we might have earned during this time, and we owe a lot of money."

"Alan Anderson Blackburn got murdered," Delia added. "Executed. He brought it on himself, and we didn't have anything to do with it, but it's terrible to us. This experience has been like a nonstop horror movie, and you can be sure of one thing. Neither of us wants to go through this ever again."

The press didn't seem overly sympathetic. "Well," asked one of the broadcast media, "it sounded as though you did, actually, intend to hire a hit man, even if the judge said it wasn't proved."

"Delia and I have a reputation as pranksters. We never meant to kill anybody. The worst we would have done might have been to tell this guy—this Alan Anderson Blackburn—about what we had done."

A reporter from the big city asked, "We understand that there was a stipulation, an agreement, to tell the jury that Blackburn was murdered, but that you had nothing to do with that. What happened to the stipulation? The jury never heard it, I guess."

"That's right." Robert answered, this time. "In any case it court, you find out all kinds of information that you may never use. As it happened, the defense never had to put on a case, because of the judge's ruling. If the judge hadn't acquitted us, we would have presented the stipulation to the jury. By the way, the prosecutor did the right thing in providing that to us. Mr. Gage is a fine individual as well as an excellent lawyer."

The next question was unexpected. "Delia, what were you going to do with the three thousand dollars?"

But Delia had learned something during this case. "That's part of the confidential case facts. I'll take the Fifth Amendment on that one."

Somebody asked, "What happened to Professor Suarez's wife? You know, the forensic linguist. His wife had breast cancer."

"I'm told they did a lumpectomy," Robert answered. "They didn't have to do a radical operation. They hope they got it all, but with cancer you never know."

And finally: "Brianna, how does it feel to be outside? Free?"

"It's awesome!" Brianna's smile was big. "It's a lovely afternoon! Now, can you lovely news reporters let us be on our way, please, so that we can enjoy this lovely afternoon . . . freely?"

42
LOOSE ENDS

Robert, you won't believe what happened," Maria said.

"Well, I guess something must have happened to get you to come all the way over to my office and take me to lunch."

"I do that all the time, silly. But I'm not taking you. I want you to take *me* to lunch. But you're always too busy. Mark that down, to make it one of your New Year's resolutions. 'Take wife to lunch. Frequently.'"

"Okay. So, what happened to make this occasion happen, so that I can take you to lunch today?"

"Carlos Leiner pled guilty. To the murder of Alan Anderson Blackburn."

"Wow! What made him do that?"

"I'm not sure I have the whole story, but here's what I understand. First of all, they put poor old Carlos in with a bunch of Aryan Nation guys, by mistake. He got insulted, spat upon, and worst of all, stabbed. Not fatally, but he was in the infirmary for over a week. Then, the sheriff's office moved him into admin seg, meaning he was single-celled for self-protection. But when they moved him into admin seg, they made a mistake again, and they moved him into the pink cells."

"The . . . pink cells?"

"Those are . . . for sexual orientation, the pink cells. They're guys who are single celled because they are vulnerable gays. Homosexuals who are classified as weak, and who might be assaulted by predators. The cells aren't really 'pink'; they're just called that. Every jail has this problem, and every jail has to do this. Some people have to be separated for their own protection. And it seems that the county jail was short on admin seg cells at the time poor Carlos needed one, and some genius who didn't know what he was doing solved the problem by putting Carlos in the middle of the pink cells."

"I'm beginning to get the picture."

"By the time they got that misclassification all straightened out, Carlos was going nuts. Besides, he apparently figured out that he wasn't going to be able to kill the witness against him, this guy Porfilio Garza, also known as 'The Comedian,' or have him killed, because Porfilio was in protective custody. Which they don't make mistakes at. Which is fortunate for Porfilio.

"And of course, the case against Carlos wasn't just dependent on Porfilio-the-Comedian; we had the gun that was found in Carlos's possession, and it tested out to be the murder weapon. On a plea of guilty, the state was willing to recommend fifty years. Which was better than what he faced, which was the death penalty. And about that time, the jail administration was ready to move Carlos to a different section of admin seg, and from what I hear, Carlos just lost it. He went nuts. He just didn't want to be moved again, because he was afraid it would turn out worse."

"How long will he be in?"

"Impossible to say, of course. What's the minimum? I guess that's what you mean, and at minimum, I'd expect that Carlos would have to serve at least twenty years. That'd make him near fifty years old. But it's deceptive to think that way, because lots of prisoners *don't* end up doing the minimum. They get in fights, they break the rules, they offer bribes, and they do stupid things. That's going to be Carlos. He won't serve the minimum. In fact, there's a substantial percentage of prisoners who serve the entire thing, the maximum: in this case, fifty years."

"Oh. Okay. But you know what? It's just a little bit weird, having a wife who is into this kind of stuff."

"Don't be a smart aleck, Robert." She laughed. "You get yourself into some prize situations, too. Why, I remember hearing that the Famous Lawyer for the Little Guy had a night visitor, recently, who had a shotgun. And whose mind was fatally bent upon mischief, such as murder."

"And guess what, Maria? I have news too. About that night visitor. Good old Elmo. I can say, 'You won't believe what happened, either.'"

"All right. I'll ask. What happened, about Elmo Naughton? Don't let it be something boring, now."

"I got a call from Detective Slaughter. You know, Derrigan Slaughter, the guy who's the partner of Donnie Cashdollar, the detective who played the part of the hit man who negotiated with Brianna Edwards. And Detective Slaughter told me that this guy, this Elmo Naughton, hasn't given up on his quest to kill me, even after his sawed-off shotgun got taken away.

Slaughter told me, quote, 'This here Elmo Naughton done been askin everybody inside the county jail, everybody he can find, to get him a hit man on the outside. To kill you, Mr. Herrick.'"

"Oh. Great. Just when I was thinking it might be safe to go to sleep."

"But Elmo's not very successful, Detective Slaughter says, because, quote, 'He ain't got no money at all. He ain't got nothin to pay to nobody, or even to hire a cheap hit man.' That doesn't stop Elmo, it seems, because he just keeps on asking people, everybody he comes across, and pretending he's got the money to hire someone. And of course, the Homicide Division has to take it seriously. Detective Slaughter says they'd charge him with this crime, too, if they could."

"But they can't," Maria said immediately, "because it requires . . . *'strong corroboration of the intent to carry out the murder.'* Just like in your case with Brianna and Delia. . . . Robert, you've helped make the world a dangerous place! If we tried to prosecute Elmo, he would be acquitted, and he'd skate out, just like Brianna. Because all there is, is Elmo asking everyone to kill someone. Namely, you."

"Okay. So. The detectives want to oblige Elmo and give him the opportunity to create some corroboration. It took them a lot of effort to figure out how to do that. First thing, they set up this phony way that Elmo could earn some money. And they put it in a so-called 'export account.' Usually, an inmate can't pay money except in the commissary, inside. But there are some situations where it's important to let inmates pay a little money on the outside. To give an obvious example, what if the inmate has to pay child support, and amazingly, he has some money in his account? Well, the jail sets up an export account for that.

"So, now, Elmo has the ability to pay the money outside. And they've got someone on the inside who's going to recommend somebody on the outside to Elmo, someone supposedly to do the hit for him, and the someone on the outside is supposed to be the hired killer, and they've set it up to tape-record Elmo and this inside guy talking, and then, for Elmo to pay the outside funds to the hired killer."

Maria laughed again. "And if the funds actually get paid from Elmo to the outside guy who pretends to be the hit man, so that the hit man actually gets paid and gets Elmo's money, that makes the case different from Brianna's. And it furnishes that famous thing called 'strong corroboration.' Or . . . at least, that's what you hope."

"Fervently." He paused. "You know, this case with Brianna has changed the way I see the practice of law. Especially when it comes to Elmo Naughton. I'm a whole lot more aware of how badly the law treats crime victims. Such as, potentially, me."

"As an assistant district attorney and a law officer, I hope that some day, I can be proud to have a husband who isn't intimately involved with criminals anymore." And she laughed.

"Well, I hear that Elmo is applying himself to something worthwhile."

"What's that?"

"He's offered to give lessons to the other inmates about how to play chess. I understand that he's a little discouraged, though, because there are so few takers. I guess chess just isn't one of the more popular pastimes inside the county jail."

*　　*　　*

"Hi, Brianna. You're back earlier than I thought." Back in the office, Robert was happy to see her.

"Well, I took three days off. Got a new apartment with Delia. And moved in."

"Uh-oh. You and Delia, together again? That's a dangerous combination."

She laughed. "Not anymore. We're just normal, ordinary Americans now. We're just regular middle-class citizens who don't get the attention of the police. No more strange activities."

"That's good. But ... speaking of strange activities, I have one for you."

"What's that?"

"Something unusual. Strange, as you put it. I want us to go into the business of helping crime victims."

"Really?"

"Yes. So: Please get with our corporate people and start setting up a nonprofit that will represent crime victims. I'm not sure what to call this nonprofit corporation, yet; for now, let's call it 'Cleaning Up After Crime, Inc.' That gives you an acronym where the initials spell 'CUACI,' which could be pronounced 'Quacky.' It will be a crime victim assistance foundation."

"Clever. Very clever. 'CUACI,' which would be pronounced 'Quacky.' I suppose this way it would be distinctive, and people would remember it."

"I'm nothing if not clever. We'd have a duck for a trademark, and the duck would say, 'Quacky! Quacky!'"

"It's corny, but knowing how the public thinks, it'll probably work. How do you want it described?"

"For the purpose clause in the documents, let's write, 'For the purpose of conducting any business that is lawful for a nonprofit' or some similar kind of flexible statement, but also, add this: 'Including representing crime victims in connection with criminal prosecutions, suits against those who perpetrate or permit crimes, recovery of crime victims' compensation, reform of laws relating to crime, and other legal actions,' or something like that."

"Now, let me ask this. . . . Robert, what has brought this on?"

"I'm newly aware of the problems of crime. Actually, I'm aware from your case, Brianna. I'm glad we got you acquitted, and it was the right result, but I'm not happy with the way it happened. It's like it was a technicality, the corroboration requirement, instead of getting you acquitted on the merits of the case, by the jury."

He hesitated. "I can't quite explain it, but I think the criminal law is too full of obstacles. Pointless obstacles, that are like barnacles. Having rules that protect people's rights, that's one thing; but we've got too many rules that don't serve any good purpose. Or that do overwhelming harm that way exceeds any possible good that they could do. Too many barnacles."

"This may sound funny, but I know what you mean. Even though I'm the beneficiary of this particular technicality, and even though it resulted in acquitting me, I didn't like it. For one thing, there's that crazy Elmo Naughton, who's trying and trying beyond all reason, to hire a hit man to kill you, now."

"That's right. *I'm* a crime victim, myself, with this whacko who came to my office with a sawed-off shotgun intending to kill me, and now, left and right, he's talking to people who he thinks he can hire to murder me. And the guards know it, the deputies know it, and the sheriff knows it, but none of them can stop him. It's crazy."

"So." Brianna was amused. "One of the first assignments for CUACI, pronounced 'Quacky,' would be . . . to go to the legislature and try to get this law amended, so that the corroboration requirement isn't any longer a license to solicit a hit man?"

"Could be. Possibly. But our efforts wouldn't be limited to that. We'd represent crime victims in all phases of the system. I'm convinced that we don't do enough in this country, in America, to help crime victims. It's my spiritual growth from this case. It's what I've learned from representing you, Brianna."

"Well, me too. I'm grateful to you, Robert, for getting me out of it. But it's a poor law, this strong corroboration law, and an unjust law, and unfortunately, that's what we used to get me out."

*   *   *

An hour later, Robert found himself sitting with Tom Kennedy, talking over the idea of a nonprofit corporation for crime victim assistance. "We'd take on cases for crime victims. Against the perpetrators, or against negligent defendants who should have prevented it but didn't. And we'd shepherd victims of crime through the discouraging system in which the criminals are prosecuted. Particularly victims of violent crime."

"I understand why you want to do this." Tom was noncommittal. "But maybe we can represent more banks and insurance companies, so we can pay the bills. And then, maybe we could afford your efforts to imitate Don Quixote."

The telephone rang to provide a kind of punctuation to that sentence. He picked it up. "Hello, Maria, my love, star of my sky, and diamond in my pinky ring!"

"You don't have a pinky ring," she laughed. "But since you put it that way, you can do something for me. Me, your diamond."

Instantly, he was wary. "What's that?"

"The Museum has another exhibit I want to see. It's Kandinsky. Three weeks, upcoming. And I ask you, I want you, I need you . . . to take me to it. To the Kandinsky exhibit. Maybe before you take me to the Opera to hear La Traviata, Friday after next."

Tom looked puzzled. "Who on earth is . . . what's his name? Kandy-who? Kandy-Kane, or whatever she said?"

"Kandinsky," Robert groaned. "You remember that guy, Olitski, whose exhibit she wanted me to take her to? And I did? The blob artist? Well, Kandinsky is worse."

"Intelligent people regard Kandinsky as a genius." Maria sounded as though she thought she was one of those intelligent people.

Robert was unimpressed. "Where Olitski uses blobs, Kandinsky uses blobs together with scribbles. Blobs above, beside, under, and over . . . all these scribbles. It's abstract expressionism that doesn't express anything. It's worse than Olitski, by a mile. But they're a lot alike, which I suppose is why they both end in 'ski.'"

"You'll like Kandinsky even better than Olitski, Robert." Maria laughed.

"Another 'ski' artist." Tom Kennedy laughed too. "Robert, it's another opportunity for you to do something good, just like setting up this 'Quacky' foundation. Only this time, the good that you'll be doing will be to bring about peace in your own family."

"Great."

"And next," Tom said, "we've got to get ready for Monday. For Jimmy Coleman. That real bad accident where the eighteen-wheeler cab ran into that pickup truck. Jimmy Coleman represents that completely guilty, negligent defendant, that long-haul trucking company. He's got a dozen motions set for hearing Monday, including a couple where he's trying to get our whole case thrown out."

Robert groaned again. Maria laughed, in spite of herself. A second later, Tom laughed too. Then, finally . . . Robert laughed a little bit, even though there was pain in his laughter.

Postscript

I wanted to write this story so that the lawyering was real.

In a book of fiction, the action should create more excitement than real life does. It's supposed to grab the reader. But still, I wanted this story to be an authentic reflection of the way that lawyers handle lawsuits.

I've drawn on my own experience to do this. For example, the "strong corroboration" requirement in the solicitation-of-murder law is taken from what the law really says, in my state. I've quoted it from the Penal Code. The case precedents that the lawyers argue about are real, too. One of them appears in my Criminal Law casebook, which is used in law schools.

But I've included this postscript, which you're reading now, to tell where the demands of fiction have forced me to stray from what I think is real.

*　　*　　*

One of the most doubtful events in this story occurs early. Robert settles a medical malpractice case with Jimmy Coleman for ten million dollars. That's a pretty high figure in a case today. At first, I wrote $25 million, but I revised the figure after checking into it. Both $25 million and $10 million are high figures, even for an egregious case.

The case itself is realistic. The defendant is a physician who operated on a patient to remove a diseased lung, but he removed the wrong lung. The situation is adapted from a real case in Dallas, a horrible case, in which that's exactly what happened.

But I doubt the ten million figure that I invented, because of what is known as "tort reform." In this state (as in many states), there is a limit on recoveries, as a result of a tort reform law passed by our legislature. In other words, there's a "cap." And the cap on so-called "noneconomic" damages, or pain and suffering, is $250,000 in a medical malpractice case.

The plaintiff can still recover other kinds of damages, such as lost earnings. And the plaintiff can recover medical expenses caused by the malpractice. And so I suppose it's conceivable that a medical malpractice case could result in more than a million in damages, but ten million would still be unusual. The person injured or killed would need to be a richly paid wage earner. The costs of later medical care would have to be very high.

There's been a lot of criticism of this medical malpractice cap, and with good reason. I've often told people that if I myself were the victim of malpractice by a doctor, and if it turned me into a paraplegic, I might not even be able to get a lawyer. I could still do my job in a wheelchair, and there would be a limit on my lost earnings. I might need medical expenses, but presumably, only in a limited amount. I couldn't play sports, or dance with my wife, or run, or even take a walk, but those things all fall into the category of noneconomic damages, and they're capped at $250,000. And here's the kicker. It typically costs more than $250,000 for a lawyer to handle a medical malpractice case. I'd be in the position of asking a lawyer, "You'll lose money, but won't you please recover some money for me?"

The idea behind the cap was that it would make insurance affordable for doctors. And it would counteract a disturbing trend, which was that shortages were appearing in some crucial specialties, such as obstetrics. Plaintiff's lawyers lobbied hard against the cap, and they also begged the legislators to set a higher cap. But the forces of tort reform had the votes.

I asked my friend Jim Perdue Jr. about this, because he's done a lot of medical malpractice work. He was pretty clear in saying that a $25 million settlement with the hospital (assuming it was liable) was unrealistic today, and it was also unrealistic to expect it from the doctor:

> ... That settlement [the $25 million I had written, at first] in a medical malpractice case would be considered unheard-of-huge [after tort reform]. First, ... I can promise you [that the doctor] does not have more than $1,000,000 in liability [insurance] coverage. ... [U]nless you ... try to chase down his money for a lifetime after bankruptcy, the policy limit is what you get. Second, this is very technical and does not make for good drama but is the fact: if the patient is dead, the most the entire family can recover for a wrongful death medical malpractice case is (currently) $1.8 mil., regardless of [his]

being a Donald Trump level wage earner. So, even [for] something as egregious as that [case] sounds, I would tell you [$25 million] sounds absolutely enormous. The reality is a defendant could go try the case, confess liability, . . . and still never pay 1/10 of that amount.

But . . . I suppose I can imagine an odd chain of coincidences that might get us to a larger settlement (such as ten million, which is what I changed it to): The doctor in fact has lots of insurance (an excess policy), the hospital is also liable, and the patient is not dead and is going to live for many years—but he's no longer able to do the (very lucrative) kind of work he did before losing his only good lung, and he has millions in health-care costs.

Possible? Well . . . it's unlikely. But it's possible, and this is fiction. Along that line, Jim kindly added a word about the story: "Sounds fun. I always like your stuff."

*   *   *

There are several lawyer's tactics in the book that I should mention. Depositions are one of the most important forms of "discovery": the process by which a lawyer finds out information that other witnesses have. Depositions are oral questions asked in front of a court reporter. In civil cases, there's a lot more questioning that goes on in lawyers' offices, during depositions, than in the courthouse.

The deposition of Doctor Kapritska that Robert takes in the second and third chapters is realistic. Some people were surprised that Jimmy Coleman says the same thing—"Objection! Form!"—after every question. In my state, the only two permitted objections during a deposition are "Objection, form" and Objection, privileged." It's not that way in other states, and lawyers interrupt with long speeches. My state adopted a rule limiting the length of depositions to six hours, and it was thought that limiting interruptions was necessary to keep the opponent from monopolizing a big chunk of that time.

Robert and Tom would have studied the solicitation law much earlier in the case than they do in this story. They would have parsed the elements that had to be proved at the beginning, and they would have considered the strong corroboration requirement. My story exaggerates the difficulty of studying these laws, but that's because I found that readers didn't understand the corroboration requirement easily. It's strange to realize that a solicitation of murder on videotape isn't enough to prove the crime, and I wrote it this way to make this clear.

The indictment looks like a real indictment in my state (and indictments in other states look like this, too). But there are several differences from reality. One of them is that this indictment doesn't show the date of the offense, and a real indictment has to do that. But it's not always a good idea for a fiction writer to put in dates unnecessarily. It makes the story seem "old" after a year or two. Also, my fictional indictment includes the charge that Brianna "solicited" the murder. Ironically, the statute that defines the crime of solicitation in my state doesn't contain the word "solicit"; it says that the defendant commits the crime if she "requests, commands, or attempts to induce" another person. And so, indictments use only those words.

The cross-examinations in this story feature lawyers asking witnesses what they "now claim." This is a rhetorical tactic. Lawyers try to avoid endorsing the words of an adverse witness, and so they might not ask, "What happened?," which is an invitation to the jury to accept the adverse witness's version. Instead, they might ask, "What do you *claim* happened?" to imply, "I know you're about to lie, you sleazy witness, but let's hear it." And asking, "What do you *now* claim?" adds the suggestion that the witness is the type to tell a lot of different stories, "but let's hear what you're *now* claiming, you lying dog." Incidentally, a lawyer can ask leading questions freely on cross-examination, and the conventional wisdom is that every question should be a leading question. You don't ask, "What was the weather outside?" if your version is that it was raining. Instead, you ask, "It was coming down like a big-time *monsoon,* wasn't it?"

*　　*　　*

Then, what about Judge Winley Waddell's granting of the defense motion, in the solicitation-of-murder case? And his acquittal of Brianna and Delia—could a judge do that, and would he?

Yes, the judge has that kind of authority. The judge has the power to decide the case alone. The judge can do this in both civil cases and criminal cases. Some people ask, "But don't you have a right to trial by jury in America?" The answer to that question is yes, of course; but the jury decides only the facts, and only facts that are in controversy. The judge is there to see that the case is tried and decided according to the law. And if the law dictates only one possible outcome, the judge decides. If you think about it, this makes sense. We wouldn't want a system in which there is legally no crime, but the jury decides that there is.

The name of this kind of ruling by the judge, isn't really a "dismissal." And during the trial, the lawyers don't move "to dismiss" because of a lack of evidence. The procedure is called a "Motion for Acquittal" in a federal court or a "Motion for Directed Verdict" in some state courts. But I found that readers were confused by that. "What is a 'Directed Verdict'?" And yet, everyone understood the concept of a judge "dismissing" a case. The popular concept of a motion to dismiss corresponds roughly to the real meaning of a motion for directed verdict. I decided, finally, to use all three terms in Robert Herrick's motion. A lawyer could do that, but most lawyers wouldn't, because it would look pretty odd.

*   *   *

Then, there's this question. Am I really saying that someone could be acquitted of soliciting a murder, even if there's no doubt at all that the defendant tried to hire a hit man, and even if the solicitation is on videotape?

Yes. Because that's the way the law is.

Most states don't like people who hire killers. And so most of them have laws that make it a crime to try. But it's important for the legislature to write the law so that yelling at a football game ("Kill 'em!") isn't a crime. Or, imagine a group of actors performing Shakespeare's Julius Caesar, which includes a guy named Cassius and his henchmen plotting a murder. The actors shouldn't be arrested, even though they're speaking the words to solicit a murder. And so most states have laws that require proof of an intent to carry out the murder. Some require independent corroboration of the solicitation, too—that is, the word of the person solicited is not enough to prove what the defendant said—and some of them, in addition, require independent corroboration of the defendant's intent to kill, just as in Brianna and Delia's case.

The Texas Supreme Court Justice whose case Robert Herrick mentions—Justice Don Yarbrough—was real, unfortunately. Justice Yarbrough ran for the Supreme Court because "God told him to," and he got elected because his name resembled those of two other well-known officeholders. It was the kind of result that shows why democracy isn't perfect. Then, Justice Yarbrough was captured on tape with an undercover witness while soliciting the murder of a political enemy. But the District Attorney determined that the case couldn't be prosecuted. The tape of the solicitation left no doubt that Justice Yarbrough was really evil, but the tape was all there was; and a tape isn't enough, without something else: without corroboration. The District Attorney was right in doing what he did, however unpleasant that decision might have been.

Fortunately, Justice Yarbrough didn't have a defense against impeachment. And fortunately or unfortunately, there were other criminal charges against him. (He was a real charmer.) Seeing his impeachment moving forward, he resigned. And later, he jumped bail on the other charges and fled to the island nation of Grenada, where the United States had no extradition treaty. But the long arm of justice has ways of showing up, and in this instance, it showed up because Justice Yarbrough made the mistake of visiting another Caribbean island where Americans were able to get him. Eventually, he served his time.

The strange result of the corroboration requirement is that a person can go around soliciting all kinds of murders and still never be subject to prosecution. The best solution, for law enforcement, is to wait until the defendant pays the hired killer. That's usually enough. But it's dangerous to wait that long. There's always the possibility that the defendant might hire someone else and actually succeed in getting his target killed. In other words, Elmo Naughton's repeated attempts to hire a killer are realistic. I'd like to see the solicitation law rewritten, but I have to admit, it wouldn't be easy, and nobody can design it so that it works perfectly.

*   *   *

Here's another legal issue that causes confusion. What does "intent" mean?

It sounds as though the answer ought to be clear. And sometimes it is, such as when a murderer shoots someone in the back of the head. That's like the crime committed by Carlos Leiner when he kills Alan Blackburn in this story. Carlos had the intent to kill.

But often, the concept of intent isn't clear at all. Again, this story is an example. And the issue becomes even more unclear when it comes up in a trial. Then, the definition of intent gets muddled by the high standard of proof in criminal cases. The prosecutor has to prove the defendant's intent "beyond a reasonable doubt."

There are different definitions of intent in different states. The judge gives instructions to the jury, usually, about the definition. But those instructions wouldn't help much in a case like this one.

So, did Brianna or Delia ever "intend" to get Alan killed? At one moment, they talked about the "prank" they were pulling. They just intended to "scare" Alan. At other times, their words were indeed evidence of an intent to kill. The word "intent" dissolves into uncertainty when the words shift around this way. And if there are two or more participants who change the words they use, does the momentary statement of an intent to kill prove an actual intent, or is it just an effort to sound more decisive to the other one than either one really feels?

Since the courts can't open up a defendant's head, intent usually is proved by what the defendant did. The defendant's actions, which is to say, it's proved by circumstantial evidence. Sometimes the intent is clear, such as when Carlos kills Alan. Sometimes it's ambiguous, like Brianna's intent.

There probably is enough evidence in this case to allow a jury to decide that Brianna had an intent to get Alan killed. Or, to decide that there's a reasonable doubt, which is the same as deciding that she didn't intend it. Intent is the ultimate issue, for a jury to decide. And in deciding it, every juror becomes like an amateur lawyer or judge, because every juror has to decide: What do I think the word "intent" means?

But the jury didn't have to decide that, in this case. The absence of corroboration meant that no crime could be proved, even if the intent to kill was present. Our system protects the criminal defendant, and it's debatable when the protection is too much. Or is just right. Or isn't enough.

*　　*　　*

The scene involving Maria Melendes at the court of appeals, working to get Eddie Ray Bonner executed, is realistic. Some courts get bailiffs or clerks to "cry in" the judges with three loud knocks and with the words "Oyez, Oyez, Oyez!" It's French for, "Hear ye, hear ye, hear ye." The "z," by the way, is silent, and it's pronounced "O-yay." I was a law clerk for a judge on the Fifth Circuit Court of Appeals, and once or twice, I had the duty of crying in the judges.

One way in which that scene involving the death penalty arguments is possible, but unlikely, is the elementary nature of the arguments. I have the defense lawyer explain the very basics about the selection of the jury. Jury selection is crucial in capital cases, and the judges don't usually have to have it explained in elementary ways, but I had to write the argument so that readers can follow it. Likewise, the prosecutor, Maria, probably wouldn't belabor the Act of Congress that requires the federal courts to accept the findings of state courts unless they are "unreasonable." That's a legal principle that comes up in every death penalty habeas case, and the judges have it firmly in mind.

One minor inaccuracy in my story is that different parts of Maria's role would more likely be done by two lawyers: one from the local D.A.'s office for the state courts and one from the Attorney General's office for the federal courts. But dramatic compression is necessary here, and it *could* be done by one lawyer.

The scene covering the death penalty argument shows the reality of this kind of litigation in a number of ways. First, why does it take so long—two decades or more, in some cases? Because the stakes are high, the questions can be knotty, the lawyers on both sides are determined, and the law creates judgment calls.

Second, who decides? The answer is, a jury, at first—but the jury is followed by a long string of judges, in multiple loops, both state and federal. Third, what are the questions like, the issues that decide these cases? Usually, they're bloodless and boring. The judges don't usually consider how bad the crime is; instead, they consider technical issues involving trial procedure.

And finally, the scene shows the horror of these kinds of crimes. And it shows how senseless they are. In this case, the court did have to consider how horrible the murders were. My wife told me that Maria's description of these murders was too graphic, too gruesome. But I think citizens in this country ought to confront the crimes that they expect their laws to judge. If you read the description of the crime in any given capital case, you might say, "That's the worst crime ever!" But then, you read about another capital crime, and it's as bad—or worse. In a democracy, citizens can't control their own laws unless they consider this kind of thing.

*   *   *

My story says that "Sugar Land, Texas, is divided into three parts." I always wanted to write that "three-parts" line. Julius Caesar famously wrote, "All of Gaul is divided into three parts" (*"Gallia est omnis divisa in partes tres"*), and I thought it sounded really cool.

In Sugar Land, two of the three parts are indeed the wealthy country club set and the old sugar-mill town, but the third part, the immigrants, isn't a geographic area. Immigrants are spread throughout the city. Still, they form a distinct part of the city, which isn't surprising since the county is always one of the fastest-growing in America. Sugar Land is wealthy, well-managed, and located at the edge of a major metropolitan center, so it's a magnet for immigrants. And so, my statement about "three parts" is true in an important way.

The Justice Center, which houses the courthouse for Fort Bend County, isn't in Sugar Land proper. It's in Richmond, which is a smaller city nearby. I avoided making that point in the story. Dramatic compression, again.

*   *   *

Some readers have asked me about the nervousness of the lawyers in the courtroom, and about the way the judge acts. I show Robert Herrick sweating before every procedure. Some readers say to me, he's a professional, he's experienced, and he'd be relaxed. But many real lawyers, the best of them, are scared when they start their hundredth jury trials (if there's anyone who tries that many, nowadays). Some of the most experienced lawyers have to settle themselves to avoid running into the bathroom to lose their breakfasts.

Why? Because defeat is public, and because it lurks behind every event in a trial. Nobody can know every law and fact, and everyone gets blindsided. And it's not the lawyer's money or freedom that's at issue; it's the client's. You might think, that would make it easier; but it doesn't. So, Robert Herrick hesitates, and he feels the sweat run down his back. That's the way it really is.

The judge, in this story, likes to broadcast not-so-funny witticisms. So do the lawyers. This too is the way it is. The courtroom participants may be working their way through a serious case, even a horrifying, tragic, or gruesome one, and yet, there will be moments when they kid around with each other. Even weak humor takes the edge off the tension. Likewise, humor can be a tactic, and a successful one, if it's well placed.

Some works of fiction depict prosecutors unfavorably. This is one of the aspects of John Grisham's novels that I find to be both unpleasant and inaccurate. Overwhelmingly, real prosecutors care deeply about the difference between guilt and innocence, they act within the law in performing their duties, and they try for honest results. Instead, defense lawyers are the ones who most often sponsor and argue inaccurate theories—but hey, that's what we hire them to do, because their job is to be advocates for the accused and make the government prove its case. We set things up so that defense lawyers test the state's case by making whatever arguments they can and by telling the jury the defendant's story, even if it's a story that's hard to believe. In any event, I've depicted the assistant district attorney in this case, Paul Gage, as an honest, fair individual, and that's consistent with my belief about the way the world is. I was an assistant district attorney as well as a defense attorney, and that's what I saw.

I have encountered a few lawyers who've brazenly used dishonest, unethical tactics as a matter of course—but only a few. There are some kinds of unethical tactics that are hard to prevent, and this kind of lawyer is expert at getting away with it. Jimmy Coleman appears in this novel, and he has been Robert Herrick's opponent in my other novels. Jimmy specializes in abusive tactics.

Lawyers who do that are counting on several factors. They can force delay, expense, and various kinds of misery on their opponents. This kind of "Rambo" lawyer is not the norm, but he (or she) exists, and Jimmy is a paradigm—a little overdrawn, I suppose. But I have to admit one aspect of this characterization that I think is inaccurate. Jimmy is from a big law firm, but I've never perceived that big-firm lawyers are any less courteous, moral, or pleasant than smaller firm lawyers. If anything, it's the opposite. But readers tend to think that the bad guy will be the lawyer in the big firm, and this is one of the concessions I've made to fiction.

*   *   *

Plea bargaining is different in different places. In my area, it works about the way I've shown it. The term, "plea bargaining," sounds bad, but it shouldn't. It's the equivalent of settlement in civil cases. We can't try every case, and if we attempted it, the cost would be crushing. Consider this: injured plaintiffs receive less than one-half of the dollars paid by defendants in negligence cases, because the rest goes to lawyers and costs. Imagine how little would go to injured people if we tried every case. Our system is expensive.

In criminal cases, it's even more dramatic. Think what would happen if we tried every criminal case. As of now, we try less than five percent. If we tried them all, we'd need something approximating twenty times as many defense lawyers—and twenty times as many prosecutors. Think what the world would be like, if we had twenty times as many prosecutors as we do now. Would it be a threat to people's freedom?

Some jurisdictions and some prosecutor's offices have tried to stop plea bargaining. Bad results follow. The cost of justice increases dramatically, without perceptible improvement in the quality of justice. Fewer big criminals get convicted, and small fry, who are more directly involved in their crimes, make up most of the guilty. Besides, there are people who admit their guilt because of remorse, rehabilitation, or simply preference for getting it over. Most observers think that people who admit what they've done deserve to be treated slightly less severely. But it's hard to do that if you outlaw plea bargaining.

At times, the job of the criminal defense lawyer is to advise his client to accept a plea bargain in the strongest possible terms. I have Robert and Mike doing that with Brianna and Delia, in this story. The basic principle that Robert explains—that the correct thing to do is to settle, if you get a good offer—is what I believe, and I think most lawyers believe it too.

I think that there is a (frankly, unfortunate) tendency for fiction readers to consider a trial to be morally superior to a negotiated settlement. It's less moral, in other words, to settle than to try the case—or so goes the suggestion. Well, most lawyers I know would say that it's just plain foolishness to try a case when the odds are that the result will be worse than the settlement you can make. That kind of attitude—"I ain't gonna admit to nothin'"—seems to characterize people who are either anarchists or uninformed.

In fiction, having a jury trial increases the drama. A novelist may tempt the hero lawyer and his client with a favorable settlement but have them reject it in a way that makes them appear to take the high road. It makes for better fiction, and my novel features a jury trial too. But in real life, refusing a reasonable settlement shouldn't really be considered a superior moral choice.

✻   ✻   ✻

Robert Herrick can discuss Olitski (the blob artist) and Kandinsky (the blob-and-scribble artist), but he doesn't like either one. I think the descriptions he supplies of their works are reasonably accurate, although his rhetoric may be too negative. Maria likes both of them. The average art viewer is probably somewhere between Robert and Maria. The art that Robert likes is geometric abstraction, because he mentions Noland (chevrons), Stella (stripes), and Mondrian (squares; Mondrian is the granddaddy of geometrics). These all are real artists, and they are reasonably accurately (if too briefly) described. Robert's office sports works by "Picasso, Mondrian, and Wyeth," which is a realistic list only if the lawyer is ridiculously rich.

The Gulfstream II aircraft that Robert owns is older now than when I first had him travel in it. But he's not the type of guy who would get rid of a fine airplane just because there's something newer. The flight path to New Orleans is realistic, I think. I'm not a pilot, but at one point I consulted my former student, Captain Bill Harger, who is a pilot.

It's been a while since I've played chess seriously, but I think Elmo Naughton's chess strategies are realistic. The Italian Opening or "Giuoco Piano" ("quiet game") is real, and it allows the player, usually White, to develop the big pieces stealthily, while keeping the king protected, in a position to castle. The Italian Opening is a natural for leading into the Evans Gambit, which is a fast way of taking control of the center board. It requires a willingness to sacrifice pieces and is defended against by the same willingness. If Black makes the mistake of trying too hard to avoid having pieces taken, Black will lose.

One thing that is controversial among people I've discussed this passage with, is the question whether a drugged-out, undisciplined criminal like Elmo Naughton could be a chess competitor. I think so. Once you learn how to play chess at a decent level, you've learned it, whether you grow further or not. Keeping your skill doesn't require a lot of study. It does require discipline during the actual play, but that's different from the discipline that lets a person live a drug-free life. And although it's controversial, I don't believe that you have to be brilliant to become a fairly good chess player. You have to have a good memory for sequences of moves, but you don't have to be inventive, unless you plan to be a grandmaster. But I wouldn't know about that, and neither would Elmo Naughton.

*   *   *

I'm no expert in the drug trade. But there are several aspects of drug traffic in this story that are realistic. For instance, the violence doesn't stop at the border. This country is in for a miserable future if we don't recognize this fact. Also, the drug trade uses every mode of transportation, not just trucks, contrary to what Detective Cashdollar suggests. Smugglers use homemade submarines, cross-border tunnels, and commercial aircraft. Not to mention the bodies of humans and animals. It is a pernicious business. I don't know how frequent it is for citizens of countries south of the border to partner with North Americans, as Carlos Leiner did with Alan Anderson Blackburn, but it happens.

The detectives' description of fingerprint analysis is accurate, I think. The more accepted terminology refers to "islands" rather than "dots," and to "whorls" rather than "circles," but it is a surprisingly simple kind of expertise. The real art is not comparing prints, but rather dusting for prints, or using the chemical called Ninhydrin on paper, or applying other reagents or techniques to different surfaces, ranging from wooden boards to human bodies. The method by which computers compare prints is different, including the National Crime Information Computer system (the NCIC). I didn't try to describe how the computer does it.

About the science of forensic linguistics, yes, there is such a thing, and it uses discourse analysis to determine various kinds of facts about a message or a speaker. The principles that Professor Suarez describes would be generally recognizable to linguists familiar with the subject, I think, although I don't pretend to be the kind of expert that he is. At one point, I have Professor Suarez saying, "The formal equivalence relations within a coherent discourse can become explicit when a transformational grammar converts the text into a canonical arrangement." All of the phrases in this sentence can be found within the writings of expert forensic linguists, although I have to confess, I'm foggy on what it means. As best I understand it, in plain English, this sentence means something like, "You can find different phrases within a meaningful message that mean the same thing, if you can figure out ways of defining what makes different phrases mean the same thing." But I never promised to give any reader a great insight into forensic linguistics.

On the other hand, using experts to do word-by-word analyses of messages is not unknown to courtroom dramas. One famous case involved John DeLorean, who started his own automobile manufacturing company to make DeLorean cars, thirty years ago. DeLorean fell onto hard times, and at one point he apparently considered the drug trade as a source of funds to keep his business afloat. His image appeared before a jury's eyes, holding a container of cocaine and exulting over how much money this commerce could bring in. This stuff was as "good as gold." His defense lawyers used textual analysis to convince a jury that there was doubt about what the conversations meant, and they secured his acquittal.

Which is more or less what Robert Herrick did in Brianna Edwards's case.

*   *   *

Probably the biggest question people ask about my story is this. Would the motion that Robert and Mike filed really *work?* Would the judge really acquit their clients?

The answer is easy for Delia. Yes, she would be acquitted. There's nothing in the evidence about Delia, except that she withdrew $3,000 in cash from a bank. Some readers ask, "But didn't she really conspire with Brianna? Didn't she agree with her about contacting Elmo Naughton, and about meeting with the pretend hit man?" Well, unfortunately, that's one of the misleading aspects of fiction. As a writer, I can show you what Brianna and Delia discussed privately in their apartment. This creates the illusion of evidence, because you, as a reader, know it. But in reality, no one else would know what was said inside that apartment, and no one would be able to make it part of the evidence. The case against Delia, really, is nonexistent.

In real life, it's unlikely that Delia would ever have been indicted. The District Attorney's office screens cases before they enter the system. And the D.A.'s office has every motivation to avoid dumping cases into the system that can't be successfully prosecuted. Bad charges not only harass innocent people; they also squander police and attorney resources, and they elbow out provable crimes. An assistant D.A. seeing the case against Delia would compare the evidence against each element of proof required for conviction. In a few cases, screeners make mistakes, but it's extremely unlikely that a case like the one against Delia would progress as far as this fictional one did.

This is an important point. The requirement of proof beyond a reasonable doubt is a real burden. It means that many cases involving serious crimes cannot be prosecuted. A lot of bad, bad people, who have committed bad, bad crimes, can't be convicted in our system, and they continue to prey upon innocent people. We also give every defendant the right to remain silent: to take the Fifth Amendment. This means that a fact known only to the defendant isn't really a fact, in the sense that it can't be proved. It may be that, in her heart of hearts, Delia is guilty. But we can't make her tell us, if she is. Many other countries, including advanced countries that respect individual rights, do not recognize a privilege against self-incrimination, and they expect the defendant to talk. Many European countries, for example. Their idea is, a citizen obtains benefits from society, and the citizen owes a duty to give an account if there is evidence of a crime.

In America, the requirement of proof beyond a reasonable doubt, together with the Fifth Amendment, creates a substantial obstacle to crime control. That's just the way we've set up our criminal justice system. We obtain benefits from these laws in the form of protection of the individual against government, but we suffer a high cost in the form of crimes committed by some of the people we protect.

Here's the odd thing about all of this. Very few readers seem to notice, during the first parts of this novel, that the evidence against Delia isn't going to permit our government to convict her. As a society, we assume that convicting people is easier than it is. We don't understand our own criminal justice system very well, because our understanding is based on fiction, and that's unfortunate.

*   *   *

What about Brianna, then?

There's an incidental issue about Brianna, and it concerns the interrogation by Detective Slaughter. Although Delia was smart and remained silent, Brianna blabbed about everything. Which was not smart. The voluntary statements made by Brianna, after hearing the *Miranda* warnings and waiving her right to remain silent, wouldn't be excluded by the Fifth Amendment; they would be potential evidence of guilt. (It's possible that state law might exclude them, but that's a complexity that's beside the point.) If Brianna's statements had included evidence of an intent to kill, the case against Brianna would be much stronger.

But remember: Brianna and Delia were prosecuted together, in a joint trial. This means that the prosecution couldn't use Brianna's responses to interrogation. The reason has to do with the Sixth Amendment to the Constitution, which gives every defendant the right to "confront the witnesses against him." If Delia is also on trial, the earlier statements by Brianna make Brianna a "witness" against Delia. The jury inevitably would use Brianna's confessions to consider Delia's guilt, and it would be impossible for Delia to "confront" Brianna by cross-examining her. The United States Supreme Court has followed this line of reasoning to decide that, in a joint trial, the statements of a single defendant can't be used, because the other defendants can't "confront" that defendant. So, the prosecution can't use Brianna's statements in this story.

A more likely scenario would be for the prosecution to decline to prosecute Delia. After all, as I've explained, the prosecution really can't convict Delia, anyway. Then, Brianna's interrogation could be used against her. But that's not what happened in this story.

Then: What about the case against Brianna, as it's shown in this novel? I think it's right on the edge. A judge might grant the defense lawyers' motion and acquit Brianna—or, the judge might not. The cases interpreting the "strong corroboration" requirement in the courts of appeals aren't completely clear. There would have been a better case for conviction, if Brianna had retrieved the money from the bank herself, but I had Delia do it because that way, it's a better story. Of course, it would have been more strategic, on the part of the homicide officers, if they had waited for Brianna to receive the money and pay it to the hit man, as I've already explained. But as I've also explained, that's risky, because the defendants might find someone else to kill the victim. The officers want to wait for the money to change hands, but they also need to interrupt the crime early by arresting the person who's soliciting the hit. This kind of factual background is entirely possible, in a case like this.

And so, the acquittal of Brianna *could* have happened this way. But it's unclear. It remains an open mystery. But, hey: isn't that what makes a good story?

A preview of *Conflict of Interest*

1
DISASTER

The headlines called it the Propane Truck Disaster. For years, it was front-page news. Maybe that was because of the place where it happened, or because of how violently it happened, or because of the carnage that was left behind. Everybody saw those gruesome pictures on television. There wasn't much for the medical examiner to work with when he tried to identify the bodies.

A few days after it happened, the lawsuits started to hit the clerk's office. They made the front page, too. And every time, the newspapers reminded their readers about the reckless, just plain inexcusable negligence of the man who drove the propane truck. He was pushing his rig too hard on the home stretch, and he got in too much of a hurry.

But maybe it wasn't fair to blame the whole thing on the truck driver. Some people pointed the finger at the construction companies—those billion-dollar corporations that had built the roadway. That overpass was a death trap, designed by white-collar criminals who sacrificed lives to boost their profits. It was an accident waiting to happen!

Now, at last, it was almost time for the real verdict. The television anchors exploited it breathlessly: "A battle between giants of the legal profession! Over the greatest tragedy this city's ever seen!" On the Internet, the chat groups grew from five to twenty-five. And finally, a talk-show host unleashed the ultimate hype: "This thing's gotten bigger than the O.J. Simpson case!"

The lawyers felt their adrenalin surge, and reporters fought for courtroom assignments, because the trial of the propane truck disaster was about to begin.

2
THE JURY

All right, Mister Bailiff. Bring them in!"

"Yes, your honor." A buzz of excitement arose from the spectators.

Robert Herrick scrambled to his feet the moment the jury panel started to enter the courtroom. His stomach twitched and bubbled, and the custom-tailored hundred dollar shirt he'd chosen for this trial was soaking wet. "My God," he murmured to no one in particular, "I've already sweated through my clothes."

He knew that it was his fear that made him sweat. He tried to settle himself by remembering that he was the immediate past president of the bar association, chairman of a blue ribbon committee appointed by the Supreme Court, and leader of the local bar's project to represent the poor. He had a brilliant career. His clients adored him. He was rich beyond most people's imagination.

But nothing could erase the memory that he had lost three of his most recent jury trials. He was afraid he had lost his touch—and his luck. His hands started to shake, so he jammed them into his jacket pocket, hoping no one had noticed. As he watched the line of randomly-selected citizens shuffle in, he struggled to project confidence, because that could make the difference for his clients between winning and losing.

The bailiff pointed. "First ten of you on the front bench, please. And then let's start the second row."

These were the sixty citizens from whom the final twelve jurors would be selected to try the propane truck case. Not only his clients' fate but Robert's whole career rested in their hands. And that was what terrified him.

"It's not surprising that you're nervous." Tom Kennedy was a five-year attorney, here to assist with the trial. "But Robert, you're the best lawyer for this case."

"Thanks, Tom." He managed a tight smile.

Across the courtroom, his arch rival, Jimmy Coleman, also stood. "Look at Coleman." Kennedy's whisper was heavy with disgust. "Biggest Rambo lawyer in town. Mister Slash and Burn. But here he is, smiling and looking cuddly for the jurors, like an overgrown teddy bear."

Robert usually managed to stay on friendly terms with his opponents, but he couldn't help disliking this one. Jimmy Coleman was the head of litigation at the biggest firm in town, the gigantic Booker & Bayne, with almost five hundred lawyers. He carried a map of his life on his face, punctured by eyes so pale and dead that witnesses turned away when Jimmy cross-examined them.

"Guy's a real street fighter," Robert agreed. "But you're right. He'll make sure the jury doesn't know it."

There wasn't any rule of courtroom procedure that required the lawyers to stand, but Robert stretched to his full six-foot-two-inch height, because he was trying to read as many of the sixty faces as possible. Women jurors usually responded to his youthful looks, with the shock of dark brown hair that fell over his forehead, and the men were impressed when he could speak without notes for hours at the end of a long case. Still, he wished he didn't always feel nervous— not just nervous, but scared!—at the beginning of every trial. His blue eyes grew dark, now, as he searched every juror for some kind of omen.

The first citizen wore a gray suit, gray shirt, gray tie. "Look at that, Tom. The guy's an accountant, of all things. And all dressed in gray." This wasn't the sign Robert had hoped for.

"He wouldn't be a good plaintiff's juror at all," Kennedy whispered back. "In fact, he'd be terrible."

Then, there was absolute silence—a brittle, self-conscious silence— until all sixty citizens had taken their seats.

*   *   *

"Good morning, ladies and gentlemen." Judge Barbara Trobelo's smile seemed a little bit forced, probably because she had to run for re-election soon. "The case now on trial is the one that the public calls 'the propane truck case.' The formal name is *Gutierrez versus Maxxco Construction Corporation and Louisiana Trucking Company*, but I'll explain what all of that means later. This is a civil case, and it will be tried before a jury."

The lawyers weren't listening. They alternated between scanning the jurors' faces and sneaking looks at the jury questionnaires, and all the while, they tried to look relaxed. But Robert found that it was harder and harder to do that.

"This is an awful jury panel!" He showed the list to Kennedy. "It's not just the gray accountant. The whole front row is crammed with types that the psychologists warned us about." This was the luck of the draw, but he wished it hadn't happened now, in the biggest case of his career.

The judge was still reading instructions to the jury panel. "When you begin your deliberations, it will be your duty to elect a presiding juror." She looked up and smiled. "We used to say 'foreman,' but today we say 'presiding juror,' because it's less sexist."

The feminists in the jury panel beamed at that. The men laughed good-naturedly.

But Robert was too wound up to laugh. That string of losses had hurt him badly, even though he tried not to let anyone see it. His latest defeat was the worst: a medical malpractice case where complications from a broken metal rod in a bone had killed Robert's poor client in a cruel, painful way. And that case, coincidentally, had been against this same opponent. This same Jimmy Coleman! "Thanks, Herrick, for refusing our settlement offer and making us try this piece-of-shit case of yours," Jimmy had exulted after the jury brought in a zero verdict. He'd won the case by pulling one dirty trick after another, all artfully concealed from the jurors.

And now, here was Jimmy again, eager to administer another thrashing. Robert valued his reputation for representing injured people with skill and integrity, but these days, his faith in his most cherished talents was shaken.

He was about to ask the jurors to award his clients a billion dollars. A billion, with a "B." But his stake in this case wasn't tied to the money. He also believed passionately in the power of juries to compensate innocent people for the damage that the careless rich did to them. But this case had hooked him at a level even deeper than that.

"You know, Tom, I need to win this case." He turned suddenly toward his younger associate. "For myself, as well as my clients."

Kennedy's voice was even. "We can do it, Robert. Just take it slow and steady."

The judge was beginning to read aloud the names of all the plaintiffs. Her voice was stern: "If any of you, as potential jurors, are acquainted even slightly with any of these parties, you must raise your hand." There would be more than a hundred names, because Robert Herrick's law firm represented all of the survivors of the propane truck disaster, and yet he listened to every one. He knew their pain, because thirty-three people had been killed instantly, and even more had died later. Robert had had to learn all of their life stories.

His drive to win this case had become a raw and primitive energy.

So far, this was the most bizarre case he had ever handled. The investigation had forced him into contact with all kinds of unsavory characters: heroin dealers, murderers, and prostitutes. It also had carried him into high society: luxurious boardrooms, glittering balls. Along the way, there had been a triple murder, a cop-killing, and a shooting in which Robert himself had been wounded.

The judge was warning the panel, now, about jury misconduct. "Do not mingle with or talk to the lawyers or the witnesses . . . . Do not accept any favors from them, such as rides, food or refreshment . . . ."

"If I lose," Robert thought, "I'll hang it up for good." Maria might be pleased by that. She would love him no matter what. His kids would like to see more of him. "But obviously," he reminded himself, "I don't want to go out with my tail between my legs."

*　　*　　*

Suddenly, the judge ended her speech. Jimmy Coleman was on his feet. "Your Honor! Before we start the trial, I have a motion to make on behalf of my client, Maxxco Construction Corporation!"

"What the hell's he up to?" Kennedy whispered.

Robert had a sense that he ought to know the answer. But somehow, disastrously, all he could say was, "I don't have any idea!"

"Your Honor, we respectfully ask that you realign the parties." Jimmy's motion was all phrased in high-sounding language. "Otherwise, Maxxco would be denied an impartial trial, in violation of its most precious right—the right to due process of law."

What *that* meant, it turned out, was that Jimmy wanted to renumber the Louisiana Trucking Company as the first-named defendant, instead of his own client, Maxxco. "All Maxxco did was, it built the intersection. Mister Herrick's trying to say Maxxco was negligent, but the fact is, it wasn't. And anyway, the case against the truck driver ought to be the one that gets the jury's attention." This seemed like a waste of breath, because it simply didn't matter which defendant was named first. Robert had never heard of a motion like this, and he was sure the judge hadn't either.

And then, he realized that the sixty citizens were listening to Jimmy with rapt admiration. For them, this must have sounded better than *L.A.*

Law. It finally dawned on Robert: "Hey, Jimmy's making a jury speech, disguised as a legal argument to the judge!"

Jimmy's hoarse voice was a bellow and a whisper, both at the same time, like the dignified anger that might ooze over the courtroom if Marlon Brando were to play a big-firm lawyer. His words rose and fell half an octave as he made his real point. "Your honor, at the end of this case, the jury will see that the truck driver was the *only* person responsible for this tragedy. Not Maxxco! *Not* my client! Not anybody but the truck driver. And that's all there is to this case!"

Robert lost control for a moment. "No, your honor! That's not what the jury will see. At the end of this case . . ."

But Judge Trobelo's eyes clouded, as she quickly interrupted him. "The motion is denied. And both counsel are way out of line. I won't tolerate any more of this kind of argument in front of the jury." She chose her words carefully, because Robert's outburst meant that it wouldn't be fair to concentrate her irritation on Jimmy alone.

The jurors smiled and nodded their heads. One or two even clapped.

"I guess these are the kind of legal fireworks they've been looking forward to," Tom Kennedy whispered.

But Robert was disgusted with himself as he stared at Jimmy across the courtroom. "First impressions are going to be all-important in this trial," he whispered back. "The consultants warned me that the jury's likely to form its attitudes sooner than in most cases." And now, Jimmy had struck the first blow. Or rather, the first thrust of the stiletto.

"He fooled me so badly, I just wasn't able to stop him." There was anguish in Robert's voice.

Kennedy nodded. "Typical Coleman! But it looks like the jury fell for it. Isn't there at least something we can do?"

Herrick shook his head. "We make a big fuss, and we'll lose more than we can possibly gain."

And so, finally, when that respected plaintiff's lawyer, Robert Herrick, stood up to address the sixty citizens who held ultimate power over the biggest case of his life, he had the discouraging feeling that he was starting from behind.

The trial had only just begun. But already, he was losing.

And he couldn't afford to feel like a loser. He would need to use every bit of his skill in this case, all the way through to the final witness. He dug into his lungs to take a breath. Then he turned to face the jurors. He stared at them for a long, awkward moment as he got ready to take them back to the beginning.

*   *   *

"It all started more than two years ago," he said slowly, "when a truck driver named Louie Boudreau ended his final run."

Robert Herrick's law firm had spent hundreds of hours reconstructing Boudreau's journey. By the time he was finished, Robert knew much more than the route of the propane truck. He knew the personality of the truck driver better than he knew most of his friends. He had come to understand Louie Boudreau's thinking, his hopes and dreams, as well as if he had crawled inside the truck driver's own skin.

And now, he was ready to draw a picture of that strange, disastrous day for the jury panel. He wanted to put the jurors right there in Louie Boudreau's cab. Or better yet, inside his head.

"Let's go back in time." Robert forced himself to keep his voice clear and calm. "Let's go back, ladies and gentlemen of the jury panel, to that horrible day a little over two years ago. Because that is when this case, this story, really begins . . . ."

3
BOUDREAU'S RUN

He was a tough, street-smart Cajun redneck, Louie Boudreau was, with a longshoreman's shoulders and arms, but at just five-foot-six, he was too sawed-off for that line of work. Instead, he'd gotten his leathery face mostly from working deep offshore on platform oil rigs, across from southern Louisiana towns like Houma and Lafayette. And also, of course, by doing what he was doing right now—driving hazardous cargo for the Louisiana Trucking Company—which he often regretted, because he was built so much like a fireplug that he had to rise up out of the seat every time he made a turn.

In the past, Boudreau had made a good chunk of his living smuggling cocaine, making the trip from Texas to Chicago, which he liked because of the easy money and flexible hours. But he'd given it up. He wasn't very religious, but if you grew up in South Louisiana you got used to talking to the saints, and anyway, like most truck drivers, Boudreau was superstitious. He'd quit selling cocaine because something had told him the next trip would be the one when he'd be unlucky. He didn't have enough patience to keep from getting busted forever. When he was younger, in his early twenties, he'd done a deuce plus six months in the state prison at Angola for aggravated assault. He'd been in a barroom brawl over a woman he didn't know except for the fact that he wanted her because she was drunk and she stood about four inches shorter than he did.

As a matter of fact, Louie Boudreau wasn't in a very patient mood right now, either. The big sign on the side of the tank that said "Louisiana Trucking Company—Hazardous Cargo" was barely visible as the rig plunged ahead in the midday darkness and rain. He'd made his run from Lake Charles all the way down to Laredo, just as he was ordered to do. But after almost two days of driving, he still wasn't finished, because every-thing that could have gone wrong, had gone wrong.

"Forty hours on the road," thought Boudreau. "Forty straight hours! And judging by this weather, every saint in heaven must be mad as hell." The rain had closed in to make a solid wall at the same time that the clumps of chain restaurants and strip centers had come together to signal his entrance into the city. And now, a strange summer hail pounded the roof of his cab as Boudreau struggled to push his eighteen wheels east-ward toward Houston. He was heading back home, to Louisiana, on a stretch of Route 59 that the local population called the Southwest Free-way.

He wiped his eyes with his thumb and forefinger. The instant he opened them, the lightning burst in his face, crackling from the top of the sky to the horizon. Suddenly, a blast of wind pushed his rig sharply right-ward, like an invisible hand poking a toy truck. Boudreau grabbed the wheel, and he wasted a few choice expletives while the whole rig shivered. "Lord help me," he thought, "if I shift this load." A skid would make him jackknife, maybe even roll over. And if that happened, it would vaporize Louie Boudreau, together with everybody else who was on the road. He remembered the red-lettered warning plastered on the back of his rig: "Danger. Liquified Petroleum Gas. Contents under extreme pressure."

Then, with that little dance of the tires that lasted a second or two, the trouble was over. Boudreau took one hand off the wheel and jammed it into the middle of his hair. Then he pushed it back through the Vaselined grooves until there were shiny black chunks sticking straight out from his head. The cab was hazy and stale with smoke, but Boudreau chain-lit another Camel. It wasn't safe to smoke around this cargo, but he was tired, frustrated and sick of driving, and he didn't give a damn.

*   *   *

This trip hadn't been a good one. Oh, it had started out well enough when he left Lake Charles two days ago. It was amazing, Boudreau thought, how much he missed Elyse and the kids, and how much he missed the little shotgun house that flaked paint chips under the mildewy air of South Louisiana, after he'd been without sleep for two days.

"Propane to Laredo," the foreman, whose name was Pointevet, had told him in a Cajun accent, back at the yard. "It's a nice day for drivin', so you can have some tacos for lonch and be back to have crawfish for breakfas'."

Well, this particular run hadn't worked out that way. Just west of Orange, when he was barely across the Texas border, Boudreau had begun to hear an unpleasant whine from the engine. He'd tried to ignore it, but the noise had gotten louder, until finally, it was a circular, scraping nightmare. Lou Spoda, at Spoda's Truck Stop, thought it might be the air conditioner belt. So Boudreau had tightened all of the belts and sprayed them with anti-slip compound.

The noise had gone away—for exactly two miles. Then it started again with a scratchy wail. He'd stopped two more times along the road, fiddling with the belts, until finally, somewhere just short of Vidor, Texas, he'd pulled way off the Interstate and limped into Ray's Garage. After two hours of looking, Boudreau had finally found it, with the help of a shade-tree mechanic named Joe Bill Heatley. The distributor rotor was busted.

Joe Bill had a genuine burr haircut, less than a quarter-inch everywhere on his head, and black spaces between his teeth. "Look at them circles in that sorry damn thing," he had said, as they both stared at the inside of the distributor cap. The rotor had dug deeply into the metal points.

But that wasn't even the worst part of the trip. When Boudreau steamed into Laredo, it turned out that the buyer of this load of propane was some company on the Mexican side called Petroliferos y Gas de Chihuaua, and they hadn't put up the letter of credit that was required before Boudreau could drop his load. "It's just typical Mexican business," said the man in charge of the terminal, whose name happened to be Sanchez.

Four hours later, Louie Boudreau had gotten to know Sanchez extremely well, and he had long since jolted Pointevet wide awake back in Lake Charles. "Jus' bring de whole damn t'ing back here," Pointevet had told him finally. "We try to settle up wid dose fucking Mexican bastards later, or else we blackball 'em." And so Boudreau had backed the fifth wheel into place and connected the hoses for the trip back to Louisiana.

"I guess I be goin' home," he announced, "an' takin' my propane 'long wid me!"

Sanchez thought all of this was hilarious. "Haulin' propane back to Lake Charles, as if they didn't have enough of it," he roared. "That's a hell of a note, even for a dumb coon-ass like you, Louie!"

As tired as he was, Boudreau had to laugh when Sanchez went on to suggest various unnecessary cargoes that he might consider importing into Louisiana. Maybe a load of crawfish? A trailer full of Blackened Voodoo Beer, which was brewed in South Louisiana? "Or how about taking back a couple hundred a them doggy-lookin' strippers with the little titties, only when they get it all off it turns out they're these female-impersonator-type guys, instead? Surely they didn't have enough of those down on Bourbon Street," said Sanchez.

Boudreau was cracking up when Sanchez waved him out of the yard, yelling, "Stick with me, Louie, and I'll make you the richest coon-ass in all a Lake Charles, even if you are dumb enough to haul propane to Louisiana!"

*   *   *

Now, Boudreau wasn't laughing, as he pushed the rig toward the city. The hallucinations, he knew, couldn't be far away. Bands of color would focus into red, green and blue figures that would cavort across his windshield like a drive-in movie. The way they always did, after forty hours on the road.

Boudreau came closer and closer to his favorite shortcut. His favorite illegal shortcut, in fact. The lightning crashed again, this time behind him. He would take the long, looping ramp that connected to Interstate 610, and then, a few blocks north, he would turn east again on Interstate 10, and that would take him clear to Lake Charles without another turn.

It was illegal as hell. Boudreau would sail right under the bright green sign that banned hazardous cargoes from the inner city. It was marked on all of the Louisiana Trucking Company's maps, as Pointevet had shown him with the stub of a cracked greasy fingernail when Boudreau first had started driving for the company. But the shortcut would save him a good half hour. "If any cop can catch me in this weather," thought Boudreau, "he deserves to write a big-truck ticket."

The Transco Tower, tallest building in the world outside a metropolitan center, rose out of the darkness on his left. The building was spooky, with shiny black surfaces and a pointed hood. Just past it, Boudreau saw the silhouette of the Galleria Mall. When he turned the corner, he would be a few hundred feet from Neiman Marcus, Tiffany's, and the hundreds of other glittering merchants-to-the-wealthy that linked this patch of Houston to Fifth Avenue and Rodeo Drive. Maybe that was why hazardous cargo wasn't supposed to be here.

But still, Boudreau pressed his foot on the accelerator. His speedometer needle bounced over fifty-five. He downshifted and dodged the concrete blocks that marked the exit ramp off of the Southwest Freeway and onto Interstate 610. Immediately, Boudreau was in a spaghetti bowl of concrete and steel, with a commanding view of Transco Tower. He braked as the ramp began to turn northward, and he coasted under the Hazardous Cargo sign.

On the radio, Don Henley sang about "Forgiveness." "Maybe there's something a little more cheerful on another station," Louie thought. He watched the freeway with half his attention while he turned the dial over to kikk, which was one of Houston's many country stations. Instantly he was rewarded by Mary-Chapin Carpenter's voice singing, "I wanna dance to a band from Lou-si-anne tonight." For the first time in five hundred miles, Boudreau actually smiled.

And then it happened. The thunder, and the lightning, and the aftermath, so fast that it was all one event.

The thunder was like a bomb; the lightning, white hot and incandescent, seemed to ride right on top of his hood, burning through Boudreau's dilated eyes. Ahead of him was a Toyota painted the same silver color as the rain. It skidded and revolved as the driver panicked. In the instant before he braked, Boudreau rode almost on top of the Toyota. That was when his own wheels locked and his cab began to skid.

As he struck the left side of the Toyota, Boudreau's propane tank burst the railing and sailed off the ramp, the way a child's yo-yo breaks free from its string. He felt his fifth wheel tearing loose as the tank pulled his cab off the ramp. There was a sickening silence as the rig fell, and Boudreau saw Sanchez's face appear in front of him, then his wife Elyse, and the kids, then the foreman Pointevet, followed by red, green and blue figures of the Bourbon Street transvestite strippers that Sanchez had conjured up. Then, for an instant, the images faded, but finally, Boudreau's spinning nightmare came back into focus with the transvestites transformed into all of the saints of heaven, bending over each other in an orgiastic Roman holiday while the clouds shook with lightning and rain.

The propane tank hit first. It slammed across the three inside lanes of the Southwest Freeway. The pressure found a pinhole. Inevitably, there was enough of a spark to ignite the bullet stream of escaping gas. The cab separated and flew to the other edge of the road, but before it did, the earth and sky exploded. The incoming cars skidded and flipped as their drivers desperately tried to stop. But the whole freeway was blocked, and the momentum of sixty miles per hour hurled them into the holocaust.

Later, shaken witnesses would describe a huge orange fireball that they thought was taller than the Transco Tower. And one even insisted—against all of the evidence—that there had been hundreds of cars twisted in the wreckage at its base. On the Southwest Freeway below the ramp, investigators found fourteen vehicles with melted dashboards and tires exploded from the heat. Parts of the cars actually had vaporized, and there were more than thirty human bodies, several of which were impossible to identify by conventional means.

And the last thing that Boudreau had seen, before his cab hit the freeway, was the sweet face of the Virgin.

* * *

David Crump's novels *Conflict of Interest* and *The Holding Company*, featuring Houston trial lawyer Robert Herrick, are available in quality paperback and eBook editions from leading booksellers.

Visit us at *www.qpbooks.com.*

www.ingramcontent.com/pod-product-compliance
Lightning Source LLC
Chambersburg PA
CBHW051639260626
47170CB00004B/1239